# Texas Crossfire

## A Billionaire's Deadly Obsession

Stephen L. Thompson

# Texas Crossfire

## *Books by Stephen L. Thompson*

### The Crossfire Series

Colorado Crossfire
International Crossfire
Israeli Crossfire
Believer's Crossfire
Spirit Crossfire
Faith Crossfire
Chinese Crossfire
Texas Crossfire
Dark Crossfire
Island Crossfire
Jagged Crossfire
Violent Crossfire
Russian Crossfire
Nuclear Crossfire
End Times Crossfire
Revelation Crossfire
Gates of Hell Crossfire
Assassin's Crossfire
Albatross Crossfire
Global Crossfire
Far East Crossfire

### The SFO Series

Station Force One - Onset

# Texas Crossfire

In *"Texas Crossfire"* The Crossfire Team is drawn into one man's delusions and torments that are set destroy an entire people to ease his bitterness. Once again the enemy of mankind has a far more dangerous end to his hidden agenda. The Crossfire Team is drawn into the maelstrom of riches, politics, and warfare in their effort to stop the enemy's plans.


-   Stephen L. Thompson

# Texas Crossfire

**Published by**
Stephen L. Thompson
Facebook.com/CrossfireNovelSeries

ISBN- 978-1-943879-03-8

Electronically Published in the United States of America

# Foreword

*To my Christian readers –*
The Crossfire continuing series of action-adventure novels include depictions of violence which are unusual in Christian literature. It would be nice if there were no conflict or violence in our world. But we live in a time when evil is increasing instead of diminishing, when some men seem to be controlled by selfishness, madness, or evil forces. When the enemies of decent mankind are bent on subjugation of other men and women, righteous men and women must stand against evil. The yoke of oppression is not lifted by prayer alone. God is our shepherd and we are his sheep. As long as there are wolves about, God will use some of us as sheep dogs to defend the rest of us. These stories are about people like that and the forces they fight against. The stories describe violence because it occurs in the real world and it is active in the lives of all people whether they recognize it or not.

*To my non-Christian readers –*
The Crossfire series include depictions of spiritual warfare and spiritual activity with which the non-Christian reader may not be familiar. These stories describe the realms and activities of both God and Satan because they're real and active in the lives of all people whether they recognize it or not.

*Steve Thompson*

# CHAPTER ONE

Jack Malone and Mark Connelly walked down the aisle towards the witness table in the Congressional committee room in Washington, D.C. Everyone was watching them with interest. These two people, along with their team, had almost single-handedly stopped a terrorist attempt to detonate a nuclear weapon in Denver, Colorado three weeks ago. They were here to enlighten the committee and everyone else on how they accomplished such a feat.

Jack stood six-foot, four in height and was solid and muscular. He moved with a grace and economy that was indicative of a martial arts master. It came across as a total and confident domination of the space he moved through. His good looks and blonde hair were highlighted by his gray-green eyes and firm face lines. To the women in the audience he registered as a good-looking man they would like to know. To the men he seemed like someone who would be a good friend.

Walking step for step next to Jack, Mark Connelly projected an image of an unstoppable force. He was a couple of inches shorter than his best friend but made up for it by his rock solid mass. He had a wide chest and heavily muscled arms that rode over a trim waist and powerful legs. His dark hair was a solid contrast to Jack's lighter blonde and he had the honest face of a soldier.

Reaching the witness table, both men took a seat, arranged their papers, and faced the committee members.

The Chairperson of the committee, Senator Joan Caldwell had both men sworn in and sat there for a few seconds gathering her thoughts. Those thoughts were less than clear about the role this "team" played in the events of last month. The administration had declared them heroes and even given them medals for their efforts. But, Joan had her doubts about a great deal the administration did and she wanted to see if this wasn't another put-up deal to paint themselves and this Team as the shining white knights of anti-terrorism. She had heard input about a miscalculation on the parts of the Homeland Security and the FBI regarding this attack. She was fairly certain that the President and his administration were taking credit for a fortunate turn of events that they didn't earn. She, and her committee would expose the incumbent party and any mis-steps right here on national television. This "team" would be the place to start tearing off the veneer of glamor of the Government's case.

She looked at Jack and opened the hearing, "Mr. Malone, I understand that you are private citizen yet somehow you are also a one-star general in the U.S. Air Force. Can you explain that incongruity?"

Jack could discern her intent and had, in fact, been warned to expect it. "Good Morning, Senator Caldwell. Yes, I believe I can explain the dual role for you. Last year my Team was working in coordination with the United States Government in a confrontation with a terroristic group that was in the last stage of demanding world capitulation through nuclear blackmail. We were the point group in the attempt to prevent a large number of ex-Russian nuclear warheads from being detonated around the top of the world. Since several different national armies were involved, not all of which liked us, a Presidential order was generated promoting myself, Mr. Connelly, and four others to the rank of General to allow for effective command and control."

The Senator stared at Jack and asked, "I take it you were successful in this endeavor?"

Jack smiled at her. "Yes Senator, we were successful. The scientific determination of the amount of explosive involved suggested that if we had not been successful then the planet itself would have fragmented and there would have been a complete end to all life as we know it." Jack let that hang there for a few seconds. "The President was pleased that we were able to give his administration a full term."

Slightly rankled by the comment the Senator shot back, "Is that why he never rescinded the Presidential Order?"

Jack smiled at her again. "No Senator, the reason that we retained our rank is because it has provided our Team with the necessary authority to continue our anti-terrorist work for our country."

2

The Senator decided she wasn't going to make this man tremble with fear concerning her lofty position so she went with the smooth approach instead. "Mr. Malone, can you enlighten this committee as to how your Team has become so important to this administration's anti-terrorist activities?"

Jack scanned the other members of the committee and saw a real interest in his answers. "Yes Senator, I can. We have been extremely successful in rooting out and destroying the evil that is attempting to destroy this country. We did not ask for this role but have been given it by events in the last few years. We have been able to surmount the enemy's efforts and contribute to the overall protection of the country due to our unique capabilities."

The Senator was about to look for another angle when the number two on the committee voiced the general opinion of the other members that they needed to get on with the business of the recent attack. "Senator Caldwell, the credentials and reputations of Mr. Malone and the Crossfire Team are not on trial here. They have been gracious enough to come here today to speak to us about the attack on Denver and I believe we should listen to them on that issue."

Realizing she was not being seen in a good light, the Senator gave the committee the floor to discern the details they wanted to discuss.

Seeing the look on her face, Jack could tell that Senator Caldwell would be digging and attempting to find something to hold against them. But, the Lord was in charge and Jack would trust Him to keep her out of their way. He started to answer the first question about the attack on Denver.

# CHAPTER TWO

Laura Malone sat quietly and considered their present accommodations. Set deep in a granite mountain outside Denver, the Crossfire Fortress was a quiet and cool retreat, serving as the nerve center of the team's operations. From the military protection on the outside of the mountain to the NovaStar security systems and formidable defense capabilities inside the structure, the Team was as safe as humanly possible from enemy attacks.

Laura and Sarah Connelly were handling the operations while their husbands were in Wonderland at the committee hearings. Laura knew she had traveled a long way from the finance executive and housewife she had once been. She had learned martial arts, weapons, and warfare in a hands-on school of hard knocks.

She had also learned to walk with the Lord and was anointed to do battle with the forces of darkness in a unique way. She knew she was definitely in love with her husband and attempted to be a kind and compassionate wife. But, she went where her Savior, Yahshua, directed and did what was asked of her without question. While she was talented, she knew that she had to depend on her God for the understanding and intelligence to keep pace with her husband and the rest of the group.

She was dressed a light green blouse, dark green shorts, tan sandals, and had her hair up in a pony tail as she went over the latest reports of turmoil around the world.

Laura sat back and studied her second best friend, after her husband, standing across the room from her. Sarah Connelly was a dark-haired deadly beauty. She was dressed in cut-offs which showed off her long legs and a fatigue blouse that complimented her figure. Two inches shorter than Laura's six foot height, Sarah was lithe and muscular. Laura smiled to herself. Sarah's career as a top Mossad field agent and assassin had taken a new twist when she met the Malones and Mark on an operation in Houston, Texas two years earlier. Since then she had become a Christian, left the Mossad, and married Mark Connelly, the man who she said impressed her more than any other in her lifetime. On her own admission she said that since joining the Crossfire Team she had increased her capabilities beyond the level of her previous career.

The phone rang and Laura punched it up at her workstation in the War Room. The large room with the semi-circular table was quiet today with only the two women working there. The quiet background flow of the conditioned air added to the ambiance.

The Caller ID showed that the caller was Joe Sobbel, one of two new Directors of the FBI. His voice came clearly over the link. "Could I talk to Jack Malone please?"

Laura responded, "I'm sorry Director Sobbel, Jack is not here right now. I'm Laura, his wife. Is there anything I can do for you?"

In Washington, D.C., Joe Sobbel had studied the records and accomplishments of each one of the Crossfire Team and was acutely aware of their effectiveness. It was their efforts that had led to his being promoted to his present position. His predecessor had discounted the team's warnings about the possibility of a second nuclear weapon targeting Denver and after that he had been convinced that early retirement was just about his only option.

He said, "Yes you can Laura. In my position one of my jobs is to determine if there are any demonic elements to any of our operations and contact your group if I feel there is sufficient cause. I know I've only been on the job for two weeks but in my review of one of our on-going operations in Dallas, it seems to be running into the same type of interference we had with the group at Denver. I was hoping your Team could check this out for me."

Laura had been praying about the request as she listened. "Why don't you E-mail us the particulars and we'll field a Team this afternoon. We should be able to give you a report before the weekend."

Joe Sobbel agreed and transmitted the file to the Fortress.

Sarah and Laura reviewed the file. A newly popular Christian evangelist was drawing large crowds and apparently performing miracles of healing and financial largess that had thousands flocking to his crusades. Nothing unusual about that except that the FBI had determined that the primary use for the funds raised by the evangelist was a shadowy organization called the "Arrow of Vengeance" that had some definite terrorist leanings.

From the records Sarah pointed out the FBI's problem. They couldn't seem to actually track the funds to the Arrow group. The agents were mysteriously losing their quarry and were being blocked at every turn. Financial probes were blunted and turned away. Direct contact was impossible as the group involved was a paramilitary organization with a tightly controlled and restricted list of personnel. The FBI could not get anyone into the organization and no one that knew anything about it would talk.

The one informant that they had that had originally led them to the Arrow group might have been insane because he kept talking about the wall having ears and things that moved in the night. He was a nervous wreck and died the second night he was in the FBI's custody. The strange part was that he died in a secure room of severe fright. His heart stopped from fear of something no one else or the cameras saw.

Laura looked at Sarah and asked, "What do you think?"

Sarah finished reading the report. "I think we ought to go down there and see what we can see."

Laura called Su Li, the Crossfire Team's primary pilot, and told her to warm up the corporate jet for a hop down to Dallas, Texas in the next two hours.

In the dark of interstellar space, the small cloud of meteors moved in silence at a speed of one hundred, sixty-one thousand miles per hour. This group of small rocks had broken off of a planet thousands of years ago when a giant meteor, more like a small planet itself, had struck the airless planet at meteoric speeds. This group of rocks had been a tiny part of the mantle of the planet that had been violently hurled into space. The angle of the collision had caused the debris to slowly separate. Most of the debris was held by gravitational attraction to the larger pieces. This little group had been blown at an angle to the majority of the mass and had moved away.

Accelerated and directed by the tremendous gravity wells of the stars, the ten-ton cloud had roamed the endless darkness for eons. Its long trajectory was presently intersecting the path of a small solar system. The huge gravity well of the primary star exerted enough attraction to slightly angle the path of the cloud. As it had done for millennia, the small group of little rocks continued on its way through the solar system. It had been noted and given the name "body XA12435".

# CHAPTER THREE

The Reverend Matthew Kloss peered out from behind the main curtain behind the pulpit in the American Airlines Center auditorium in Downtown Dallas. The crowd was filling up nicely and the pre-crusade music ministry was warming up the crowd. He stepped back from the curtain and checked his diamond-studded watch. He was due to make his appearance in exactly forty minutes. He went back to his dressing room and checked his image in the large mirror. He looked good by God! Well, he looked good anyway. He stared at his reflection carefully looking for any trace of the loser he used to be. He couldn't see any sign of the weak, moralistic, slob he had been not too long ago.

Shaking his head he thought about those years. After two decades of attempting to follow the Christian way of life and suffering mightily without anything, he'd finally seen the true light. All the talk about Jesus had left him broke and without any real hope of enjoying this life. The voice that had whispered to him every night had finally explained his miserable state. He was never supposed to do without when so many that didn't deserve it had everything. He had been deceived all along by the senior pastors and teachers. They did that so that he would never amount to anything. Why would they do that? Because they were afraid of what he could become if he knew the secrets for success.

He had agreed with the voice and soon he had found the real path to enjoyment and success wasn't in preaching a dreary, seriously unfunny life of old Christianity. The new power in his life changed his looks, his outlook, and his success. He started telling the people what they wanted to hear and how to be successful themselves. Yes! Invest in his crusade and they were guaranteed a 30, 60, or 100-fold return on their investment. Their seed would bring in a big harvest in no time. There were wonderful witnesses to that fact every night of the crusade. People had been made overnight millionaires after depositing thousands of dollars into his coffers.

One thing was for sure, it had brought him a 10,000-fold harvest. For the first time in his life he had a luxury car to drive, a million-dollar mansion, and all the female company he could handle. Men he had envied fell to the right and the left while he prospered without end. Every night he counted the audience and realized he'd just gotten richer and more powerful. He loved it.

Tonight he would heal many people and get the crowd's undivided attention. He would then preach the powerful prosperity gospel that would lead the people to generously contribute to his crusade tonight. He guessed the take would be around three million. And God would just have to be happy with all the people who suddenly wanted to know the riches of Jesus.

He felt the power building within him and knew that it would be another powerful night of the awe and reverence he so richly deserved. Secretly inside he felt that he could ride this wave until he was content and then jump off.

As Laura and Sarah approached the main entrance to the arena, Laura felt a shiver run down her spine. She sought the Lord for the source of the warning and felt an unease rise up in her spirit. She looked at Sarah and saw that she was feeling the same things. They were at the booth where they paid for their admission. Laura felt that this was unusual for a Christian crusade. But people were almost fighting to buy tickets. Normally the admission was free. She paid the fifty dollars for each of them and took the tickets. As they walked along with the press of enthusiastic people heading for seats she felt the shiver again. She could feel the demonic eyes watching them. This wasn't good, not at all.

The ushers showed them to a pair of seats on the main floor that were only thirty rows back from the open area separating the seats from the podium. The music ministry started up with an upbeat hymn and everyone stood to their feet and started singing and clapping their hands. Laura and Sarah did the same and watched the throng as they truly worshiped the Lord and sang songs of praise.

After thirty minutes the music leader brought the festivities to an end with a foot-stomping version of "What the enemy stole from me". The lights in the audience area dimmed and one spotlight picked up the Reverend Kloss as he came out of the curtain behind the podium and raised his arms, Bible in one hand. His voice, amplified by many thousand watts of power rang out over the crowd noise and applause with his motto saying. "Are you rich and healthy in the name of Jesus? Well, You SHOULD BE!"

The crowd went wild and only settled down when he motioned for everyone to be seated. He then preached on the right of every believer to be rich and that God wanted them to have more money than their neighbors. God wanted them to be affluent so that everyone would know that Christianity was the right way to go. This assault on God's riches went on for twenty minutes. Then he changed his approach. "Christ doesn't just want you to be rich in finances; He wants you to be rich in health too. Who here needs a healing touch tonight?"

Hundreds of people flooded out of their seats and ran to the altar to be healed by the Reverend. Laura felt sick to her spirit by the false doctrine the Reverend had spewed out concerning wealth. Jesus wants everyone to be "spiritually rich" and if it is to God's glory and in His plan then a person will have financial "wealth". But those riches are given to people who have been tested and will use the money to help others in many different ways to better God's Kingdom on earth. The money wasn't to be hoarded or to be used just for the person who He enriched. This Kloss guy simply said that God was an ATM in the sky. Put your tithes and offerings in and get a financial reward. The more you put in, the more you got back. This wasn't the way God works. If selfish people try to get riches to make their lives more opulent then God doesn't hear their prayers nor accept their bribes. The heart and the attitude have to be right first. This Reverend didn't even allude to repenting of a person's sins or being right with God. He simply hit on man's greed and how to get God to give them personal wealth.

The Reverend went down into the crowd and began to touch people. If they were limping, they started walking without a limp. If they were in a wheelchair, they got up and walked. If they were blind, they got their sight. Every one of his touches resulted in a healing. A man on crutches with only one leg suddenly had two good legs and started dancing and praising the Lord. Cancer, high blood pressure, malignant sores, hair loss, you name it. It was healed immediately.

Sarah looked at Laura to find her in prayer and crying. She waited and watched the continuous healings up at the platform. Laura touched her on the arm. Sarah saw the tears in her eyes and felt worry and compassion for her friend. As Sarah turned and gave her a hug, Laura spoke quietly to her. "He's healing each person by the power of Satan. The Lord told me that when he lays hands on a person he is assigning a demon to that person. The demon makes the person "well", but Sarah! It is only temporary! Every one of those people will have a relapse sometime in the future when it is no longer in Satan's interest to maintain their healing."

Laura broke the hug, turned to go and was attempting to leave when there was a shout and everyone tried to get to the aisle at the same time. Looking up she saw that the Reverend was coming up their aisle and laying hands on people as he came. Laura attempted to draw back but the crowd was pushing forward and she couldn't move.

Laura wanted to pray for protection from God but was concerned that her armor would appear. She then hoped he would pass her by and not attempt to demonize her. She sat down to make herself less accessible.

Laura watched the man approach and knew that in the spiritual world they had already been spotted by the demon riding the Reverend. Laura knew that in the demon's world where faith and purity to God was abhorrent, she and Sarah stood out as bright beacons of righteousness that repulsed the demon and probably made him nervous.

She watched as the Reverend, unknowingly, was drawn by their anointing. In the natural, she could tell he saw her and Sarah as a pair of desirable women, Reverend Kloss' attention settled on them. She suddenly realized that since she was sitting down he probably thought she needed some kind of healing so he headed directly for her.

As he reached out to touch her, he recoiled and jerked his hand away from her shoulder. He was surprised as were the people around him. Thinking quickly he said, "Sister, you have a powerful spirit on you that needs special prayer. I want to give you some personal attention."

He signaled two of the catchers who normally caught people who fell under the power of the spirit and told them to take her to a "meditation room" off of the main floor area. They moved forward to take her arms and she looked directly at the Reverend. The power of the Lord was in her eyes and she said clearly, "You really don't want to do this."

Laura saw the sudden fear in his eyes but, the Reverend was adamant. "Oh, yes, I really think I do." He motioned again and the men moved forward to physically remove her from her chair.

Laura put up her hand to stop them, stood up, and walked down the aisle without allowing them to handle her. She felt that she would create less of a spectacle if she went without an argument. The Reverend looked up to address the other woman but she was no longer there. He shrugged and smiled and put his hands on a woman crippled with arthritis. Since arthritis is frequently demonically caused it was an easy for the demon now attached to the woman to "heal" her of her condition. She stood up for the first time in years and threw her cane away. The crowd roared its approval.

Laura walked out of the main arena area, away from the crowd and into a roomy alcove that was separated from the main floor by a curtain. The two men stopped just inside the curtain.

Laura felt sliminess come into the room. Fear, dread, sickness, pain, abandonment all assailed her mind. Knowing who she was in Jesus, Laura knew these were demonic thoughts being impressed on her. She quietly said, "I bind up this evil spirit of fear, pain, and sickness in the name of Yahshua who came in the flesh and ask God's Holy angels to take it to the abyss where it is to remain until the end of time when it will be judged."

The fear and other emotions were gone as if they had never existed. With a simple prayer of commandment through the authority and righteousness of the Son of God the demon was defeated.

Then Laura prayed that the Lord would guide her so that she would serve His will in this matter.

# CHAPTER FOUR

Sarah had eased back into the crowd as the confrontation between Laura and the Reverend escalated. She went to a new vantage point and watched Laura walk out of the seating area and head for a curtained area to the back of the arena. Using her field craft to keep people from noticing her, Sarah managed to reach the area just after Laura walked through the curtain. She was contemplating what course of action she would take when another of the large "catchers" came up and took up a position outside the curtain. He stood there with his arms folded over his massive chest signifying that no one was allowed to pass.

Inside the alcove one of the men shoved Laura towards the center of the room. Laura got a response to her prayers. The Lord led her to understand that she could be His instrument to stop the false gospel that Reverend Kloss was spewing out over the Christian believers. God was giving her the choice to put herself in harm's way, go against the huge crowd, and denounce the false leader, or she could choose not to be involved.

Laura understood that when God put such a choice in front of one so clearly, that the stakes were huge. She thoughtfully considered the idea of staying out of the action and protecting herself, for about two seconds. She then humbled herself and her future to God's will. She felt the power of the Lord sustaining her as she turned around and headed back for the curtain.

The man on her right stepped in front of the split in the curtain and raised a beefy hand. "You're to stay right here, ma'am."

Laura contemplated his Texas drawl, his eighty-pound weight advantage, and the male inclination towards violence and other testosterone-fueled activities as she closed with him. Rotating to her left on the ball of her left foot she leaned to her left and sent her right foot crashing into the locked knee of the man's right leg. The knee broke backwards from the force with a loud "crunch". The man went from big, bad, dude to wimp in less than a second as he collapsed to the floor with a wail.

This quick strike brought Laura parallel to the other man on her right, who was turning towards her. Continuing to rotate to her left, she pulled her right leg back to her and then slammed her right foot into the second man's gut. The hours and hours of intense training had been effective and Jack was an excellent martial arts teacher. Laura had studied very hard on her striking and kicking techniques. This kick had significant power in it.

The air flew out of the man's mouth as the diaphragm forced it out of his lungs from the kick. In one smooth movement, Laura turned more to her left and was now facing the same direction as the second man who was bending over from the pain of the kick. She whirled to her right and whipped a right hand back fist into the side of the man's head. He didn't have any air with to scream with so he just grunted and fell to the floor unconscious.

Laura could feel that she was building up a real case of righteous anger about the Reverend Kloss and his treatment of God's children. Her green eyes flashed as she reached up and captured some loose strands of hair and flipped them back out of her eyes.

She went to the curtains and ripped them open. She found Sarah standing calmly on the other side looking at her with one eyebrow raised. Stepping out she noticed a third man crumpled on his face to one side of the opening. Nodding, she started back towards the podium.

Sarah started subtly working the kinks out of the remaining muscles she hadn't used already. After one look at the expression on Laura's face Sarah knew that whatever the woman was going to do, it was going to happen. Sarah decided that she would just back Laura's play. Actually, it had felt good to beat that smug, out-of-practice macho ape into a sack of rags. Looking at their direction of travel, Sarah thought to herself, "This should be really interesting."

Laura emerged from the seating area into the open space before the podium with a full head of steam. Sarah was right behind her quietly grinning in anticipation. The Reverend was still basking in the glow of admiration from the crowd. He had finished his healing walk and had the crowd take their seats. Walking around the podium with his hands raised to the cheers of the crowd he was unaware of the two women approaching the platform from his right.

Three of the "catcher/bouncers" converged at the foot of the stairs to the podium. They came together to stop the women from going up on the stage. Unaware of the previous damage to their ranks the first two went down with almost no effort. The third one was ex-military and an ex-police officer. He pulled out a collapsible baton and extended it. Carrying it professionally in his right hand he approached the dark-haired woman cautiously. He feinted with the baton and executed a quick snap-kick with his left foot assuming that her concentration would be on the baton and he could catch her unaware.

Sarah knew the damage a metal baton could do in a fight. She'd used them herself several times. She went into combat speed which makes everything apparently slow down. She saw the kick developing and kicked first with her right foot. Her skirt flipped up as her foot slammed into his left shin bone with sufficient power to break the leg. Quickly stepping into the man she drove a full power palm-heel strike to his chin. Reaching out with her left hand she twisted the baton out of the weakened grasp of the man and swung it up and around and caught him at the back of the head. Falling forward from the third step to the concrete floor of the arena he landed like a side of beef. One bounce and he ceased moving. There was a collective gasp from the crowd on that side of the podium at the ease with which she had dispatched the man.

Sarah flipped the baton and it landed on the unconscious man's back. She started climbing the stairs. Laura walked up onto the brightly lit stage area with Sarah only a step behind her. The cameras which had been focused on the Reverend swung over to catch the sight of the women and the three men lying at the bottom of the stairs.

Laura ignored the Reverend and walked up to the microphone at the podium. She addressed the crowd without bothering to wait for full silence. She let God's Holy Spirit do the talking. "My Christian brothers and sisters! The Lord your God has a word for you. *"There is nothing concealed that will not be disclosed, or hidden that will not be made known. Watch out! Be on your guard against all kinds of greed; a man's life does not consist in the abundance of his possessions."* Yahveh God has listened as this man has perverted the glorious gospel of His Son and will allow it no longer."

The crowd had fallen silent as she spoke. One man yelled at her, "Oh yeah, what about all his healings? Isn't that God moving through him?"

Laura eyed the man, "Do you want God to show you the truth of Pastor Kloss' healings?"

Many in the crowd thought to test her and shouted agreement. Laura prayed out loud, "In the name of The Master Yahshua Messiah, who came in the flesh, may the will of God be shown in this place concerning the healings done by Reverend Kloss."

There was a sudden commotion throughout the crowd as the demons that had been impressed on people were suddenly gone. People that had been healed of many things suddenly found themselves sick again. Screams issued throughout the people as the lame collapsed again without their crutches, walkers, or wheelchairs, the blind lost their sight, and the sick were stricken again. The man who had received a new leg fell to the floor with only one leg again.

The Reverend, sensing his financial empire in jeopardy, pushed forward and grabbed the wired microphone from the podium, pointed his hand at Laura and told the people, "This woman is a witch and she has used Satan's power to rob you of your healings!"

The demons still present used all of this to turn the crowd's anger and hatred towards the woman that had prayed to eliminate their healings. They cursed her and then hundreds of men and women charged the stage area.

With the crowd attacking, the demon controlling the Reverend wanted him to lead the assault and pushed him to attack Laura who had begun to pray quietly. The Reverend picked up a microphone stand and swung it at Laura. Sensing the demonic-inspired attack, Laura's golden armor of God appeared along with the sword of light. The light from the armor and the sword flaring outward drove the remaining demons that still had a hold on people to flee in all directions. That included the demon that had been dominating the Reverend for years. Caught in mid-swing with a look of astonishment on his face the Reverend's eyes widened when Laura swung the sword and it cleaved the microphone stand into two pieces. The Reverend dropped the pieces to the stage. As the demonic presence left the arena, the bitterness and anger drained out of the people. Many pointed at the stage and said that Laura was an angel as her armor and sword gleamed in the bright lights on the platform. Laura lowered her sword when she saw that the Reverend wasn't a threat anymore and her armor faded out of sight.

The Reverend had dropped to his knees and was sobbing. Free from the demon and the voice that had battered and mislead him for years he realized the truth of his folly. Worse yet, he realized his greater sin as a Pastor in leading other Christians in ungodly ways. He got up and looked around in a daze. He walked to the reserve microphone lying on a chair and turned it on. He walked to the edge of the stage and addressed the people with tears running down his face. "Flock, friends, and guests, listen to me. I have a confession to make to you before God". He paused and prayed that the Lord would give him the strength to confess and ask them for forgiveness.

The crowd was very confused, some were leaving and others were arguing with each other. They all quieted down and stopped moving when they heard the Reverend. Again, Kloss pointed his finger at Laura. "Sadly, everything this woman is saying is true." The silence of the people was complete. "I have been led down a dark path through my own weaknesses and left the path the Lord had for me. I gave control of my life to the evil spirit of Mammon and have spent the last six months trying to have you do the same. God will deal with me in time but for now I want to ask your forgiveness and to ask you to pray for me and every person I have hurt with this false doctrine. I will attempt to return the funds I have been given and seek the Lord for repentance. I will find a way t....BLAM"

The shot rang out loudly in the arena. The Reverend's head snapped forward with the impact of the bullet and he fell face first off of the stage into the open area. Laura and Sarah spun towards the shooter who aimed his gun at Laura and pulled the trigger.

There was a flash of gold and white in the air between Laura and the shooter. The bullet was stopped in mid-flight and fell to the stage. The angel Rose appeared floating above the stage with her sword drawn. The crowd collectively took in one huge breath in astonishment. While Rose was beautiful, the terribly awesome visage of God's wrath was on her and it was enough to made brave men cower.

The gunman cursed at the angel and emptied his automatic at her without effect. She pointed at him and her voice rolled over the crowd. *"You have been judged a brute beast, a creature of instinct, born only to be caught and destroyed and like a beast you too shall perish. The Lord knows how to hold the unrighteous for the Day of Judgment, while continuing their punishment."*

A blast of light emitted from her sword and there was a clap of thunder as the man disappeared and the air rushed in to fill the void he left. The purity of that energy carried God's conviction and the first ten rows of people fell to their knees in total repentance. Rose swirled into a flowing mixture of gold and white and disappeared.

# CHAPTER FIVE

In the confusion of the crowd, as it reacted to the angelic visitation, Laura pulled the cordless microphone off of the microphone stand she had cut in two and spoke calmly to the crowd. "People! People! Please settle down!

The people in the crowd quieted and listened to her. "Remember that God is in control and He loves each one of you very much. Please exit the arena in an orderly fashion, back rows first. Reverend Kloss' ministry will see about having your ticket price refunded in the next few days. Please pray for the Reverend, that his repentance was acceptable to God and that he be forgiven. Thank you, and good night."

She turned the microphone off and motioned to the technicians. Breaking out of their state of shock, they turned on the arena lights and turned off the bright stage lights. As the lights went down, Sarah took Laura's arm and headed her off the stage through the curtain in back. As they left the area, one of the ministry managers grabbed Laura's arm and said with great anger, "You can't leave! It is because of you that the crusade was ruined and Reverend Kloss is dead! The police will want to talk to you."

Laura whirled on him and he backed up. "You sniveling coward! You were standing right next to the gunman and didn't do anything to stop him from killing the Reverend. Try to remember also, that it was one of your people that shot him. If you are a believer and I seriously wonder if your heart is for God, then you'd bettered start praying about all the money you fleeced from these people and where it has gone. The police are sure to ask you those questions very soon."

The man thought about those questions and realized that he could be in serious trouble. He decided that it would be good if he wasn't there either. He turned and ran for an exit.

Laura and Sarah found an exit from the building in the back of the arena and stepped outside. Working their way anonymously through the exiting crowd, they found their rental car and inched their way out of the parking lot. They finally reached an on-ramp to Stemmons freeway which led north to the LBJ freeway. Sarah got on LBJ heading east.

Sarah, true to her training, had been watching the vehicles around them and told Laura, "We've got a tail on us. Big, black SUV, two lanes to the left and three cars back."

Laura was praying that the Lord would help all the people that had lost their perverted healings. She hadn't quite gotten over her irritation either. "Lose them." was all she said.

Sarah watched for an off-ramp and was able to cut through two lanes of slower moving vehicles and get off at Preston Road. The SUV forced its way over to the off ramp through honking and hand-waving traffic that had to avoid a collision with the bigger vehicle. Sarah took a left and went under the interchange and saw the Galleria shopping center to her right. Spinning the wheel she shot into the multilevel parking structure. She slid to a halt and got an automated ticket. The arm went up and she took the first up ramp to the second level. Spotting an open parking place she drove into it and stopped using the emergency brake avoiding the flare of brake lights.

She told Laura to get out and they ran through two rows of cars to the railing that separated them from the up-ramp. The SUV was coming up the ramp at that point. The women ducked down behind the cars that were up against the wall and watched the SUV as it unerringly homed right in on their car. The SUV stopped and both men got out checking it. One of them held a small device he kept looking at. Sarah tagged them both as mercenaries, ex-military types with mean attitudes.

After checking the rental, one of the men took out a knife and slashed two of the rental's tires. Two more SUVs, identical to the first, pulled up. Eight more men got out and huddled up with the men from the first SUV. One of the new men passed out papers to the others. They all studied the papers and then left the vehicles, each with a driver, and broke into five groups. They headed for the store entrances on that level as the three SUVs started cruising around the parking structure.

As everybody left the area, Sarah ran, doubled over, down the aisle to the up-ramp with Laura right behind her. They then walked down the ramp to the street level and exited the structure. Walking away from the shopping center they headed south on Preston Road and back under the Interstate.

Reaching a family restaurant they went in and sat at a booth that gave them a view of the parking lot and the exit to Preston Road. Laura had calmed down enough to be more like her normal self and asked Sarah. "Now, what is that all about?"

Sarah remembered the FBI data and made an assumption. "I'd guess that the "Arrow of Vengeance" isn't too pleased with us terminating their source of funds that the Reverend was supplying them, not to mention getting the Reverend terminated at the same time."

Laura thought that over for a few minutes as she drank a cup of tea. Then she shook her head. "Well Sarah, I think we can tell the FBI that we checked out the Christian fund source and that there was definitely a demonic involvement. I think we need to get back to the aircraft and Su Li as quickly as possible."

Sarah dropped a couple of dollars on the table. "I agree but the SUVs turning into the driveway here might try to stop us. What I don't understand is how they keep tracking us no matter how we try to get lost."

It was obvious that Sarah was getting irritated about this. They got up and left by the door away from Preston Road. Laura followed Sarah as she walked around the restaurant until they could see the two black Ford SUVs sitting in front of the building. Sarah put out a hand to restrain Laura and then walked up to the first SUV in its blind spot. Carefully checking to see that the other men were busy checking out the patrons in the restaurant and that the other driver was occupied, she made her move. In a rush she closed to the side of the SUV and went up on the running board. Using a left-handed knuckle strike to the temple, she cold-cocked the driver before he knew she was there.

Stepping back down Sarah went around to the other SUV and repeated the attack on the second driver. Sarah was good at her trade. Two for two without an alarm. She opened the second vehicle's door and pulled the driver out of the SUV and pulled the unconscious form back into the bushes. She then motioned for Laura to get in that SUV. She moved the driver of the first SUV onto the floor by the rear seats and got into the driver's seat. At her signal they both backed up and drove out of the parking lot.

She led Laura down the half block of Preston to the east-bound on-ramp of the Interstate. Sarah looked in the mirror and saw some of the other mercs running down the embankment trying to catch the vehicles. Sarah and Laura drove for two miles and then exited the freeway. They dumped the second SUV behind a building across the interstate from the Texas Instruments site.

Laura joined Sarah in the first SUV with the unconscious driver. Laura drove as they headed south on the Central Expressway through the Highland Park district. Sarah stripped their hostage of his weapons and gear and used some duct tape she found to secure his wrists together and his ankles. She set him up in the back seat and started slapping him to bring him back to consciousness. He moaned and then grunted. His eyes flew open and he attempted to get loose. Settling down he looked at the two women who had taken him captive. "What do you think you're doin?" He asked in a Texas drawl.

Sarah poked him in the forehead with a finger, making him jerk back. "We'll ask the questions. The first one is why are you and your mercenary friends tracking us?"

The man sneered at Sarah, "I ain't talking to you." He turned his head away in a deliberate action to show her he wasn't concerned about her.

He jerked his head back with fear showing around the whites of his eyes when he felt the sharp edge of Sarah's knife cutting through his pants at his crotch. Sarah hadn't changed expressions and didn't verbally threaten him. "I asked you, why are you and your mercenary buddies are tracking us?" She pushed on the knife gently and some blood ran out on the blade.

The man paled and rethought his earlier statements. "Look, I'm just doing a job. Don't cut me up because I'm following orders."

Sarah pushed a little harder and the man screamed, "Agghhh! Okay, okay. I'll talk. Stop! Please stop!"

Sarah didn't change the pressure or her look. She waited for him to continue. He knew then that he really didn't have a choice. He had to talk or she would kill him. It was obvious in her eyes and he read it loud and clear. "We were given your pictures and told to find you."

Sarah nodded, "Okay, how do you keep finding us?"

The man tried to look cooperative and superior at the same time. It wasn't a good effort. "One of the people at the arena fixed a tracker unit on you."

Sarah asked him, "What kind of tracker unit?"

He looked at her with worry. "It is a clear plastic button about the size of a nickel."

Sarah checked herself over and then checked Laura as she drove. She found it on the bottom of her loose shirt on the side. Carefully pulling it off Sarah threw it out the window. The man had decided that he wanted to live bad enough that he was cooperating. He said, "That don't matter now. They can track this vehicle six ways from Sunday. They know right where you are right now."

Sarah nodded, "Yeah, I kinda figured that. Now, why do your bosses want us?"

He looked hesitant, "I don't really know. They don't tell us grunts what the drill is about."

Sarah knew that well enough. "Okay, what did you hear from the others?"

He smiled at that, "Well, they say that you ruined the Reverend's deal and our boss wants to find out how and why that happened. We're not supposed to kill you, just acquire you and bring you to him." Laura asked, "Who, exactly, is your boss?"

# CHAPTER SIX

The mercenary wanted to lie but Sarah moved the knife towards him again and he blurted out, "Barton Severon. He is the man that calls the shots! He's the one with the money and the guy who hired Major Pickett. He's the one who tells us all what to do"

A mental countdown clock in Sarah's mind had reached zero and the mention of Severon's name made her blood run cold. She smiled at the man and said, "Thanks". Reversing the knife, she smacked the mercenary in the head with the hilt hard enough to knock him out.

Turning to Laura she said, "We need to lose this vehicle, now!"

Laura saw a shopping center off of the freeway and exited. Pulling into a busy store's parking lot, she shut off the SUV and opened the door and got out. Sarah had already exited the passenger door and together they walked into the store. Five minutes later they were two stores away and Sarah took out her cell phone to call Mark. A whine in the ear piece made her look at the display. She slapped the unit closed. "They've somehow figured out our cell phone numbers and they can track this phone by its GPS signal." She pulled out the SIM card and threw the phone into a trash bin. Laura did the same.

Looking around Sarah spotted a pay phone and placed a call to the number of Mark's hotel in Washington, D.C. which she had memorized yesterday

Mark answered on the second ring. He was glad to hear his wife's voice. "Hello, lady spy, why the land line?" Mark was ebullient that they were done testifying and could head home the next morning.

Sarah sighed, "Mark, we've got problems." She outlined the events up to the phone call and asked him for advice.

Mark's happiness vaporized in listening to his wife's tale. "Okay, it sounds like you've got a tiger by the tail. You've probably ditched them by leaving the SUV and getting rid of the homer on Laura's shirt. But, they now have a good fix on what your capabilities are and will not make the same mistakes again. They're probably doing a store by store walk-through making a visual search for you guys with the vehicles roaming to form a perimeter. Can you get back to the plane?"

Sarah said that they would try and if she was able to get airborne, she would call him back on the satellite system. If they couldn't make the plane, that would mean that Su Li would be in the mercenary's hands. She told him that she would call from another phone when she found out what was going on.

Mark told her, "Don't use the cell phones. If they have the plane, then they probably got Su Li's phone and that has all the numbers in it. I'll get them changed immediately.

Hanging up the phone she looked at Laura. "Mark says to try to get back to the plane. We're only several miles or so from Dallas Love Field down the Dallas North Tollway. Let's call a cab."

Keeping a sharp watch out for their pet mercenaries; they caught a cab and got to Love Field. Getting out at the terminal entrance they paid off the cab driver and then looked around. Each woman separately attached themselves to another group for camouflage as they walked inside.

Once lost in the hustle inside the terminal they linked up and found a phone. Calling the plane resulted in a man's voice asking who was calling. Laura hung up without speaking. Getting Sarah's attention she said, "They found the plane and are in control of it. How can we help Su Li?"

Sarah was about to answer when the woman in question appeared at her elbow. Su Li was calm and her eyes sparkled. "Hi guys. You didn't happen to irritate anyone while you were out, did you?"

Laura smiled at the pretty, black-haired Asian. "Possibly, what's the situation with the plane?"

Su Li frowned. "I went to get a soft drink and on the way back I discovered we had big, mercenary rats all around the plane. So, I came over here because I figured you'd come here if there was trouble. I've been here for about thirty minutes."

Sarah spotted a pay phone. Laura and Su Li went to the ladies room. Sarah called Mark again. While she was talking to him, a man walked up behind her, shoved something hard into her back and said "Hang up the phone, now!"

Looking at the image of the newcomer in the reflection of the chrome phone housing, Sarah said, "Honey, I've got to go." She twisted to her right, arched her back, and swung the handset of the phone back into the man's face hard enough to break the hard plastic in two. A bullet skimmed across her back and smashed into the wall under the phone. Blood and flesh flew against the wall as the man's nose and gums took the beating. Turning quickly, Sarah then kneed him in the groin. As he folded up with the pain she struck him on the back of the neck with the remainder of the handset. She used all the force she had. He'd tried to kill her and so he didn't deserve any mercy. He collapsed to the floor and the gun he'd been holding fell out into the open. It was a 9MM automatic with a silencer screwed into the barrel.

Sarah calmly stooped and picked up the gun and slid it into her waistband all in one easy motion. She stepped away from the man's body and walked over to Laura and Su Li as they reappeared. "Time to fly, ladies". Laura saw the body lying on the floor and agreed.

The three of them walked quickly apart and worked their way out of the terminal through several of the passenger exits to ground transportation. Sarah stopped at the Hertz counter and rented a car with a Mossad credit card. Nervously she rode out to the lot to pick up the car. Once she had gotten it, she cruised back to the door they had left by and picked up both Laura and Su Li. Coming out of the airport she worked her way back onto Interstate 75 north and then went west on LBJ freeway towards Carrollton. It seemed that they had slipped away from their trackers for the moment.

# CHAPTER SEVEN

Barton Severon heard the phone on the other end ring once and then it was answered, "Yes?"

"Thomas? It's me, Barton. What's the hold up on those two women? I wanted them out here by now."

Tom Pickett knew people saw him as a ragged rock of a man. He stood six-foot, four-inches tall and had a weight-lifter's build with a thick chest, large biceps, and a slim waist. He also knew that his face was permanently darkened from the sun in too many hell-holes in Africa and South America. His close-cropped hair may have still been black but it was hard to tell as short as it was.

His blue eyes had seen too many good men that in his opinion had simply been wasted in the U.S. Marine Corp. Even though he was a valuable asset to the Marines he had taken his skills elsewhere. He had earned his pay as he had risen through the ranks of mercenary wars and now he had a gig that paid very well and needed a real leader. So, he appointed himself as a Major.

As he started fielding his own troops Pickett only took the most lucrative jobs and he only hired the best people who he vetted himself. Tom Pickett had heard that Barton Severon was offering a major mission. Tom also felt that he and his men were the only ones up to the task to implement it for the Billionaire. It really didn't matter to Pickett if he didn't he agree with the rich man's obsession but, his Team were the best. Tom was clearly aware that Severon knew that Tom Pickett wasn't afraid of anyone. Beside that fact was well known that Pickett charged more than other teams but had a solid record of successes. In reality, Tom Pickett didn't care about money other than what it could do for him.

When he'd been hired by Barton, Tom knew that the man demanded results and that he had more money than skills, but the two of them complemented each other. Together they had forged a powerful team to accomplish the Billionaire's goals. They also understood each other and got along well without threats or bravado. But trust was a wavering goal. Both men kept a sharp eye on the other to see if they had a knife in the hand that was patting them on the back.

Tom answered his boss. "We're running into complications. So far these two broads have destroyed Kloss' ministry, beat up six of his flunkies, and then eluded my men more times than I can count. At that point, they got creative and commandeered two of our SUVs and captured one of the drivers."

Barton was stunned. "What did your driver know?"

Tom shook his head, "Nothing of value. He wasn't one of the brightest lights on the tree so we left him in the dark. We've got both of the SUVs back and both drivers have been dismissed as unworthy. We caught up with the women at Love field, apparently attempting to get to a corporate plane. When we broadcast a picture of these gals, we got a call from our guy at the airport. He'd seen these two get off of the bizjet this afternoon. We confiscated the plane. It's licensed to a private corporation in Denver called Technology Alternatives, Inc. We're looking into that now. We got a cell phone and blocked the numbers when they tried to use them."

Barton thought about that. "Well, that's good work. Do they still have a tracer on them?"

Tom replied in the negative, "No. We found it on the roadside off of Interstate 75."

Barton said, "Keep looking for them. They seem very capable and that worries me. Tell your man at Love Field I appreciate his being on the ball."

Tom frowned at the phone. "I can't do that Barton, he's dead. Apparently he tried to take one of the women captive by himself rather than waiting for us. He lost."

Barton thought for a few seconds. "Listen, since you've lost them, I'm going to bring the police in on this. I'll get them to believe that the two women are suspects in both the murder of Reverend Kloss and also your man at Love Field."

Tom asked, "Do you think that's a wise thing to do? Bring the cops in and you could well get the Feds. They know the history on the guy at the airport. Right now he's just a John Doe because he never carried any identification and his fingerprints aren't on file locally. Also, if the cops catch them, then they have a chance to tell their story. I really advise against any involvement by the police. My men will find them and we will get them for you without any Government entanglements."

Barton didn't like the limitations but then Tom knew a lot more about this stuff than he did. "Okay, but don't mess this up. Those two women are just too capable to just be housewives and that really concerns me. If they are connected to the military or the Government, I've just wasted twenty-two million dollars."

Tom agreed with him that it was imperative that they find the women and neutralize their threat. He hung up and went to find some troops.

Barton sat there in the quiet luxury of his country home and stared sadly at the beautiful countryside for a while. Then a tear formed in the corner of his right eye as he whispered, "Donny, oh, Donny, they'll be sorry. I won't let anything stop us."

# CHAPTER EIGHT

Tom called in three of his best men. He maintained a military posture in all his organizations. The three men stood at ease with their hands behind them. Tom stood before them and spoke quietly and commandingly. "I have a new lead to help find these two women. We found out that they rented a car under an assumed name at the airport. He handed out a flyer. "The descriptions of the vehicle, both women, and a list, ^&@@!" He waved the papers in the air. "A list of all the men they've beaten so far. Don't let me down on this. Call all our contacts and backers. Have them get their runners and cars out looking for this rental. I don't care what you have to spend to get cooperation. Just get it and find them. Your job, and possibly your lives depend on finding them and neutralizing them. We need at least one of them alive for questioning. Now get out there and make me proud of you."

Within twenty minutes, hundreds of pairs of eyes were looking for the black car all over Dallas. That number would grow in less than an hour to over two thousand people in the hunt with a ten-grand reward as the prize.

At the moment, the subjects of this manhunt were hunkered down in a hotel room on Belt Line Road just off of the Dallas North Tollway. They had parked the car two blocks away at another hotel's parking lot that they could watch from their tenth story window on the off chance their enemy traced the rental.

Sarah punched in a cut-out number and waited. When she got a dial tone again she quickly punched in an eighteen digit number. When a voice asked what she wanted in a Midwest American accent Sarah answered back in Hebrew. In three seconds she was connected with David Zahavy. The man had been her boss in the Mossad and was still a good friend. He had managed to move up again even though he openly admitted that he was a Messianic Jew who loved Jesus. He was very good at his job.

His precise voice was like music to Sarah's ears. "Shalom Sarah. What is the crisis this time?" There was a note of humor behind the serious words. Sarah knew that the humor was there because David was literally a dead man walking. The Lord had restored him to life after he had been shot dead by a radical PLO member as he prevented the man from killing Sarah and Laura in Israel.

Sarah said, "Barton Severon".

David said, "Ahh, I see. Hang on a second while I pull up his file.

After he scanned the report he said, "So! You've gotten yourself tangled up with a real anti-Semite that is certifiable and has a lot of money. Not a good combination. What do you need?"

That's one thing Sarah always admired about the man. He was always straight to the point. "It seems that he has acquired a Para-military organization in Dallas, Texas, in the U.S. And this organization is also somehow involved in some demonic activities. The problem is that Laura, Su Li, and I have backed into this buzzsaw and this rich nutcase seems to want us dead. They have tried four times to kidnap us and once now to kill me. They are good enough that they have compromised our communications by cell phone and found and took control of our jet at Love Field. We may have shaken them for a little bit but I have the feeling that they will be on our heels soon. I need you to give me a reason for this open display of aggression against us, assuming that they don't know my background."

David thought for a few minutes. "I would suspect that you have interfered with a project he has underway, or he assumes you will interfere with one. I would have a better idea if I knew who was running his little army."

Sarah said, "The name I have is a Major Pickett."

David typed the name in his computer. "Ahh, Thomas Pickett, a very able and courageous mercenary. Quite honorable in a person who doesn't care who he works for or how many people his operations kill. A generous man but very methodical in his operations. I do believe that the man is totally fearless. This, of course, as you know, is a weakness that can be exploited. Hmm, Severon and Pickett, that's quite a package."

Sarah let him ramble on because she knew that he was actually thinking of all the angles and possibilities of the situation. She had trusted David with her life more times than she could remember and the fact that she was still alive was proof that he had never let her down.

Sarah added to his mental calculations. "David, I believe they're using the name "Arrow of Vengeance" this time."

David came back with, "So, it's the Severon and Pickett combination that calls themselves the Arrow of Vengeance? Good, we weren't aware of that information.

David finally cleared his throat. "Sarah darling, I think that you may have stumbled into something momentous. There are several reports that the experts in the Mossad, the American CIA and NSA  suspect that the Arrow of Vengeance was responsible for an attack on a Pakistani military outpost. The attackers killed everyone at the outpost, including women and children. The death count was over two hundred."

Sarah asked, "What were they after, and, did they get it?"

David sighed, "A ten-kiloton nuclear weapon. And yes, they did get it and got it out of the country somehow. I must remind you that his group is only "suspected" of being the ones to do it. There were no military witnesses left alive in the outpost."

Sarah asked him, "Then why do the experts feel it was the "Arrow of Vengeance"?"

The reason they believe it was Pickett's group is because they killed only three of the four people in one of the outposts. Pickett is hyper-critical on his planning. He plans his attacks down to the last bullet. It was just one of those things that screw up the best plans. One of the soldiers was sweet on a young woman and had smuggled her into his outpost. The other two men there must have known about her but she kept hidden so that her boyfriend didn't get into trouble with his superiors. When the attackers raced through the outposts they knew there were supposed to be three men there. They killed three men and moved on.

After they were gone she crawled out of her hiding place to find everybody dead. She looked at the main post and saw bodies everywhere. She got the guard's high-powered binoculars and looked at the camp to see if she could find her sister. Her sister had apparently already been killed by then but was inside a building. While this young lady was looking around, she saw the attackers bringing out a large crate on a skid. That was the nuclear weapon. She got a really good close-up of the man giving the orders. When she reported all this to the authorities after the raiders were gone, they had her look through pictures of known mercenaries that could have pulled this off. There was only a handful in the world still alive that could do it. She positively identified Pickett as the man in charge. But, no one knew where he is, or was, until this call."

Sarah had been reviewing her mental files and asked David, "I don't believe that there is a large enough Jewish population in Dallas to warrant such a raid or such a weapon."

David laughed, "Don't jump to conclusions little one. There are a whole lot of places in the world Severon would be able to use his new little toy. It doesn't have to be local."

Sarah laughed back, "True, but Severon is here, Pickett is here, and we seem to have stirred up a hornets nest."

Sarah's new cell phone beeped twice in her purse. She told David to hang on and answered it. "Yes?"

Mark's voice sounded very comfortable to her ear. "Hi Spylady. I've got all the phones but Su Li's reprogrammed now. Your new number is on your display. Jack and I are twenty minutes out of DFW Airport. Where can we find you?"

Sarah laughed, "I've got David on the land line and he has a lot of information that we needed. Let me keep talking to him and I'll let Laura tell you where we are." She handed the phone to Laura who had been listening to the conversation.

Talking to David again she brought him up to date. "I just heard from Mark. He and Jack will be here in less than a half an hour."

David laughed again, "I'll bet that Barton Severon doesn't know what he's messing with and I think the shoe will be on the other hand fairly soon. Keep me informed ayshet chayil. (This meant a woman of valor). Shalom."

Sarah answered, "L'chaim Chochom, shalom." (To life, wise one, Peace).

Su Li chimed in with, "Heads up ladies, we have enemy action at the rental vehicle."

Laura was still talking to Jack on the cell phone as she and Sarah joined Su Li at the window and watched the black SUV pull up near the rental car in the parking lot two blocks away.

# CHAPTER NINE

There was a knock at the door to the bedroom. In one fluid motion Sarah stepped away from the window, dropped the cell phone on the bed, turned and drew the silenced 9MM pistol. She took a two-handed Weaver stance aiming at the door. Su Li went to answer the knock. Laura told Jack what was happening and made herself scarce in the coat closet alcove.

Su Li opened the door and squealed in delight. She jumped out of sight and then came back in leading Captain Wollard of the Crossfire Sensitive Operations Group (SOG). Sarah safed her weapon and Laura came back out into view.

Captain Wollard spoke into the combat microphone just barely visible under his collar. "Quarterback to team, softsides located. Home on my signal."

Laura raised an eyebrow, "Softsides?"

The Captain smiled, "You'll have to talk to your husband about the codenames General Connelly. Do you have any contact with the enemy?"

Sarah indicated the window and they walked over to it. The black SUV had been joined by two more just like it. Two of the mercenary personnel were looking at the rental car and others were coming out of the hotel it was parked at.

Captain Wollard pulled out a set of combat binoculars and studied the men. "I saw two of those boys in the service a few years ago. Shame." He keyed his combat microphone and pushed a button on the binoculars. The picture he was seeing was being transmitted to the rest of the SOG along with the GPS coordinates. "We have approximately twelve hard cases in the parking lot of the Hyatt Regency. Jam all cell phone and radio frequencies and see if we can get them all."

The small crew in the bedroom watched two armed Humvees pull into the parking lot from either end and confront the mercenary troops. Since the Humvees each had soldiers manning an M-60 heavy machine gun and two

SAWs, the bad guys were way outgunned. The SOG troops put the mercenaries on the ground and cleared them of weapons. Then they used riot cuffs on them and got them back on their feet. Needless to say, the normal citizens were very impressed by the military hardware and all the armed men. Several Dallas County Sheriff's cars accompanied the Humvees and the police were involved in the bust advising each of the mercenaries of their rights.

Captain Wollard's bone conduction speaker vibrated and he turned to Sarah and Laura, "General Connelly and General Malone have arrived and should be here in approximately one minute."

True to his prediction, Jack and Mark opened the door and came into the room in less than sixty seconds. They first got a situation update from the Captain. After explaining the situation, he saluted, basically, the whole room, and then left.

Jack and Laura hugged each other and Jack kissed her. "Boy, we can't leave you gals alone for one day without you stirring up a hornet's nest." Sarah hugged and smiled at Mark, "Boy, you are a sight for sore eyes. I thought we were going to have to keep dancing with these bozos for the next day or so."

Mark smiled a grim smile. "Thank God you won't have to, but I want to talk to a few of them."

Checking out of their room the whole crew went downstairs and out the front door of the hotel. Two more Humvees were waiting for them out front. They boarded and in twenty minutes they were at the Sheriff's station. Jack went to the Sheriff and discussed their options.

The Sheriff was a trim, white-haired officer in a tailored uniform. He set his coffee cup down and looked at the paperwork in his hand. "I don't know General; these guys have concealed handgun permits and weren't really breaking the law. I doubt that you have grounds to hold them over twenty-four hours." He looked at Jack to see how he wanted to proceed.

Jack looked at his watch and told the Sheriff. "We appreciate your cooperation and thank you for allowing us to operate in your county. There should be federal warrants for each of these men delivered to you in the next twenty minutes. Several of these men are wanted on multiple murder warrants by Interpol and on International warrants from the nation of Pakistan. It has been confirmed that six of them were at a Pakistani outpost where a nuclear weapon was stolen. The raiders killed over 200 men, women, and children on the raid. The other six men are possibles and the U.S. Government wants to interrogate them and see if they were part of the raid. Homeland Security will be holding them all on terroristic warrants."

The Sheriff was nodding, "Yep, I'd say that would do it. We'll hold them until I get the warrants and then we'll transport them where the warrants dictate."

Jack frowned. "Sheriff, I would like to recommend that you request the military transport them. There are probably a lot more of them out there with heavy weapons and no compulsions. They wouldn't hesitate to attack this station or your transport if they can overwhelm your officers."

"Crap!" The Sheriff spit out. "What have we got here? The beginning of World War Three?"

Jack sighed, "I don't know, but I hope it won't be that bad. There is the possibility that they have brought that nuclear weapon to Dallas."

That thought made the Sheriff blanch. He went to his desk and sat down. He took a big drink of his coffee and shook his head. "Once I get those warrants, I want to get these fellows out of here as quickly as possible. My SWAT Team isn't geared to handle military attacks.

Jack smiled a grim smile. "Don't worry, while the prisoners are in here the Crossfire troops will keep things quiet and they are more than sufficiently armed and ready if the other mercenaries try anything.

Mark walked into the Sheriff's office. "Sheriff, I would like to interrogate two of the prisoners if you'll assign an officer to accompany me."

Eyeing Mark's physique the Sheriff nodded. "Loomis" he yelled. One of the deputies stepped into the office. "Sergeant Loomis, accompany the General here and assist him in interviewing two of our new guests. Remember gentlemen, they may be scum, and murderers, but under our system of law they have rights. Don't touch them unless it is allowed by the rules or in self-defense. Do I make myself clear?"

Mark nodded since he knew this lecture was for his benefit. "Don't worry Sheriff, I know the rules." The two men left and Mark pointed out the one he wanted first. Taking him out of the cell and to a holding room, Sergeant Loomis handcuffed the man's wrists behind him and to a lock ring on the chair. The chair was bolted to the floor.

Mark shut the door and sat down across from the prisoner. Five minutes later he got up and motioned the deputy to follow him out of the room. After closing the door, Mark nodded and said, "Good, just what I expected."

The deputy looked at the ex-SEAL with confusion. "He didn't say a word, how can that be good?"

Mark smiled at the younger man. "I didn't expect him to crack or help us at all. He's really just stage dressing for the main act. Now, do me a favor. I saw that you've got a medical dummy in your back room for first-aid practice. Get that for me, please, and don't let the other prisoners see it.

While the deputy was getting the dummy, Mark went into the holding room and took the prisoner's shirt and pants off of him. This required unlocking him briefly but Mark told him that if he even thought about doing anything except what he was told to do, he would personally break his neck. It was obvious that Mark wasn't bluffing. After he locked the man down again he taped the man's mouth closed, went out to the hall, and closed the door leaving the man in his underwear.

The deputy got back with the full-body dummy through the back corridor and helped Mark dress it in the borrowed clothes. Then Mark had the deputy bring some of the stage blood they used to make the dummy realistic during medical training. He rearranged the limbs to look like both legs and one arm were broken with compound fractures and then made it look like there were three gunshots to the chest. Arranging the dummy on a litter so that the face was covered Mark stood back and admired his handiwork. It would do. He told the deputy to wait a minute. He went back to the Sheriff and explained what he was doing. After the Sheriff agreed, Mark went to the shooting range in the back of the facility but left both doors open. He then fired three rounds in rapid fire down the range. The echoes of the shots were heard throughout the jail.

Mark got Jack to help with the little play and walked by the main cell area with his automatic out and still smoking. Behind him, Jack and the deputy carried the litter with the dummy on it out of the holding room area and past the main cells. Every one of the prisoners saw the body on the litter leaking blood from the gunshots and the mangled and broken limbs.

Mark pointed at another prisoner and said, "Him next!"

The man had just seen what happened to the strongest of their group and didn't want to go. The deputy took out his night stick and the man finally stood up and allowed himself to be handcuffed and led from the cell.

The deputy took him to a different holding room and locked him down. Mark sat down across from him and smiled. "I just asked your friend these questions. He was reluctant to answer. That was just too bad for him. Now, I will ask you the same questions. I have ten more people to ask after you. Where is Tom Pickett and what are you planning to do with the nuclear weapon you stole?"

It was obvious that Mark wouldn't hesitate to torture and kill the prisoner. Heck, he'd just seen what had happened to the first man. These people didn't play by the rules. Probably working under military permission to do whatever it takes to get their information. The man just knew one of the others would talk and any sacrifice he made would be a waste. So he might as well be the one to save his hide. "The Major works out of a ranch just north of the Colony near Frisco. Just off of highway 423 on Stewarts Creek Road. The house is an empty front. The operation is run from the big barn in back."

Mark wrote down the information, including the address. "You know if you're lying, I'll be back?"

The man nodded. He was dead anyway at this point and he just didn't care.

Mark asked him, "How many men has he got?"

The man thought for a few seconds, "Without us he's probably got ninety to a hundred more troops."

Mark wrote again. "What heavy equipment and weapons does he have?"

The man chuckled, "He don't have any tanks if that's what you're asking. He's got everything else though. He's got everything from rifles to Stingers. A few heavy machine guns, M-60s, a classic twin .50 setup, and a bunch of LAWs. Most of it is carried by SUVs and eighteen wheelers."

Mark wrote and then asked the real question. "What is he going to do with that nuclear weapon he stole?"

The man looked Mark in the eyes. "I really don't have a clue. He had a select crew get it and then went doggo on any information after that. I thought they were going to sell it on the black market but I haven't heard anything, really I haven't."

Mark believed him. But his comments confirmed the fact that it was Pickett that stole it from Pakistan. "Okay, one more question. What time lines are you aware of?"

The prisoner knew that Mark was familiar with these types of operations because of his detailed questions. No use in trying to snow him. "We have to be done with our operation by the end of this month."

Mark thought about his answers and nodded to the deputy. "Take him back to the cell."

After that was done, they redressed the other man and took him back to the cell too. That raised some eyebrows and a strange mixture of happiness to see him and disappointment that he hadn't really been killed. Mark locked eyes with the talkative prisoner and slightly shook his head. The prisoner knew he had been conned but could keep his lips shut and no one would know he talked. He gave the barest nod to Mark.

Mark looked at the other prisoners in their cell. He commented to the deputy. "These guys aren't talking so I'm just going to let the troops at Guantanamo have a crack at them.

# CHAPTER TEN

Mark met with Jack and Laura as they talked to the Sheriff. Mark held up both hands with his fists clenched in a victory symbol. "Well, our little charade worked. I got whatever the man knew. It confirms that Pickett was the man that stole the weapon from Pakistan and that Severon was behind it. But he didn't have any more than that. They're playing it close to the vest so that we can't get the information from the soldiers."

He looked up. "Sheriff, could you have a car check this address? It's in your county and where the merc said that Pickett is working out of right now."

The Sheriff looked concerned. "I know every one my men personally and I don't want to send one to get killed on a fool's errand."

Mark smiled, "Don't worry; I just want to confirm that they are gone from there. Its standard operating procedure to abandon a base that could be compromised by troops that have been captured or gone missing. I know Pickett and he is a stickler for conformity to operational guidelines. I'd bet they were pulling out twenty minutes after they lost contact with this bunch. But, tell your man not to try to open the barn or anything else. I wouldn't put it past Pickett to leave a few nasty surprises around. Like a Claymore mine for example."

The Sheriff told the dispatcher to send a car and to advise the deputy what to be careful about.

Jack moved aside and asked Mark. "What do we do now? We've stung Pickett and now he knows we have military capabilities. He won't be caught like this again."

Mark nodded in agreement. "True, but if I can predict what he is going to do then we have an edge. The real worry is the deadline. We still don't know what he is going to do with that bomb. We need to brainstorm this with the others including David Zahavy."

The Sheriff interrupted them. "My man says that the place is deserted and a neighbor said that eight big trucks loaded up and left to the north an hour ago."

The federal warrants came in and a detachment of Army troops showed up to escort the prisoners to an unnamed federal facility. Homeland Security was imposing the Patriot Act policy of terrorist apprehension. These guys were not allowed to operate under civilian rights. They took the twelve men and left.

Laura and Sarah had dictated their statements about the events at the Reunion Arena and Love Field so that the police could be looking for someone other than them.

Thanking the Sheriff and his people for their help, the Team took the SOG and drove to the old Carswell Air Force Base which had been decommissioned and was now the Naval Air Station Joint Reserve Base in Fort Worth. The base was secure from Pickett or Severon's spies. The base is home to a fighter squadron and a Marine Air Group. The Crossfire Team was housed with the 14th Marines of the 4th Marine Division on the base.

Collecting together in a really large ready room, the combined Crossfire Team and the SOG numbered forty people. Mark explained the situation to the entire group and asked for ideas or concepts for locating and eliminating the mercenary group and if possible, finding the weapon. David Zahavy had left Mossad Headquarters and wasn't available right then.

Many suggestions were made and the top three were decided upon. The group was broken into three groups, one to follow up on each of the ideas.

Laura and Sara were complemented by twelve of the SOG warriors and were to try and lure Pickett's men into trying to capture them again. If the mercenaries came after them, then the Team could possibly track them back to their base. This concept probably had the least chance since the mercenary leader had lost twelve men the last time he tried it and would be leery of a trap.

Su Li and fifteen of the SOG were going to work with other agencies to see if they could track the movement of the mercenaries to their new base.

Jack and the remaining seven SOG personnel were going to research Severon's activities and see if they could determine anything about the bomb or Pickett's operations.

Mark made the assignments and then left to follow up on an idea he had. Before he left, Sarah stopped him and reminded him of what happened to Jack in Denver when he left on his own to investigate a lead.

Mark looked thoughtful for a minute. Then he took her in his arms and told her, "I know the risks honey, I'll keep my tracker on me and I'll check in often. But, if what I suspect is true of Pickett, I might be able to get a lead on him by talking to the mercenaries in the area that he hasn't hired. Jealousy is big in that field and the left outs will be eager to see him fail because he didn't take them along. If I can find one that has information it could cut down our required efforts considerably. I have to do it alone because these types are street smart, suspicious, and won't talk to many people, definitely not more than one at a time." Sarah nodded and kissed him. "Be careful, please? I love you and don't want to keep fighting if you're not there to fight next to me."

They split up and each group started their projects that afternoon and through the evening.

Su Li and her Team contacted the alphabet agencies and worked with them for information concerning Pickett, Severon, or the mercenaries working for them. Captain Wollard called the NSA in Mark's name and explained the situation. The NSA did a search of any recent passes over the north of Texas. Isolating the proper tracks they did a time search and were rewarded by a Keyhole satellite that was over the proper area at the right time. Analysis of the photos showed the arrival of the trucks at the ranch, loading, and departure. The trucks went north on 423 to Highway 380 and then east to Interstate 75. The trucks turned north and drove out of the scanning area. The NSA couldn't find a parallel track that showed where the trucks went. The next scan of the northern part of Texas was thirty minutes later and the trucks could not be seen.

The Captain's next call was to Homeland Security to register the possible nuclear terrorist threat and seek assistance in tracking it down. They took the information and told him they'd get back to him in the next two hours.

The other agencies were each willing to share what they had on the mercenary and the Billionaire. The definite identification of the Arrow of Revenge as the Pakistani raiders kicked several operations into gear to find them.

# CHAPTER ELEVEN

Sarah arranged for a television interview at their hotel room concerning the events at Reunion Arena. The interview didn't give away their location but Sarah was sure that Pickett had the brains to get the location from the TV people by hook or by crook. The trap was baited but to make it realistic they had to actually be there so that a soft probe could confirm it. Then when an attempt to get them occurred, the SOG soldiers that were charged with watching from a distance would attempt to track the raiders back to their lair.

Sarah and Laura would have to fend for themselves during any such attack. The SOG could come to their rescue but only after the attack started.

Su Li and the inter-agency Team started fielding phone and email leads and sending out teams to see if there was any truth to the lead. So far nothing had checked out as being Pickett's hideout.

Jack and his group started tracking Severon's activities and attempting to determine if there was any link they could follow that would lead them to Pickett and the stolen weapon. They got federal warrants and started monitoring all of Severon's phone calls and emails. They also instituted a 24-hour surveillance of Severon's known haunts such as his home.

Mark started circulating throughout the mercenary world looking for men that hadn't made the cut with Pickett. Two days later he struck pay dirt in one Lenny Goldman. Goldman was a good mercenary soldier with a good record of combat in some of the worst hellholes that attracted mercs. He was fairly smart and very talented, but he was of Jewish descent. His father had been Jewish and that was an absolute killer where Severon was concerned. Even if Lenny was a "failed" Jew, he was still genetically a Jew.

Mark sat in a dimly lit bar with Lenny and discussed Pickett. "Yeah, I wanted to join up with him too, but he said I was too old."

Lenny laughed a low chuckle. "I wasn't too old, I was too Jewish. The schmutz!" (filth, scum).

Nodding his agreement Mark picked up his beer and said, "L'chaim Lenny. I couldn't agree more. The thing that irks me the most is that he wouldn't tell me what the gig was about, since I wasn't qualified to join his elite little group."

Lenny shook his head. "Oh, I know what he was hiring for. Buy me another drink and I'll enlighten you."

Mark called for another round on his tab.

Lenny got his new drink and took a sip. Setting it down the mercenary moved closer to Mark. "Listen, this needs to be kept quiet, but, if you have any loved ones in Dallas make sure they are a long way away on the first of next month. Hear me?"

Mark just nodded and played dumb. Lenny looked around to make sure no one was listening. Satisfied that they were alone he looked at Mark with severity. "Pickett has stolen a nuclear weapon from Pakistan and plans to bring it to Dallas and set it off in the downtown area on the first!"

Mark acted amazed, "But why? What's his motive for killing so many people?"

Lenny took another sip and laughed again. "So that everyone will think that the Israelis did it, why else?"

Mark shook his head and asked him, "How is he going to put the blame on Israel?"

Lenny frowned into his drink. Looking up he said, "I don't know for sure but what I do know is that Severon is spending millions on computer wizards and high-level cryptographers. He has a whole think tank of electronics gurus and internet brains and all these other guys working twenty-four, seven. I don't know how he is going to pull it off but I know he's spending money that totally eclipses most merc contracts. And I can't have a part in it because I'm descended from a Jew."

Mark thought for a few seconds and then asked Lenny, "What if we broke in and stole some of his computer wizards or his programs and demanded that he let us in on it."

Lenny looked shocked. "Are you out of your mind? Pickett would hunt us down and fillet us over a slow fire for a whole week. Anyway, how would you pull that off? Ain't nobody knows where those guys are located."

Mark said, "Oh yeah, I didn't think of that, sorry."

After another drink and a discussion as to linking up on any future contract either one of them heard of, Mark paid up and left.

Triple checking to eliminate any tails he worked his way back to his car. Thirty minutes later he was back in Ft. Worth calling a meeting of the Team and the SOG.

# CHAPTER TWELVE

After Sarah and Laura arrived, Mark briefed them on the information he had learned. Afterward he asked for comments or thoughts.

Captain Jane Maxwell raised her hand. When Mark pointed at her she stood up. Jane had one of the highest ratings in the intelligence community. Her ability for intuitive reasoning was uncanny in that she could take a few unconnected items and often decipher a complete concept from them. She addressed the whole group of what had become her friends. "I have a concern about this information. It could be a false lead that Pickett gave to this Lenny character, just in the event he talked to someone at a later date. Or, it is only Lenny's pipedreams. Looking at the operation from a practical standpoint, it just doesn't make sense."

She addressed the leadership. "If Pickett and Severon can get the Pakistani bomb into Dallas there really aren't any ways they can disguise the nuclear signature of the explosion. It will be instantly identified as the stolen Pakistani core. If you take that into account, then they have to fabricate a story that the Israelis stole the bomb and planted it in Dallas. What for? The U.S. is the largest supporter of the Jewish nation in the world. Rogue Israeli agents attempting to drive a wedge between the U.S. and Israel because they think the U.S. has too much influence in their country? Again, why would that be believed and how would they do it?"

She raised her hands in an expansive gesture. "Even if they could provide a believable story, the resultant investigations wouldn't bear them out. The U.S. will not launch a retaliatory raid against Israel regardless of how much Mr. Severon wants it to do that. There is something wrong with this whole setup, either the information is wrong or he is planning something else." She sat down.

Mark looked around, "Comments?"

Nobody could answer the questions Jane posed because they just didn't have enough information to make a value judgment.

Jack asked the group, "What does anyone think about this "brain trust" that Lenny mentioned? What is its purpose? Why is Severon dropping millions into it? If he has the bomb, what is he researching?"

Again, no concrete concepts were offered.

Mark stood up. "All right, let's get back to work and see what we can find out with these new leads."

Jack and Mark got some coffee and sat down to think about the whole thing. Jack stirred his coffee and asked Mark, "What do you think is going on?"

Mark sat back and sighed, "I really don't know but I can tell you this. We have less than three weeks to stop it. I think we need to really bring in the Government to expand the effort. If we try to run with this and fumble the ball, then millions of people could die and it would because of our pride. During our week of prayer I told the Lord I would never let my pride be an idol again. I meant that." The look on Mark's face confirmed his resolve.

Jack nodded, "I agree with the concept of asking for more help, but let's keep it as classified as possible. I'm sure Severon has purchased eyes and ears in the Government with the kind of money he's throwing around. First, let's talk to Gary Rhodes of the FBI and see if he can help."

The Resident Agent for the Federal Bureau of Investigation in Denver wanted to wake up from a horrible dream. In this dream he had just managed to survive a nuclear terrorist attack on the city of Denver and now, less than a month later he was faced with a nuclear terrorist attack on the city of Dallas, Texas. Dallas wasn't even in his jurisdiction. But the voice on the phone, and the dream wouldn't go away. He listened to Jack Malone as he described how the Crossfire Team, responding to an FBI request out of Washington, D. C., had plunged them into a second WMD scenario in less than thirty days. Gary sighed and shifted mental gears. This was a real threat and from the information Jack was giving him, it meant that there were possible agents of the enemy within the Government.

Gary knew the double-edged sword that a national Government presented to the country. The huge amount of personnel, necessary to solve problems bigger than a single state could handle, resulted in a bureaucracy that could easily become a home for workers who would look the other way or spy for ridiculously small sums of money to supplement their merger salaries. He told Jack that he would contact Joe Sobbel and get the machine that was the FBI into high gear without compromising the operation.

Meanwhile a thousand miles away, Severon answered the phone on the first ring. "Yes?"

Tom Pickett's voice was strained. "Barton, we have a problem. We identified the ownership of the plane and discovered we are butting heads with a group known as the Crossfire Team. Both of the women we're after are on that team. They have high level connections with the Government and apparently have created a small operations group of specialized military personnel for their own use. I believe it was that group that captured our people in Dallas."

Barton thought for a few seconds. "Who is the leader of this team?"

Pickett shot back, "A guy named Malone, Jack Malone. The light-haired gal in the pictures from Kloss' operation is his wife, Laura. Malone mainly runs a small research and development company in Denver, but this Crossfire Team is apparently operating out of a secure facility outside of the city."

Barton said, "I think I know of some people who might like to take a shot at this team. It would take the heat off of us until we can accomplish our goal."

Pickett liked the idea. "I put the word out on this team to all our Government contacts, especially the big one. If they know anything I'll let you know."

After Pickett hung up, Barton called a small group of like-minded individuals and discussed the Crossfire Team. One in particular had several good suggestions. His concept was to fight fire with fire. He knew of an Asian outfit that had been pretty well mangled by the Crossfire Team and were itching to get even. It would take some serious cash but they thought that they could handle Barton's problems for him. Barton told him to work out the details and that money wasn't an object in this case.

# CHAPTER THIRTEEN

Bill Colton finished unloading the last crate off of the semi. He spun the fork lift in a 180-degree half-circle and took it to the staging area. Setting the pallet down, he parked the fork lift next to the end of the row of crates and shut it down. One of the other men came over to him and told him the brass wanted to see him.

Jumping off the fork lift and removing his gloves, Bill headed through the cavernous warehouse building to the row of offices at the side of the structure. Opening the door he walked in and stopped at the desk. He saluted Major Pickett and stood at parade rest waiting for his superior to enlighten him as to what he wanted.

Tom Pickett looked up at Captain Colton and smiled. Out of all the people he'd hired for this contract, Bill Colton seemed to be the best. The man was the first to start work and the last to quit. He was sharp and well liked by the rest of the mercs. He wasn't perfect though; he did like to party too much and had a taste for alcohol that might get in his way if the reports were true. But then, in the field he worked in, that was almost a standard vice.

Tom had watched the six-foot tall resident of Portland, Oregon in training and on operations. There was something too good about him to be a mercenary. But, while the man was a specialist with a laser-focused drive for the goal, he was flexible enough to resolve problems on a strike that allowed for success even when the parameters changed. Tom hadn't known whether to get rid of him or promote him. The latest information he'd gotten from Severon cemented his decision.

Tom sat back and asked the man, "Bill, how do you see our situation in light of this latest problem?"

Bill thought quickly about the loss of twelve men and the probable involvement of the U.S. Military as opposition. "Well sir, I am under the impression that you expected something like this to happen as we get closer to H-hour. I regret the loss of the guys but there are losses in any conflict. They were specialists but they only made up a small percentage of the force and were compartmentalized well enough that they don't compromise the operation. The involvement of the U.S. Military should cause us to tighten up our operations and make us more cautious, but I don't see that it should prevent us from achieving our objective. Whatever that is of course."

Tom liked the summation and the little zinger on the end. "Okay Bill, I think you understand the situation. Since we lost two of the other Captains in this snafu I am promoting you to the rank of Major with all pay and benefits of that rank. I need a man that can understand the big picture and help me run this outfit." He took the Major's oak leaf clusters off of his collar and got up and replaced Bill's Captain's bars with the clusters. Yeah, they did look good on Bill. Then he opened a drawer and took out a set of Bird Colonel's gold eagle insignia and put them on his uniform.

He got up and looked at his reflection in a mirror. Pleased with the new rank he turned to the new Major and told him to sit down. It was time he learned what they were doing and how he was going to help get it done.

Bill Colton wasn't shocked that he got picked for the position. He'd worked harder and smarter than any of the other men. He was a cut above the normal merc and had proven it in a dozen battlefields. He should be a better soldier than most of them. Besides normal military training he had spent three years in the Mossad honing his capabilities and his image. But something about the timing of this promotion bothered him.

His long tenure as a mercenary soldier had been very profitable for the Israeli intelligence service. He had been instrumental in blunting or completely destroying a dozen contract assignments against the little nation. But this one was the jackpot. Having been at the right place at the right time, he had been hired by Pickett right after their big raid in Pakistan.

Bill knew exactly what they had stolen and had played his part as a leader of the grunts precisely and without any undue interest in the overall operation of the group. Just like the mercenary he had been for years. His cover was real and very complete. Most of the men out there had served with him on other contracts. There were a lot more that weren't in this world any more that had known him too.

His deep cover work had paid off even though it had meant that he hadn't seen his home or family for the entire time of his mercenary career. He had gotten to go to Portland, Oregon in the U.S. to visit his "family" seven times in ten years. He had gotten a chance to relax among real friends and speak Hebrew for a few days each time. He also had been extensively debriefed each time he could get away.

This assignment for Severon was the pinnacle of his undercover career. If he could undermine this operation he could finally retire back to Israel. That was, if he survived. These people weren't idiots and they were incredibly well connected. The higher his visibility in the operation, the more vulnerable he became. So, he had to do this right and find out what was involved. Hopefully he could then turn it over to his superiors and disappear.

As he sat there and listened to "Colonel" Pickett explaining the operation, his blood ran cold. Severon and Pickett had this thing incredibly well crafted. They were on the brink of creating a terrible disaster that would be pinned on Israel with all the evidence vaporized in the bomb in Dallas. This was a much bigger threat than anyone anticipated, including the Mossad.

Bill realized that Pickett was watching him carefully and any slip would be fatal. He submerged his Jewish knowledge and life as Joseph Goldberg, into the persona of Bill Colton, mercenary. He had to be the mercenary until he could find a way to warn his country. He also realized that this promotion would bring him out of the field and into constant contact with Pickett. The chance for a slipup was terribly real and his loss would be Israel's loss.

Tom Pickett sat back and asked Bill, "What do you think?"

Bill was enthusiastic and made it clear that he really hadn't ever had a chance to be in on anything as big as this before. This was the truth. The stakes were much higher than he had ever had to deal with. He was shaking from concern that he could fail and it came across to Pickett as eagerness.

Pickett picked up a sheath of photos and paper. "Okay, here's the first thing I want you to handle." He handed the package over to Bill. "Those two broads who messed up Kloss' action have surfaced again." He punched up the VCR with a remote. The first of the interview ran for a minute and then he shut it off. "The last time we tried to get them we lost twelve men, including two captains, to a military force. I wanted these women so that we could learn what they knew, but I smell a rat here. The whole interview thing was contrived and it was too easy to find out where they're staying. I'd say they're setting us up again to capture more of our troops. "

Pickett watched Bill's eyes as he told him the next part. We now know that these two women are part of a Christian Militant group called the Crossfire Team. We don't need to know anything about them anymore. I want you to take them out without getting any more of our men captured or killed. Handle this one yourself, verify that they are dead. Consider it your "rite of promotion" assignment. I'll be watching you and how you handle this. If you can bring it off there's a permanent position with this group for you."

Bill looked at the photos of the two women and seemed to ponder. "Okay, I'll take a swag at it." He got up to leave quite sure of how he was going to handle it. He had an "edge". He and Sarah Cohen had trained together in the Mossad and he was pretty sure she'd remember him.

The phone rang as Bill was getting ready to leave. Pickett listened for a few seconds and nodded. He said, "Yes sir, I'll go see him in the next hour. You tell Mr. Lutz that we have it covered."

Joe left the room wondering, "Mr. Lutz? Hermann Lutz?" That was a name from his past that he didn't think he'd ever hear again.

# CHAPTER FOURTEEN

After making the assignments for the sniper attack, Joe had several hours to wait until dark. He chose to catnap and be rested for the night's action.

As he laid on his bunk the mention of Lutz' name caused his mind to go back to a previous assignment he'd pulled posing as a mercenary.

-----------------------******-----------------------

His control in the Mossad had identified a potential problem for Jewish people living in Germany. Following the Holocaust, Jews had resettled in Germany. The Jewish population consisted of three types: Those who lived in Germany before the war and returned to their cities and homes; displaced persons from elsewhere in Europe, who took refuge in Germany; and those Germans who had never been discovered by the Nazis, and had remained in Germany throughout World War II.

The total number was barely five percent of the Jewish population before the war. This number decreased further as many German Jews immigrated to Israel in the 1950s. By the mid-1960s, Jewish communities had solidified in West Berlin, Munich, Frankfurt, Dusseldorf, Hamburg and Cologne. They consisted of about 20,000 Jews. For a long time, the communities were primarily elderly men and women, and opportunities for Jewish life were minimal: Intermarriage became rampant. But, because of reparations paid to Holocaust survivors and their descendants by the German Government, the Jewish communities in Germany were among the richest in the world.

In the late 1980s and early 1990s, the long-stagnant communities began to change. Huge numbers of Jewish immigrants from the former Soviet Union doubled the total number of Jews registered with communities by 1993.

The influx of Soviet Jews revitalized community life, kosher food and restaurants and grass-root organizations.

The reunification of Germany, which repatriated Jews in East and West Germany, also went a long way to increasing Jewish opportunities and unity in the country. Joe's parents, actually his mother, were part of the influx from Russia. His father had been German and Joe exhibited little or no characteristics of the normal "Jew". This was why he had been so successful at penetrating Jew-hating organizations. Like the one he was in now.

Before he took the assignment Joe remembered that two years ago, the number of Jews in Germany was calculated at more than 60,000. While the German Jewish communities have traditionally observant members, the population has become increasingly more liberal.

Throughout the post-war period, anti-Semitism continued and neo-Nazi groups flourished throughout Germany. When Joe was ordered to penetrate the Kolter operation, hate crimes and membership in neo-Nazi groups had skyrocketed, and even taken on some political forms in far-right political parties. These parties, however, had been generally unsuccessful in recruiting members from among the German populace, and several had been outlawed by the Government. Hate crimes are very strictly punished by the German courts.

At the time of his assignment, Germany had been one of the most reliable allies of the State of Israel. Limited diplomatic relations had been established between the two states in 1956; in 1965, relations had been fully normalized, even though the move led to the severance of relations between Germany and most Arab states. In subsequent years, Germany had become second only to the United States in its economic relations with Israel, by importing and exporting, and providing assistance in the form of grants and loans. Germany had also played a leading role in shaping the pro-Israel attitudes of many European countries.

This new Kolter group was attempting a twist on persecution that might get past the German courts. Owned and directed by a group of radical German lawyers the group worked to find ways to reclaim the reparations paid to the Jews along with interest for the time the money had been in Jewish hands.

They had been successful in prosecuting several dozens of recipients of the reparations on obscure German laws that denied the defendants the right to receive the payments. But resistance to their investigative people had been growing. So, the Kolter group had been hiring its own mini-army of mercenaries to force the Jews to cooperate with their investigations. For that, read coercion and beatings.

The concern of the Israeli Government wasn't that they were finding ways to finagle people out of their proper and hard-won reparations. It was the multiple rumors coming out of Germany that this group had Hitlerian ambitions and were planning on building popular support by re-instituting the Holocaust.

By becoming one of the bully boys, Joe Goldberg could gauge the actual intent and probability of success of the Kolter operation.

After being accepted and signing on, Joe had been given a plane ticket to Berlin and a contact name and number.

Arriving in Germany, Joe was able to make contact with the local Mossad organization before he had to get to his new "job".

Joe remembered the events clearly. He had called his contact and was picked up at the airport. Eventually he was received by the Captain running the operation at the barracks in Berlin.

Joe knew the Captain from an earlier stint in Africa where he had been a grunt just like Joe. A grizzly bear of a man he looked up at "Bill Colton" and smiled a grim smile. "Well, well, well. Here we are again. How are you doing Bill?"

Bill saluted the man and then reached out and shook the offered hand. "I'm doing great. How are things here, Al?"

Albert Stephonus shook his head slightly. "Too much work, not enough men, too little pay, too much rain. In other words, just like normal."

They chatted about old times and where they'd been for a few minutes. Then they reverted to their military personas. Joe stepped back and stood at attention. "Reporting ready to go to work Captain."

The Captain assigned him to a squad and explained his duties. These had consisted of looking tough, acting tough, and when necessary being tough. His squad leader would walk him through the first couple duty cycles and after that Joe would be up to speed on his assignments.

Joe wondered inside if this was going to be trouble for him. He normally would not stand for soldiers terrorizing citizens. But this time he might have to keep his mouth shut until he could get the information he was tasked to do.

# CHAPTER FIFTEEN

It was far worse than Joe Goldberg could have imagined. The troops he had joined committed atrocities that would have called for court martial in any real service in any country. They were encouraged to beat normal, innocent citizens and to terrorize old men, women, and children. To destroy the keepsakes and heirlooms of any Jewish person if they didn't do exactly as the leaders told them to do.

He was part of it because if he failed to be "one of the men" he would have been sent packing and the only access the Mossad to the Kolter group would be lost. But still, it sickened him greatly. In his heart he swore revenge on each and every one of the people that took satisfaction out of browbeating, really beating, or threatening the gentle people they came against.

One time his troop had been assigned to harass a middle-aged, Jewish couple who were complaining to the authorities about the outrages performed in the name of serving the law. They had been singled out to be made examples of for the rest of the community.

As he lay in his bunk three years later, he remembered that two squads of six men each had been assigned to the family on that dark night. They had broken into the house citing a seldom used law dating back to the days of Hitler. "Unlawful assembly of dissidents". The German-speaking Sergeants browbeat the couple and shoved them around as the rest of the troops ranged through the house, breaking and spoiling everything.

One man on the other squad, named Uzbeck, was a certifiable pedophile, so Joe kept an eye on the man whenever they were assigned to the same target. As they reached the bedrooms there was a childish squeal from the smaller one. Joe stepped in to find Uzbeck pulling a young girl out of her bed with intent to do more than scare her.

Joe looked around and the three of them were alone in this part of the house. He kicked Uzbeck in the seat of his pants which made him drop the child back on the bed.

When he turned around there was the red glow of insanity or something worse in his eyes and a combat dagger in his right hand. He was silent and he came at Joe with lethal intent.

Joe's training had been thorough. He deflected the knife thrust to his left and hit Uzbeck in the throat with a full-power knuckle punch. He heard and felt the larynx break. Uzbeck was as good as dead at that point. Joe took hold of the man's knife hand and twisted the knife out of it. Grabbing the man around the neck in a choke hold, he looked at the terrified girl and told her to hide in Hebrew. As the girl slipped out of bed and into a small closet that Joe hadn't even seen, Uzbeck collapsed in his arms and died.

Joe took the body out of the room and down the hall. He saw a side entrance and dragged the body outside and threw it on the ground. Going back inside he collected the knife and went to find the Sergeant in charge of Uzbeck's troop. Seeing the man talking to two other members of Joe's troop he interrupted him and handed him the knife. The Sergeant took the knife and looked the question at Joe.

Joe said, "Uzbeck tried to knife me over a girl in the bedroom."

Knowing Joe's fighting reputation and low tolerance for fools, the Sergeant asked, "And?"

Joe kept a stone face as he replied. "I killed him and put the body outside."

The Sergeant shook his head. "I knew that idiot would irritate the wrong person sooner or later. "What happened to the girl?"

Joe shrugged, "I don't know, she must have run away."

# CHAPTER SIXTEEN

Waiting until the right time at night Joe continued to remember the German job, After Uzbeck's death Joe's popularity among the mercenaries went up rather than down. Uzbeck hadn't been well liked and many of the men had wished they could have been the one to send him on his way.

Having an opportunity to call "home", Joe summarized what he had found out and what their aims were. Actually, in Joe's opinion, the Kolter group didn't have much chance to succeed. Once they strayed away from beating the Jews in the courts they would come up on the radar of groups like BGS-9 which specialized in terror groups, local as well as foreign. This was not to mention the American CIA and other international groups.

Directed to call back in one hour Joe cleaned up his area and took a shower between calls. When he contacted his handler the second time he was told that the decision had been made to eliminate the Kolter group, not as a threat to Israel but because of their activities against the local Jews. Joe was tasked to effect the elimination. He could do this in the way he determined but was to not blow his cover if possible. A secure file was being sent to him in a birthday card containing information on the six leading members of the Kolter group.

Two days later he received the birthday card and got a lot of ribbing by some of the other "tough" mercenaries. In reality they wished someone cared enough about them to send them a card.

That afternoon, Joe took the tiny microfiche he had found and went to a printing company that allowed him to print the sixteen pages of text for a small fee. He destroyed the microfiche and during the night he studied the papers in his car by flashlight.

The controlling players in the Kolter operation were the three Kolter brothers, Kraus, Heinrich, and Fritz. All three were lawyers but Kraus was the driving force behind the Kolter group. He was the only one who incorrectly traced their lineage back to the Gestapo. The report showed that their grandfather was actually a camp guard at the infamous Tribunate extermination camp. The demonically fostered, generational hatred of the Jews continued regardless of the actual lineage. These three then made the policies and assignments of the Kolter group for the mercenaries.

The other three leaders were an odd lot. Karl Murchen was the most vocally anti-Jewish of the six. He was also the least capable of leadership and the most minor of the group. He apparently rated because of his inherited wealth. Karl was a bitter, mean little snake of a man, who everyone disliked. The other leaders remained aloof from him and the men under him, including the mercenaries, were afraid of him. This was because he was prone to nasty retaliation for any real or imagined insults. Still, the Kolter brothers kept him in the group because he was the primary bankroll for the operation.

The three Kolter brothers were, without a doubt, the legal brains behind the Kolter group and Karl was the money man. That left Pieter Stahd and Hermann Lutz.

Pieter was the advertising and political brain that brought the Kolter group special interest groups and social and political approval for their efforts.

Hermann Lutz was harder to pigeon-hole. He didn't seem to bring any unique talent to the group but was like a trusted advisor and ally. Joe was sure he'd seen the man before, either in case files or on a previous assignment. But that didn't matter at this point. All six were the power behind a march against anything Jewish which would lead to genocide if left unchecked.

Joe thought long and hard between assignments to ruin the lives of the local Jewish population on how to behead this vicious snake. It would be tricky to do without revealing his hand in the matter. Thinking back to his training days, Joe remembered a case study he'd read during his classroom time that would just about fit the bill in this case. The heart of his destruction of the Kolter group would be based on the "Zahavy Gambit". This was a ruse that had been used by a senior member of the Institute and adopted as an effective technique for destroying a terror cell. Joe thought with some small modifications it would work with the Kolter group.

He spent part of his time learning everything he could about Karl Murchen. The report he had been given included the facts that Karl had the ability to get blind, falling-down drunk yet still function, somewhat. The other fact of interest was that women disliked Karl more than the men did, despite his wealth.

Karl couldn't buy a date with a decent girl from any country. Even the professional, working girls shunned him because he was a violent psychopath that enjoyed beating anyone weaker than himself. That meant a woman didn't have a chance with him. The report showed that two years ago he had killed a prostitute, bought his way out of trouble, and bragged about it. But the word was out and he was avoided by anyone with a lick of sense. According to the file information, Karl kept a picture of a young German actress in his wallet. He bragged about his "love" for her and claimed that she was his girlfriend to anyone who would listen. Joe reasoned that he could use these facts in his effort to avoid detection in the destruction of the group.

As "Bill Colton", Joe knew he had become well-liked in the mercenary camp. He also was aware that Karl envied his popularity but was afraid to move against him because it might turn all of the mercenaries against him. Joe knew that Karl desperately wanted to share in that popularity.

During his down times, Joe kept an eye on Karl for several days until he was confident in Karl's routines. He knew that Karl spent his Tuesday evenings at the Rattskeller, an upscale strip joint four miles from the headquarters of the operation.

Making sure he was alone, Joe prepared his body and stomach for a night of drinking. The Olive oil he ingested would cause most of the alcohol to pass through his system rather than going directly into his bloodstream. The drug he took would keep him more level-headed than would normally be possible during a drinking bout.

Suitably prepared, the young Israeli Mossad agent donned his Bill Colton personae and went to the Rathskeller. He managed to run up a sizable bill before Karl arrived.

Once the influential German had been seated by himself as usual, it didn't take him long to see Bill Colton having a grand time with several of the showgirls at his table. Karl came over to Bill's table and appropriated a chair for himself. Turning the chair around backwards he sat down and stared at the mercenary. In stilted English he said, "I did not know you able to afford this place, Mr. Colton."

Joe cast a beery eye on his intended victim and slightly slurred his words. "You are probably right Mr. Murchen. But after some rough days, I am having a good time. I'll just have to ask for an advance on my salary for tonight's fun."

Karl stared at him speculatively.

# CHAPTER SEVENTEEN

In the Rathskeller, with the music pounding and scantily-clad women dancing on the stage, Joe smiled a lop-sided smile at Karl as if to say, "I don't care about the cost, I'm going to have a good time if it kills me."

Karl almost drooled looking at the women with Joe. He smiled back and said, "Forget an advance. If you'll drink with me tonight I'll cover your tab."

Joe acted like that was the nicest thing anyone had ever done for him. It took a good deal of his acting ability to act thankful, drunk, and respectful at the same time. All the while hating the man and everything he had done. But that was one reason that Joe was still alive. He was good at his trade.

Joe said, "Great! Wha'cha drinking?"

After four hours of drinking shots and watching the girls perform, Karl had become thoroughly drunk and loquacious. He and "Bill" had become the best of buddies.

Joe steered the conversation around to girlfriends by giving Karl a total fabrication of how his girlfriend had just dumped him for the affections of a chicken-livered, punk, worthless politician. Joe lamented on how she had taken everything of his and walked all over his heart in the process.

Karl was sympathetic telling "Bill" how faithful his girlfriend was. He eventually pulled out his wallet to show Bill her picture. He was too drunk to get the picture out of the holder and finally just gave the whole wallet to Joe so he could stare in amazement at the beauty of Karl's "girlfriend".

Joe gawked over the picture and palmed a gold MasterCard from the wallet at the same time. He gave the wallet back to Karl with the hundreds of Euros still intact, a fact that did not escape Karl's attention.

Two hours later after confiding their mutual secrets to each other, Joe staggered to his car while Karl's chauffeur poured Karl into his limousine. Once out of sight, Joe sobered up and returned to his barracks for a few hours of sleep.

The next morning he used the MasterCard to order a briefcase and a set of powerful, but compact, computer batteries and a charger for the batteries. He did this over the phone at a call box near Karl's residence. He had them sent to a P.O. Box he had already rented in Karl's name. He had studied Karl's signature and had become quite proficient in signing the little German's name.

Back at the barracks, Joe forged Karl's signature onto a request form for four blocks of C-4 Plastique explosive. He slipped it into the regular request file. When the order was filled by the arms dealer they worked with, Joe intercepted the package before it was delivered to Karl.

Joe went downtown and rented a cheap room. After a few minutes he looked at himself in the cracked mirror on the wall and almost laughed. He was in full surgical dress. He had scrubbed his face and covered his body and head with a surgical gown and cap. He had clear goggles over his eyes and rubber gloves on his hands. He had erected a small plastic tent on top of the rickety dining table. He had been well-trained to prevent any DNA evidence from accidently falling into his work.

Turning on a small blower motor he inflated the tent and opened the side to put several objects into the tent. The positive air pressure kept out pollen and lint that was in the atmosphere and could be used later to trace the manufacturing back to this room. He carefully opened the box containing the briefcase and took it out. Discarding the box he took the sample envelope he had used at the Rattskeller and let one or two hairs from Karl's arm fall into the briefcase's lock. He then used the C-4, batteries, and a cheap digital timer to build an extremely powerful bomb in the briefcase. Carefully wrapping the finished bomb in a clean plastic bag, he removed all traces of his being there in the room. He then returned to the barracks and left the bomb in the trunk of his car.

At three a.m., Joe got up and acted like he had sentry duty. No one noticed him or even cared. They were just glad they didn't have to get up at that hour. Pulling on rubber gloves, he got the briefcase out of the trunk in the bag. On the pretext of doing a security sweep of the conference room to be used for the staff meeting the next day, he slipped the briefcase into the room. Using a penlight he crept under the large conference room table and taking the bomb from the bag, he taped it securely to the bottom of the table.

Clearing all signs of entry, he walked sort of a beat for the next hour and then made his way over to the chow hall for breakfast. His squad was assigned to harass some more Jews that day and he wanted to be a long way away from the conference room when the bomb went off.

# CHAPTER EIGHTEEN

The six controlling members of the Kolter group met in the conference room to discuss the progress of the operation and plan new strategies. At ten minutes before 10 a.m., a woman called the guard station and asked to talk to Karl. Informed that he was in a meeting, she said that he had requested her to call him and was eager to hear what she had to say. The guard wasn't too interested in relaying the message until the woman asked for his name. He knew Karl's reputation for revenge. He went to the conference room and gave Karl the message that the woman he had asked to call was on the phone. Karl didn't remember asking a woman to call him but the meeting was boring and he was intrigued, so he left the room and went to the phone.

The female Mossad agent was coy and seductive at the same time. She said that she had been enamored of Karl for some time and was going to be out front of their headquarters building in five minutes so they could meet.

Karl immediately agreed and went out the front entrance to wait for her. As he stood waiting for her to drive up, the entire center of the building exploded into the air. Battered by the noise and thrown to the ground by the force of the explosion, Karl jumped to his feet and tried to get back into the building. But the way was blocked by fallen concrete and intense flames. He walked away from the destruction and sat down on a small wall to contemplate his future. He had completely forgotten about the mysterious woman and their "date".

With the Kolter brothers dead, the Kolter operation faltered and died within two weeks. The mercenaries were paid off and disbanded to find new work elsewhere.

As he waited for his airplane to leave Germany, Joe read the English newspaper and wondered exactly what happened that morning. According to Karl's testimony, all five of the other directors were in the room at the time of the explosion. But the authorities only recovered the remains of four people, the three Kolter brothers and Pieter

Stahd. There was no body for Hermann Lutz and no one knew where he was. Joe thought that he could have also left the meeting prior to the explosion. Still, you would have thought that he would have been vocal in his denouncement of the bombing.

The second major story was the investigation into the bombing and the arrest of Karl Murchen for the murders. BGS-9 had traced the request for the C-4 and the purchase of the briefcase and batteries to Karl. More damning evidence was the DNA evidence found in a briefcase lock that had been blown into a wall but survived to implicate the man. The fact that he had left the building just before the explosion added weight to his guilt.

The investigation was very thorough as are most things German. They had found his chopped-up gold MasterCard he'd used to order the bomb parts and the box for the briefcase in a trash can behind his house.

To his protestations that he had been lured out of the meeting by a telephone call from an unknown woman, the police pointed out that there was no record of such a call and the only person who could verify that call had been also killed in the blast. The prosecutors were confident they could get the death penalty for such a callous and premeditated crime.

Satisfied that he had accomplished his orders to eliminate the Kolter operation, "Bill Colton" moved on to other things.

-----------------------\*\*\*\*\*\*-----------------------

His remembrances came to a halt as one of his sharpshooters stuck his head into Joe's room and said, "Time to rock and roll."

# CHAPTER NINETEEN

Jack called Charlie Wu and his wife Linda in Denver, and asked them to do a research project for the team. Jack wanted them to find Severon's think tank.

Charlie and Linda agreed and set to work on the internet. This would be the quickest and easiest way to find such a high-powered group of individuals.

Jack got a call from General Howard Miles, the chairman of the Joint Chiefs of Staff of the military. "Jack, Howard Miles here, I understand that the Crossfire Team and Miles Marauders have gone from one snake pit to another. Can you come here and brief the President and his staff and several important Congressmen as to the situation tomorrow at one p.m.?"

Jack thought about what they were doing and agreed to meet them for the support they could throw behind the operation. He asked the General, "Miles Marauders? What happened to Miles 'Maulers?"

General Miles laughed, "The makeups of the personnel are way too refined to be called "Maulers". I think "Marauders" is a better name for the SOG. That okay with you?"

Jack grinned, "Yes Sir!"

After hanging up Jack looked at the clock. He had six hours before he had to get airborne. He'd sleep on the way and be ready when they got to D.C. the next morning. He punched in Su Li's code and she came back on the phone immediately. Jack had thought about the trip. "Su Li, I need to be in Washington, D.C. by ten tomorrow morning to present this situation to the President and others. I want you to fly me, but, since Pickett's people still have our commercial jet, I want you to contact Mike White and get Air Force permission to use a war bird. I think that Severon will have a grudge to settle with us about his men and Reverend Kloss. Will you handle that? I will authorize it if they give you any grief."

Su Li agreed and hung up. She called Mike White and got him the first time. He was about to go on a short flight but had time to talk to her. Su Li summed up the problem and Jack's request. She finished up by, "I know I'm not certified as an Air Force pilot to fly your aircraft but I can do it."

Mike laughed, "I'm sure you can Su Li. I'm not worried about it. Jack can not only authorize your flying one of our aircraft, he can pay for it if you break it which I doubt you'll allow that to happen. I'll make the arrangements and have you met at Randolph AFB around four a.m., okay?"

Su Li agreed and then asked the Major what she would be flying. He said, "Well, I know you're qualified on the F-22 Raptor so I'll make sure a two-seater is fueled up and tasked to go to Andrews AFB in Maryland."

Signing off, Su Li went to her room and fired up her laptop computer. Using the codes she had gotten from Mike during her training, she brought up the USAF F-22 Simulator program. Dimming the lights in her room she concentrated on the 16-inch color monitor which showed the view out of the front windshield of the fighter as well as the HUD and flight controls and screens. It didn't take her but a few minutes to be back in the plane she flew and she relaxed knowing that she was still familiar with the controls, gauges, and readouts.

She set her flight path into the computer, taxied out to the main runway and got permission from the tower. Letting the plane have the power of full throttle and afterburner she raced down the runway and into the air. She kept the chatter up with the tower as she turned into her pattern and rose to 32,000 feet. She then advanced the program to landing at Andrews AFB. She ran the program through twice and then decided to add some unknowns into the shift. Looking at her watch she saw that she had ten hours before they had to leave for Jack's flight.

Su Li called Mike's cell phone and got him in flight. He laughed, "What now Su Li, do you want a space plane too?"

Su Li stopped and seriously thought for a few seconds, "No Mike, I don't have any time in one, yet. What I wondered was, do they have an F-22 simulator I can get into in the next eight hours?"

Mike made some flight adjustments and said, "Wait one." Putting the young woman on hold he called the training command at Randolph. After a few conversations he went back to Su Li. "Yes, actually, they just started one at Randolph two months ago and I just arranged for you to get an hour of time at five p.m. Go to the base, show them your identification I got you when you were training and ask for Captain Abrams. He'll take care of you. "Look, I gotta run, bye."

Su Li was glad that she had had the presence of mind to have packed some of her stuff on the aircraft. She had that stuff brought here after they recovered the plane. She went to her closet and got out the custom-made g-suit that the Air Force had made for her. Stripping down to her underwear, she put on the silky undersuit and then put on the g-suit. She got all the connections and seals finished and grabbed her helmet. Then she took her identification and her sunglasses and checked herself out in the full-length mirror in her room.

What she saw was a petite female warrior dressed for combat aerobatics. Her short-cut black hair and the Ray-bans finished off the image. Impressive she thought, but I'm glad I took care of the bathroom needs first.

She walked through the common area on her way to the flight line. Sarah had stopped by the barracks for the latest information on Severon and saw Su Li as she left in her g-suit. "Going for a little ride?" she said with a smile.

Su Li raised her helmet in a salute. "Yes, I'm going to fly a simulator like my hair was on fire." She smiled at Sarah and headed for the flight line. She checked out the Air Cobra the Marines had on loan to the Crossfire Team while they were stationed at the Ft. Worth NAS. She checked it over and did a preflight checklist. Finding it ready, she contacted flight operations. She fired up the engines and waited until they stabilized. Arm's stores came up on her screen and she noted that she had four air-to-air missiles, two fire-and-forget Hellfire missiles and two thousand rounds of 20mm explosive ammo for the eight-barreled cannon under the nose of the aircraft. She got permission from the control center to lift off. They had already cleared her flight path with the civilian air control.

Lifting off cleanly from the pad, Su Li thrilled to the power and aggressiveness of the whirlybird. Next to a fast mover this was the way to travel. Both of her radar systems displayed her area of travel and negative threat alarms, which one would expect in the U.S. air space. It took only twenty minutes to reach Randolph AFB and she was vectored to a landing space off the main landing strip.

Shutting down the chopper, she finished her check list and exited the helicopter. She walked to the flight operations office and checked in. They arranged refueling of the Apache and for transportation to the simulator building. She got there ten minutes before five and had to wait until the earlier pilot had finished his paperwork and cleared the simulator.

The F/A-22 Full Mission Trainer was built by Link Simulation & Training. It enabled Raptor pilots to practice a complete range of tactical scenarios. Su Li had over thirty hours in one just like this during her training. Training realism is heightened by high resolution computer image generation that is projected onto a trademarked SimuSphere visual system display, which wraps around the cockpit providing the pilot with a 360-degree field-of-view.

The trainer which Su Li found herself in consisted of a fully populated cockpit on a fixed base. It simulated complex, integrated missions where she had to establish air dominance in the midst of the world's most advanced integrated air defense radar networks and surface-to-air missile environments. Setting up she told the controller of the flight tomorrow and she wanted to add in being attacked by two competitive jet fighters with air-to-air missiles. She asked for a 100% realistic program which had the same chance as reality of winning or losing.

An hour later, a confident Su Li, climbed out of the simulator and thanked the controller. Finishing her paperwork she got ready to go when a Sergeant, wearing a head-set, walked up to her and stuck out his hand. "I really enjoyed your performance today. I'm Wayne Jenkins, I was your controller."

Su Li grinned, "No, I want to thank you. That was the most challenging air combat I've every experienced. And, you had me so engrossed, I forgot it wasn't real. I enjoyed it immensely. Thanks."

She went back to the Cobra and pre-flighted it. Getting clearance she lifted off and went back to the Naval Air

Station. After the process of landing and refueling the aircraft, she went to her room to get ready for the mission.

Not far away Tom Pickett was talking to a compromised Congressional Aide sitting in Washington, D.C. "Give me that information, Gus."

The Aide repeated quickly, "My boss is going to meet with Mr. Malone tomorrow right after lunch. I checked and Mr. Malone is flying from Randolph AFB into Andrews AFB arriving at 10 a.m. Eastern time. That's all I've got." The man hung up.

Pickett called Severon who called his contacts. The information was finally relayed to the remnant of the American Liberation Association or ALA. Thanks to the efforts of the Crossfire Team the ALA was being hunted out of existence throughout the world. There were million-dollar bounties on the heads of their leaders and big cash rewards for the capture or termination of any member of the ALA.

The ALA representative called his contact. "Mr. Lutz, I need a favor." A phone call was made to an assassin named Largo. Largo was able to determine that Malone would be leaving Randolph AFB around four in the morning for his flight to Washington. The tail number on the aircraft would be 011. That was all he needed. Just as insurance he also contacted a rogue Russian military pilot who had access to his own fighter and who would do anything for cash. He explained his desire and was gratified by the response. Lutz went to a bank and forwarded two million dollars to a Swiss account number.

# CHAPTER TWENTY

Jack was tired from his efforts to track down Pickett or Severon. He'd stayed at it until time for his flight with Su Li. He also donned a g-suit and rode in the gunner position of the AH-1W Super Cobra between NAS and Randolph AFB. Jack liked the AH-1W Super Cobra. It provided full night-fighting capability with the Night Targeting System, and is armed with a 20mm turret gun, TOW, Hellfire, Sidewinder, Sidearm missiles, and 5 inch or 2.75 inch rockets. Nothing unusual happened on the flight and they transferred to an F-22 Raptor in the dark of early morning.

The plane had been preflighted and Su Li went through her checklist quickly. She taxied out and turned onto the main runway. She ran the Pratt & Whitney: F119-PW-100 engines up to full power and kicked in the afterburners. The plane had more than enough power to lift it long before the runway ran out. Su Li raised the wheels as they rose through two hundred feet altitude.

Suddenly the threat board lit up with an urgency that shot ice through both of their guts. The threat was identified as a MANPADS which meant a shoulder-launched U.S. Stinger missile. Su Li reacted as she had been trained. She cut power to both engines and ejected high-intensity flares to draw the Stinger's heat detection system away from the aircraft. She then cranked the aircraft around towards the firing position indicated on the HUD. Jack watched the horizon whirling around and the ground coming up at them at the same time. He was praying that the Lord would keep them safe from missiles and from crashing.

Re-engaging the engines Su Li stopped their fall and accelerated quickly towards the site which was in an open field. All weapons were on-line and Su Li selected the 20mm long barreled cannon. As the target appeared in the FLIR, it resolved itself into a pickup truck racing away across a field with a person trying to get a second Stinger out the passenger window. Su Li didn't give him a second chance to knock them down. She triggered fifty, twenty millimeter explosive rounds directly on the truck. It looked like a dust bowl with a violently red and yellow explosion in the middle. The Stinger and whatever else they had on-board went up at the same time.

Su Li cranked them around to the right to avoid flying through the fireball and then corrected their altitude while talking with air traffic control. Jack heard a transmission from a civilian aircraft nearby yelling, "Kick their butts Air Force, Yahh!" Su Li was attempting to avoid silos, power towers, and the lower level aircraft that her sudden dash after the target had placed them among.

The ATC told her to ascend to 12,000 feet as quickly as possible. Su Li checked her path on the HUD and lifted the Raptor's nose to almost vertical. At the same time she engaged the afterburners. The stealthy fighter rose on twin columns of white fire like a missile. She eased off and leveled her flight at 12,000 feet. The ATC directed her up to 42,000 feet and headed her toward the east coast. The President had priority, the military and civilian review of the action would take place when they got back.

At 42,000 feet, the traffic and the air were much scarcer and they could both relax. The missiles that could reach them here were few and far between and required a major installation that would have been noticed almost anywhere in the United States. Su Li checked their fuels stores and their flight condition. She'd used more fuel than expected but then combat was hard on gas. She put the aircraft into supercruise which allowed the Stealth fighter to cruise above the speed of sound with good fuel usage. Soon she was talking to the ATC at Cleveland as they were vectored towards Maryland.

As they were crossing north of Atlanta a new threat warning came on the board. Checking the listing Su Li saw that they were being scanned by air-to-air radar seeking a lock-on. It was hard to get a lock-on on the F-22 but someone was trying pretty hard. The threat warning also indicated at least two air-to-air radar missile seeker heads were active at the same source.

Su Li was unconventional in her aerial warfare. Instead of following normal procedures she cut her power to almost zero. Their rate of travel and altitude started dropping rapidly. Because they got even stealthier at low power output, the following aircraft overshot them without realizing they were now below and behind him.

Jack was watching the output of a satellite which provided radar tracking that had their plane and the pursuing fighter in a top-down view. Su Li reapplied power and came up behind the other aircraft. As soon as she locked onto his aircraft he attempted to outfly the much superior fighter behind him. Unable to shake the lock-on that Su Li had on his aircraft, the pilot attempted a dangerous maneuver. He tried to dive out of the pursuit. The Mirage 2000-5 is rated at Mach 1.5 but the full-power dive quickly exceeded Mach 2. The pursuit ended when the wings overheated, melted and fell apart. The plane was tumbling when it exploded. There was no sign of an ejection by the pilot.

Jack hit the intercom and told Su Li, "I don't think someone wants me to talk to the President."

Su Li came back with some anger, "True, but they seem extremely well informed as to our flight plan."

They managed to finish the trip without further incident.

# CHAPTER TWENTY-ONE

Jack and Su Li were ushered into the conference room where the President was holding their meeting. Jack noticed immediately that the climate in the room was definitely chilly, socially speaking. The President did not look happy. General Miles looked positively irate but was holding it in and there wasn't a friendly face to be seen.

Taking his seat, with Su Li sitting behind him, Jack addressed the President. "President Bollen, I wish I could be here in a more pleasant time. I would like to introduce a member of my team, Su Li. She is our pilot and has proven valuable to the team's activities."

President Bollen smiled at Su Li, "Pleased to meet you Su Li." He turned to Jack, "Jack, I'd like to introduce you to Senator Lorch from the State of Maine."

Jack had heard a great deal about Senator Lorch. He was a far-left leaning liberal and held a powerful seat as the Chairman of the Armed Services Committee. He was an obstructionist in the worst way. His presence at this meeting could only mean trouble. Jack politely said, "Pleased to meet you Senator Lorch."

The Senator was in his sixties and grossly overweight. His feeble attempt to hide his baldness with an expensive toupee was almost laughable. His florid features spoke of prolonged alcohol abuse and his spirit spoke of demonic forces. He fixed a watery blue eye on Jack and cleared his throat. Speaking in the Boston accent with a nasal twang he replied, "You may not be pleased at the outcome of this meeting, sir. I can tell you right now that you are in big trouble and it ain't going to get any better!"

That confused Jack for a few seconds and he prayed for wisdom. God grants wisdom to any who ask for it and do not doubt that He will give it to them. Jack's normally low threshold for idiots and dumb actions dropped off the low end of the scale and was replaced with a sanguine feeling of peace. Smiling he said, "I don't understand what you mean Senator."

The Senator waved a batch of papers in his hand. "I mean this, young man! To start with I have Senator Caldwell's summation of your sworn testimony concerning that fiasco in Denver last month!" By now the Senator was building up his usual head of steam and was turning red in the face and neck. "Sheer poppycock and slight-of-hand theatrics. I'm not sure how but I think you and your "team" staged this whole thing so that you could get the publicity."

Jack evaluated the Senator's statements and replied. "What publicity, Senator? We deliberately stayed out of the limelight and let the FBI take credit for preventing the nuclear attack on Denver."

That enraged the Senator even more. "Whatever, don't try to confuse the issues Mr. Malone. I know what I've read and it looks like you could be facing a bunch of federal and state charges. Such as deliberately introducing a nuclear weapon onto U.S. soil, detonating said weapon on U.S. soil, and a host of other charges. I plan to seek a full investigation of every one of your little stunts.

Jack glanced at the President who looked like a man who had to eat an unpleasant meal. Jack returned his attention to the Senator. "Senator Lorch, regardless of your personal take on our activities it is imperative that action be taken against Barton Severon and his mercenary army before they set off a nuclear weapon in Dallas."

The Senator waved his paperwork around again. "Most likely just more of your little grandstanding! I know Barton Severon personally and he is anything but anti-American. I am bringing your little play to an end Mr. Malone. You will not use anymore of my country's military assets or money!"

Jack calmly raised one eyebrow, "Your country? I thought it was our country Senator, and I thought you were elected to serve, not to rule."

The Senator turned a darker shade of red, if that were possible. "I've heard enough!" He turned to the President, "Not one more cent! If you want to get any legislation through this Congress again! I will not stand for this unmitigated slander and vile rhetoric against my good name!" He got up and his aides with him. They all glared at Jack like he was the devil himself. They stormed out in a high snit. The door closed silently behind them.

The President shook his head. "I'm sorry Jack, Su Li. The man is completely wrong and out of line. Unfortunately he is also very powerful. He can shut us out of accomplishing anything this term if we provoke him. He has taken a lot of half-truths, innuendo, suppositions, and outright untruth and created a picture that makes the Crossfire Team the bad guys in both the Denver and Dallas operations."

Jack looked at the President. "How do you see this, Sir?"

The President frowned, "I see it just like it happened and just like your Team explained it. So do most of the people in the Government. Unfortunately, Senator Lorch has been here a long time and has pressure he can apply to almost everyone in the Senate and the House. He is wrong, and we will prove him wrong. But, by the time we do, it may be too late for Dallas or your Team."

Jack thought about the situation. Turning to the Chairman of the Joint Chiefs he asked, "Tell me how this Congressional pressure is going to hinder our operations, General."

General Miles smiled grimly. "Just about everything we are doing to help your operation is going to have to go away, for a while." He looked at his notes, "Miles Marauders is my line item and they can't disband it, but they can stop us from letting the Crossfire Team use them. I will reassign it to a nasty little hostage situation in South America. That way they won't lose their edge." He was obviously going to go to the wall for them but he was going to do it the smart way.

General Miles continued, "The Fortress was built with your own funds and it has been deeded to you so there is nothing Lorch can do about it. He can't even complain about the troops exercising there with their missiles and helicopters. You are allowing them to train on your property at no cost, so he should be thanking you. Don't look for a pat on the back from him unless he has a knife in that hand.

All four of your Team is going to lose their ranks as Generals for the time being. The ranks are only being inactivated, not eliminated. Your cooperation with the FBI, CIA, NSA, and the other agencies is also being disallowed for the present. We will also have to rescind our permission to use our aircraft or base facilities. By the way Su Li, at the risk of Congressional censure, I want to congratulate you on your combat skills in the F-22. I have reviewed both incidents and pronounced them righteous. There will be no Congressional meddling in those two incidents. Also, Jack, we took the liberty to forward two care packages to your Team at the naval air station in Ft. Worth. You will get twenty-four hours to vacate the base as far as your operations go."

The General shook his head, "I know the real facts in both the Denver and Dallas terrorism acts. That pompous airbag is trying everything he can to hand this country over to its enemies and convince us that they are right and we are wrong. At times I wish we weren't so governed by laws that can be twisted by people like him. The sad part is that if a nuclear bomb is detonated in Dallas, he'll try to find a way to blame us for not acting quickly enough and your Team will be tagged for triggering it."

Jack could not believe how little the situation bothered him. He thought, "God really does grant one peace if they ask for it". "Mr. President, General Miles, let me bring you up to speed on what we have discovered so far.

Jack completed the briefing and then he and Su Li left the White House. Jack was on the phone to Mark during their ride to the airport. "Mark, we will go over the situation when I get back, but for now, plan on the SOG leaving and our contacts with the other federal agencies terminated."

Mark simply asked, "Why?"

Jack had thought about the situation and then prayed about it. "Satan is pulling out all the stops on this one. He has his favorite Congressman, Senator Lorch, running full-speed to denounce us and have us tried as the terrorists involved in both the Denver missile and this bomb thing in Dallas."

Mark laughed harshly, "I would guess he would be upset at our attacking Severon. In looking into the billionaire's affairs to find links to Pickett and his think tank we found that he gave over five million dollars to Lorch's reelection campaign. I wouldn't doubt that he'll call Severon a patriot."

Jack laughed back, "Yeah, he did that in front of the President. Listen, there are two "care packages" coming from General Miles, also we are civilians only for the time being. All four of our Presidential commissions to the rank of General have been deactivated."

Mark thought, "That's not going to sit well with Sarah. She kind of liked being a boss in military matters."

Jack had a sudden shock. "Mark, get Sarah and Laura out of that hotel, the SOG is being called back and if Pickett does go for them they don't have any backup! When you're done with that, call this number." Jack gave him a Dallas telephone number. "This is a friend of mine who has a six room suite on top of a major hotel in Dallas. We'll move our base there but use his name. Make it harder for Pickett to find us once we leave the NAS."

Mark said, "You two had bettered hurry back, you're now forty percent of our total force in Dallas."

They hung up and Jack called to another friend of his and asked if they could use his corporate jet, for a substantial fee of course.

# CHAPTER TWENTY-TWO

In the dark, the three men carefully slid over the roof and looked down and across at the hotel room that was their target. Joe, as Bill Colton, used his night binoculars and studied the two women sitting on a couch, probably watching the ten o'clock news on television. He saw a gleam on the face of one of the women. Smiling to himself he slid back down and told the two men with the sniper rifles. "They are sitting there like two ducks in a pond. Remember! Both shots have to be as one. Okay?" They both nodded and took their positions with their silenced sniper rifles. Quietly one called out, "On three; one, two, three!" Both men were experts and each shot hit the forehead of the women the man was shooting at. The lights went out in the room as the two women fell to the floor. Both men gave Bill the thumbs up sign.

Bill told them to wait there and back up his recon of the hotel room to make sure they were dead. The two men agreed and stayed hunched on the side of the roof, watching the room through their telescopic sights.

Bill made his way back to the side roof that led almost directly to the other building. Taking a weighted line out of one of his utility pockets he swung it around until he released it. The weight flew up and wrapped around a large vertical pipe on the other building's roof. Bill tested the line and then stepped out into space, twelve stories above the ground. He swooped over to the hotel and landed on a small porch that led to a window. Seconds later he was in the hall and stopped next to the door to the women's room.

Knocking quietly he said, in Hebrew, "Sarah, Sarah Cohen?"

A female voice came back in the same language just as quietly. "Who are you?"

Bill looked carefully around, "It's Joey Goldberg."

There was silence for a few seconds. Then the voice asked, "How do I know it's you Joey?"

"Remember the time I tried to kiss you in basic spy school? Remember how you slammed me into a wall and then kissed me on the cheek and said, "You get points for the effort."?

After a second there was a quiet chuckle and the door was unlocked. Joey slid into the darkness and felt Sarah's hand on his pistol in his holster. He heard her whisper, "I do a lot worse to people that try to kill me."

He started to sweat on that one. "I knew it was a mirror reflection, that's why I told them to shoot! That way I could come over here and tell you I'm still in love with you."

Sarah's whisper said, "Sweet, but I'm married now. Why did you really come?"

Joey got serious, "Because they're watching me like a hawk. You can get word back to the Mossad that Severon and Pickett have really got this bomb in Dallas set to go off below the Pan-Arab summit at six in the evening on the first. They're setting the stage so that all the Arabs will blame us for the explosion and deaths of their people. This could be the worst disaster that our country has ever faced."

Sarah said, "You're right about the anger it would generate not to mention the loss of American support if they think it was Israel doing it on their ground. Where is the bomb now?"

Joey whispered back, "Pickett say's it's already in place and will be triggered remotely. He has twenty five of his troops protecting it until just before H-Hour. The summit is going to be held at the American Airlines Center in downtown Dallas."

Laura said, "There must be something about that place they like."

Sarah said, "Okay, I've got the message. Are you going to go with us?"

Joey thought about it, "God knows I want to. But, no, I need to keep tabs on those characters in the event they change things. Listen, one more thing. I need a four-star Intel investigation into a character once named Hermann Lutz. I thought I'd blown him up in Germany a couple of years ago, but I think he's involved with Pickett and Severon somehow. He should be dead!"

Sarah agreed and reached out in the dark and kissed him on the cheek. "That's for everyone in Israel."

Joey said, "Keep down and I'll signal them that you're both dead. Then I'll leave and get them. Give me three minutes and then you can split. Shalom!"

Sarah said, "Shalom"

The women crept closer to the door and stayed down on the floor. Joey acted like he was looking at two bodies and then stood up and gave the thumbs up sign to the window.

Four rounds crashed through what was left of the picture window and smashed into Joey's head and body. He was flung against the back wall and slid down it leaving a long bloody trail. By the time he was sitting on the floor he was quite dead.

The rest of the glass disintegrated as round after silenced round blasted into the room. Sarah and Laura stayed down amid the flying glass and wood chips.

Eventually quiet returned and Sarah crawled to the window and surveyed the roof across the way. "They're gone." She said. Looking sadly at Joey's body she shook her head. Then she got a strange look on her face. Going over to her small makeup case, she took out a tiny instrument. Running it over Joey's body she saw a small pin-head LED light up. Carefully scanning that area again, she shut the device off and took Joey's insignia off his uniform, wrapped them in three layers of cotton. Then she wrapped the cotton in two layers of aluminum wrapper she had. Then she put them in a small plastic bag and dropped them into her pocket.

Using a prearranged path, they got out of the room and the hotel and eventually made their way back to the NAS and Mark.

They related what had happened and Mark took his wife in his arms and held her. Sarah was sorry that she couldn't cry over her friend's death but the nearness and warmth of Mark's embrace felt so good and important at this time. Kissing him on the neck she backed up and told everyone to be silent. She reached into her pocket and brought out Joey's oak leaf clusters she had taken with her.

Going over to one of the electronic radio encryption stations, she opened the door to the wire mesh surrounding the station. This prevented any radio frequency signals from getting in. It also prevented them from getting out. She signaled the others to come in with her. After they were in and the door was shut, Sarah turned on the receiver in the station. Taking the insignia out of their wrappings she told everyone to keep talking to each other. As they talked she let the autoscan feature of the receiver run. It locked up on a 900-MHz frequency. Sarah turned up the volume and they could hear themselves talking. She turned to Mark and said, "I thought so!"

Sarah turned off the receiver and picked up a paperweight and smashed both of the insignia until they were dust. She then swept the dust into a trash bin and walked out of the wire mesh room.

Laura asked her, "What was that all about?"

Sarah sighed, "It means that Pickett knew Joey was a spy all along. They deliberately fed him a story and then let him tell us while they listened to all of it. Then they killed him and made it look like they wanted to kill us too.

Laura smiled at that, "They certainly threw enough bullets into that room to kill us."

Sarah shook her head, "No, if they wanted us dead, a grenade would have worked better."

Mark then told them some of what Jack had told him. They then started packing the important items in preparation to leave the NAS.

Captain Wollard came in and reported that the SOG was ready to leave. He also told Mark that if he would say the word, every man and woman would resign their commissions or take an early out and leave the service. They would then be a permanent SOG without Congress pulling their strings.

Mark smiled and told the Captain to tell the entire SOG that everyone on the Team appreciated their dedication and would miss their expertise for the near future and their company. Mark sat on the corner of a work station. "Captain, tell your men and women that the Crossfire Team values their contributions and if and when they leave the service they are in, they have a place with us. The hours are worse, the dangers are greater, but the pay is much, much better."

The Captain smiled, saluted them all and left.

There was a message from the base's front gate. Two packages had been delivered by military courier for Mark. Mark went to the gate and took the packages back to their area.

Opening the first one, he found it was full of the latest in military surveillance equipment from night vision to miniature cameras and wrist-watch monitors, a lot of audio surveillance equipment and hand scanners to detect other people's surveillance equipment.

The second box contained six handguns and ammo to go with them. A note from the General suggested that they use these for the time being. Mark pulled one out and inspected the weapon. "Aah, caseless ammo. We can carry thirty rounds in each pistol." He handed one to Sarah. She said, "Umm, baby rocket bullets. This should be interesting."

Sarah smiled. "I think we have a friend. She then typed a coded message to David Zahavy and told him of Joey's death and his message regarding Hermann Lutz."

# CHAPTER TWENTY-THREE

After Jack and Su Li returned to the barracks at the NAS, Jack called a meeting of the team. The five of them met in the same conference room that their original meeting was held with the SOG. It looked deserted with thirty-four less people in it.

Jack related what happened on the way to Washington and in the meeting with the President. Sarah smiled and told Su Li, "We always knew you were a great pilot and a good friend, but now you have shown everyone how good you really are."

Su Li actually looked embarrassed. "I normally would be very grateful for your comment, but I have to tell you that the only reason we lived through that flight is because I prayed before we left and it was God that made the missile miss us and it was He who told me to drop below and slow down when we were being chased. Standard procedure dictates a high-speed Immelman turn. We would have flown right into his sights if we had done that because he too, knew what we were supposed to do. If the Holy Spirit hadn't told me clearly what to do, neither Jack nor I would be here right now."

Mark sat back and laughed a hearty laugh. "Su Li, don't feel you're less of a pilot because you listened to God. All the good pilots, and soldiers, who are still alive, listen to God to know what to do. That just makes you an obedient servant that God can and will use. Your admission that God is on your side increases my admiration of your skills rather than diminishes them. Thank you for your humility and honesty. You'll go far in this business."

Jack's cell phone chirped and he answered it. It was Frank Barrett, a friend from college who had become very successful in the oil industry. He remembered Jack and his advice upon graduation that led to Frank's first "risky" investment in the oil field. In a way, he owed Jack for everything he had now. His penthouse suite at the top of a major hotel in North Dallas was Jack's for as long as he wanted it, no questions asked. He agreed to leave it in his name so that "undesirables" wouldn't know who was staying there.

Jack thought about the obstructionists in the capital. "Frank, where are you going to be on the first of the month?"

Frank checked his calendar. "Right here, buddy."

Jack thought for a second. "No, you're not. I have a friend I'd like you to go see on the first. You might be able to leverage some incredible new business with him."

Frank said, "Who are you talking about, Bill Gates? I hate to break this to you but he doesn't deal on my level." He laughed at his own joke.

Jack laughed with him, "No, somebody better, Victor Chamberlain. I will arrange for you to meet him on his island in the South Pacific and discuss things of mutual interest. That okay with you?"

Frank had gone cold sober. "You're not pulling my leg are you Jack? Victor Chamberlain is way out of both of our leagues you know."

Jack chuckled, "Not really Frank. He just adds a bunch of zeros to his transactions. He actually is a very likable guy."

Frank coughed, "You know him?"

Jack looked at his Team mates, "You might say we spent some quality time together not too long ago. He is like a brother and is actually a member of my Team when his skills are required. Go see him. You'll like him and I think you two have a lot in common."

Frank laughed and said, "Keep the suite man. If you can get me an appointment with Victor Chamberlain I'll give it to you."

Jack put Frank on hold and dialed Victor's number. It was just after two a.m. in the mansion on Chamberlain's island when the phone rang. It was answered by Victor himself on the second ring. "Hello Jack, good to hear from you."

"Hi Victor, did I wake you up?"

Victor looked at the clock, "No, but you should have. I've just gotten into studying the Bible and praying to all sorts of hours in the morning anymore. I have you to thank for that you know."

Jack laughed, "Okay, I'll take the blame for that. Listen, I have a friend from Colorado University that I would like to have come out and visit you on the first of next month. He's in oil field financing and I think you two would give each other some new ideas. His name is Frank Barrett and I'll fly him down and back if you can make time in your schedule."

Victor got serious, "Jack, Listen, my life is so awesome now that I'll give him his own island if you want me too. Sure, I'll make time on the first and I'll be glad to see him."

Jack said, "I've got him on the other line, hang on and we can all discuss this together." Jack clicked the conference call feature on the phone. Frank came back on the line.

Jack said, "Frank Barrett, allow me to introduce you to Victor Chamberlain. Victor, tell me what airline you want me to send him down there on."

Victor responded, "Hello Frank. I'm glad to meet any friend of Jack's. Don't worry about the details. Jack, I see that you're in Dallas. Frank, just be at DFW at the private aircraft hanger around 10 a.m. on the thirtieth of June. I'll have a man there whose name is Carlton. He will see to your flight arrangements and you should be here in time for breakfast on the first."

Frank was awed but didn't let that interfere with his business. "Thank you, Mr. Chamberlain; I really appreciate your efforts on my behalf. I'll try to justify your time and expense."

Victor laughed, "Frank! Call me Victor. Mr. Chamberlain was my father's name. If you're half as sharp as Jack says you are in your volatile field, then there are several areas where we could help each other and it will be my honor to have you here as my guest. I'll send you a letter detailing some areas to think about until then. Let me have your e-mail address."

Frank gave it to him and Victor grew serious again. "Jack, are Laura, Mark, and Sarah there with you?"

Jack said, "Sure they are Victor. You know how we tend to stick together."

Victor felt an urging from the Holy Spirit to inquire about the unstated emotional stress he heard in Jack's voice. "Is there anything I can do to help you at this time?"

Jack hadn't really thought about that. He said, "Hold one." He turned to Mark. "Is there anything that Victor could provide that we could use?"

Mark thought for a few seconds. He nodded and held out his hand for the phone. Jack gave it to him. "Victor, this is Mark. If you can spare it, we're going to need some funding for the next several weeks. We'll see you get it back with interest."

Victor came back with, "Mark, my money is as much yours as it is mine, how much do you need?"

Mark said, "Fifty million dollars, U.S."

Victor chuckled, "Is that all? I thought you needed some serious money. Go to my bank in downtown Dallas, Jack knows which one. The money will be there in your name tomorrow morning. Can I do anything else?"

Mark told the billionaire, "Thank you Victor, but that should take care of the situation." Mark handed the phone back to Jack.

Jack said, "Thanks Victor. We're good. Just talk to Frank on.... Just a minute, Frank, have you gotten married or anything since I talked to you last?"

Frank laughed, "I've got a lovely wife for the last three years and no kids as yet. I think I sent you an invitation to the wedding."

Victor quickly picked up on the vibrations from Mark and Jack. "Frank, why don't you bring your wife with you? The plane can handle twenty and I have some fantastic scenes on my island she can tour while we talk business."

Frank was impressed. "Thank you Mr. Cham... Victor. I know she will be thrilled to come with me. Now about my mother in Wichita..." He laughed. Seriously, I really appreciate this, both of you. We'll be at DFW on the thirtieth. He hung up.

Victor said quietly, "Jack, I'm worried when you start sending your friends out of the area. Can you let me know what's going on?"

Jack thought about it for a few seconds. "Let's just say that we need your prayers. We are in a situation with a guy named Severon and there are possibly nuclear dangers."

Victor was quiet for a few seconds. "I see. Listen, give me your email address where you'll be tomorrow morning, I might be able to help you."

Jack gave him is email account number and they hung up after Victor told them all to be careful because they meant a lot to him.

# CHAPTER TWENTY-FOUR

Severon talked with Pickett on the phone in the quiet of the early Texas morning. "Did you get rid of that Jew spy?"

Pickett said, "Sure did, if you want to see the gun photos they are digital and I can send them to you."

Severon liked the idea and told him to do that. "Do you think the Crossfire Team women swallowed the tale he told them?"

Pickett thought for a few seconds. "I don't know if they did or not. Their conversation with Colton seemed to indicate that they did, but they're not idiots and they might have figured out that it was a setup after we killed him."

Severon thought for a few more seconds. "Okay, I think we have to assume that they believe it. I have pulled their teeth anyway. They are completely cut off from the Government and have only their own resources now. We can crush them whenever we want to. Basically, unless they interfere again I think we should leave them alone to suffer the accusations of our agents in the Congress."

Pickett didn't like leaving any enemy alive but had to agree with Severon that if they were no longer a threat, then they weren't important to their plans anymore. "I agree. Let's make sure the data is correct and that we have every angle covered. This week we are going to do the run throughs in the mock up. If your guys have the right software and net controls, then my guys will get you in there to do your business."

Several miles away from where Pickett sat, Jack was running through the information that the SOG had collected before being extracted from their operation. He called the others into the large bedroom in the suite that they had decided to use as a war room.

Jack threw the paperwork back on the table. "Something doesn't add up with this operation of Severon's."

Sarah nodded, "Lots of things aren't adding up."

Laura sat down on one of the beds in the ornate room. The gold and silver brocade bed cover looked beautiful but unimportant considering what they were facing.

Mark put his feet up on the table and rested his head back in his hands. "I don't understand the military setup of Pickett's at all. You're right, this whole thing doesn't add up to a simple plan to nuke the Jews and Arabs in Dallas."

Jack said, "Let's review what we've got. First, we know they have a Pakistani nuclear weapon. We believe it could be somewhere here in Dallas. We think they are going to use it to take out the Pan Jewish and Arab Conference on the first of July in downtown."

"We know that Severon is a rabid anti-Semite and has a lot of money. He apparently established a think tank that has a bunch of electronics, cryptographic, and network experts and has spent a great deal of money on them. They are in an unknown location at this time.

We also know that Severon has hired Tom Pickett and a force of approximately one hundred mercenaries to accomplish his goals. We also know that they are aware of us as an enemy and are using their control in the Government to isolate us and prevent us from interfering with their operation."

"In addition to that, we know they were getting funding from the Reverend Kloss' crusades until Laura and Sarah got involved and Pickett's men killed the Reverend, apparently to prevent him from ratting on them. Now, what don't we have?"

Sarah started, "Well, we don't have a good reason for Severon to blow up most of downtown Dallas just to kill some Jewish and Arab leaders and thinkers. According to our shaky Intel on this, it is to blame Israel somehow for the attack and degrade the relationship between the U.S. and Israel."

Laura jumped in, "We also are missing any new demonic warfare. Possibly the people in Congress who are out to get us are being controlled but, ever since we braced Kloss' demons it has been far too quiet on that front."

Mark had listened and imagined how he would use strategy if he was Severon and Pickett. "I have a real problem with the fact that Pickett has over a hundred mercenaries but is only going to use twenty-five of their men to protect the weapon until just before it goes off. What are they paying for an extra seventy-five men to do, protect Severon?"

Jack added back into the discussion, "I don't understand the purpose of the think tank that is costing, supposedly, millions of dollars. The Pakistani bomb is not too complicated according to what the SOG determined. One nuclear scientist could rig it and set it off. Why have all those network wizards and cryptologists for?"

Mark swished it all around in his mind. "Okay, what we have here is Déjà Vu. This is so much like the Denver misdirection it's scary. It's obvious that they are going to bomb Dallas but I now believe it's only a smoke screen for the real action. The think tank and the other seventy-five guys have another target and it is something that will hurt Israel for sure. But, what is this loftier goal? Can we call David Zahavy in on this and see what he thinks?"

Sarah nodded and got her phone out. David wasn't in at the moment but he would call her back soon.

They discussed the possibilities for the next hour and twenty minutes but couldn't come to any serious conclusions because they didn't have enough facts.

David called back and Sarah explained the situation in general terms without any names. David was quiet for a while and then told her that he would be in Dallas in the next twenty hours. He'd call her and they could pick him up at the airport.

# CHAPTER TWENTY-FIVE

For the last three days Jack had been trying to contact Charlie and Linda Wu. Their continued silence bothered him and there was no way he could get back to Denver to try and help them.

For the tenth time that day he tried their number. He was actually surprised when Linda answered the phone. "Hi Linda, where have you guys been?"

Linda chuckled, "Many places but, I'll let Charlie tell you."

Charlie came on the phone, "Hi Jack. Listen, we have some good news for you. Linda and I have finally tracked down the hideaway for Severon's group of experts. They are only a couple of hours east of Dallas in a town called Tyler. They are in a small business building, single story, off of Troup Highway which is numbered 110. They are housed on the east side of 110 just north of Edna St. You'll need to be careful as they have at least thirty armed men around the place."

Jack wrote down the directions and thanked Charlie and Linda for their efforts. Then he thought again about all the misdirection involved in this operation. "How did you ever get so much detailed information?"

Charlie laughed, "We tracked down all new centers of internet game players that were really, really good. There were only twenty-seven new groups since last year. We checked them out and were pretty sure that *brainboys.com* was our think tank. The reason was the accuracy of their game playing and their all-inclusive hours of play. It takes a lot of people that are smart and talented to play at all hours of the day. It indicated a twenty-four hour operation."

"Then we tracked down the registration of brainboys and got an address in Chicago. Checking that out we determined that they were a front but had information about the listing. It took two days but we found a disgruntled employee who liked Linda's looks and was willing to have a few drinks with her in hopes she would go farther than drinks. He was pleasantly surprised when she bought the drinks so he helped himself. The more he drank, the more he talked. Linda played him like a harp. She told him how brave he must be to do such illegal activities as register sites that other people used. He puffed up like the pigeon he was and got conspiratorial with her. He told her all about this soldier group that needed an anonymous set of email addresses and that he had fixed them up and took them for two thousand dollars. She did her little girl worried routine and he assured her that they were no where near Chicago. Two more drinks and he had to prove that he wasn't making it up and he gave her everything. He went to sleep on the next drink and we took the next flight to Dallas and connected to Tyler. We just spent the last twenty-four hours counting all the mercenaries guarding the place. It isn't easy to count them, they all look alike and they keep moving around."

Jack was surprised, "So you guys are in Tyler now?"

Charlie said, "Yes, we expect you would want us to keep an eye on these bozos for you, right?"

Jack realized that he was talking through a relay or to a roaming cell phone. "Okay, we'll be there in about three hours, where shall we meet you?"

Charlie told them to meet at a Mexican restaurant on the corner of south 323 Loop and Highway 69. "The loop is the major highway around this town and 69 is the main north-south road."

Jack asked, "Is it a fairly small town?"

Charlie laughed, "Yeah, basically but it has about a hundred thousand or less people, one mall, and rush hour is a pain like anywhere else."

Jack told them that they were on their way.

He relayed the information that Charlie had given him and everyone packed up weapons and clothes. Not knowing why but feeling led, Su Li decided to add her helmet to her luggage.

They went downstairs to the garage and got the large Chevrolet Suburban they had rented and packed it. Jack looked at a map and they headed for Tyler.

On the way Mark brought up a good point. "What, exactly, are we going to do when we get there?"

Jack said, "Let's wait until we talk to Charlie."

Two hours later they were seated in the restaurant with Charlie and Linda and they had ordered dinner. While they waited for the food they discussed their options.

Jack made a suggestion. "Why don't we eliminate enough of the mercs so that we can get inside and question some of the "experts" as to what they are doing?"

Mark laughed, "I like it, but, it is totally illegal. We may think that we're on the trail of terrorists and a nuclear weapon but we couldn't prove anything in a court of law. The "remove" some of the mercs, break and enter without permission from the owners, to coerce some of the employees are all crimes that Lorch and his crew would love to lay on the press about the bad, bad, Crossfire Team."

Sarah asked, "What if some of us gals were to "entice" one of the experts away from the place for a little one-on-one time? We could definitely question him then."

Charlie shook his head, "No can do. They are walked to and from the working building to their apartments by the mercs. They don't seem to come out at all."

Laura had a thought. "How about after dinner we cruise over there and study the lay of the land?"

Everyone agreed and the food came at the same time.

Sixty minutes later they were parked in a parking lot with a clear view of the business building in question. Jack used his binoculars and studied the building and the surrounding area. "I think there is something wrong here. I don't see any 24/7 activity at that building and I can't find any of the mercs."

# CHAPTER TWENTY-SIX

Moving closer, Mark brought out a thermal scope and checked the building. "Well, it looks like they moved out between the time you left for the lunch and now. I'm registering computer heat sources and little else. Let's check it out."

Walking boldly up to the door they knocked on it. There was no answer and it was locked. While the others stood around him, Mark quickly picked the lock and opened the door. There wasn't any audible alarm and Mark doubted that there would be a silent police call with everything shut down. They went in and found the place cleaned out except for the computer terminals which were rented and would probably be picked up in the next day or so. There wasn't as much as a slip of paper to be seen. Mark indicated Sarah, Charlie and Linda Wu and pointed at the systems. These four people had training and a lot of history of looking for clues that didn't seem to exist.

Charlie and Linda started making sure that all the links had been removed from the systems. The systems had been thoroughly gone through by experts. There wasn't even a hint of anything on the hard drive on each local unit. All data had been erased from the hard drives except the basic operating system functions. The internet server hard drive was also erased which left no sign as to what web sites the computers had been communicating with when they were working.

Charlie fired up the server and connected it to his system in Colorado. He downloaded three programs developed for this exact scenario. Running the programs on the server work station and on one of the slave computers he was able to capture quite a lot of the data that the people before him had tried to hide. He uploaded all of the data to a safe storage area in his domain where any software worms or traps the enemy had left behind wouldn't be able to infect his systems.

Sarah had found a series of numbers taped to the bottom of a keyboard that had been overlooked and she took those with her.

But, that was the extent of their finds and they erased their presence from the building as they left, locking the door behind them.

Back in their vehicle, Charlie explained how he had been able to procure the information that the preceding group had erased from their hard drives. "You see, unless they took the time to do a low-level debug of each hard drive when they removed their data, all they accomplished was to eliminate the file allocation table or FAT table. This is the outer rings of data that tell the operating system where the files are on the hard drive. Without the FAT table it looks like there is nothing there. But the data is still there but without a directory. Any new data recorded to the hard drive would simply write over what was there before. My program simply records the data regardless of its location. I don't think we will get much from the individual, or slave, computer's hard drive I recorded, but, we should get a bunch from the server hard drive."

Mark asked him, "How long before you can get usable information that could tell us what they were working on?"

Charlie thought for a few seconds. "We should be able to see that by the time we get back to your base in Dallas. My programs are working on the data as we speak. The organization program should sort everything out and eliminate false leads so that we can make sense of what we got."

Laura asked Charlie, "If these guys were such computer and internet geniuses why would they leave the data on the drives and only erase the directories?"

Mark answered her. "That is because the bright guys weren't in charge of the security. The mercs were probably the ones that came in and hustled the brains out without advance warning. Then the security types sanitized the place. I would have expected them to destroy the computers but something must have prevented that. By now the "experts" are probably scattered back to their individual homes or businesses with the warning not to discuss anything they saw or did while they were working on Severon's business."

Everyone thought that over as they collected the Wu's belongings and turned in their rental car. The Team could use two additional people at this point. Jack aimed the big Suburban back towards Dallas in the dark in the piney woods of east Texas.

# CHAPTER TWENTY-SEVEN

In a small, quaint cafe in Jaffa, Israel, David Zahavy continued to be dismayed by the thick-headed, stiff-necked attitude of the people that seemed to comprise the majority of the Jewish race. He had lived here most of his life, had been an exemplary Jew, and had protected the nation for decades as a member of the Mossad and he still couldn't believe their stubbornness.

The man in front of him was a prime example of that mentality. He was a leader in his religious sect, a highly-respected man and forward thinker. Yet, he couldn't accept the concept of Christians defending Jews for any reason or despite any proof.

Abe Barzelai's concepts of the world included a temple-reinforced distrust for anything Christian and a radical viewpoint concerning the future of Israel. He would hear of no other thoughts. David remembered hearing Gary Eisenthal say, "His mind is made up, he doesn't want you to confuse him with the truth." How very true in this case.

David was here following a lead his agents had turned up concerning Barton Severon and his money. It seemed that he was conniving in Israel even though he professed to hate the country and the people. Some of Severon's millions had been traced to the radical Israeli group that based itself out of the temple in which Abe Barzelai was a Rabbi.

When David had originally walked into the cafe he had felt a catch in his spirit. That bad feeling was suddenly back as he was looking at this man. There was something going on that wasn't right. He smiled at the Rabbi and prepared to say goodbye when a dark, fabric hood was pulled over his head from behind and he felt a needle poke him in the neck. He tried to react but whatever was in the hypodermic was very fast acting and he lost control of his limbs and couldn't hang on as he slid into a great darkness. His last conscious thought was confusion as to why the two agents backing him up hadn't prevented this.

Outside the cafe, the two agents were beyond caring about anything. Their bodies were slumped down in their car with multiple bullet wounds. Three men openly carried the unconscious body of David Zahavy out of the cafe and roughly threw him into the back of a small truck which had a topper over the truck bed in back. They climbed into the cab and the truck sped off into the back streets of Jaffa.

As the truck turned down a narrow street they found themselves stopped by a handcart with sweetmeats on it. Blowing their horn and complaining about the blockage they were unaware of the three men closing on their truck from both sides.

All three new men opened fire with silenced pistols. The three Arabs in the cab died as quickly as the two Mossad agents they had killed moments before. The three men went to the back of the truck and opened the door. David was still lying crumpled in the back. They closed the doors and went back to the front. Pulling the bodies out of the cab the new men cleaned it out quickly and got in. Backing up to the intersection they turned and headed a different direction leaving the three Arab bodies in the street.

Sam Nelson smiled at the other two men. "It was certainly nice of those terrorists to collect Mr. Zahavy for us, don't you think?"

Bob Bullard laughed quietly, "Sure was. They certainly acted quickly on the tip we gave them, didn't they?" All three men laughed. Bob continued. "What do you think their rag head group will do when they find their guys dead and Zahavy missing?"

Sam shook his head. "It should be a while before they find out and by then, we'll be long gone!"

Sam wouldn't have been so confident if he had known about the Arab man on the rooftop a block away from their ambush site. He'd been watching with binoculars and speaking into a cell phone as the hit went down.

Sam took another corner at an intersection that led down toward the water and suddenly slammed on the brakes. He yelled, "Ambush!" and opened the door of the truck. Diving to the ground he rolled to the side of the road and behind an old French sedan sitting at the curb. Bob and the other mercenary went out the other door and sought shelter on that side of the street.

The cab area of the truck started taking rounds from what sounded like five or six Kalashnikov AK-47s. The roar of automatic rifles filled the street. The glass in the truck disintegrated in a shower of bullets. One of the rounds snapped the shift lever off of the steering column and shattered the column itself.

The mercenaries returned fire with their pistols and scored two hits. The volume of gunfire crossing between the merc's positions and the local rooftops was immense and made all the residents of the area flee to their homes or out of the area. Sirens were already responding as the Israeli Police homed in on the battle.

Freed of its parking prawl, the little truck started to roll downhill by itself. Smashing into the side of a parked car caused the truck to veer to the left as it left the battlefield behind. It deflected off of a building and rambled down a side street as the unconscious Mossad agent lay in the back.

Noticed by both sides of the battle, there was nothing that could be done about it as the bullets were keeping everyone pinned down.

The truck continued down the street, occasionally ricocheting off of other parked vehicles until it rolled across a larger avenue causing several other cars to swerve to miss it. Reaching the other side of the street, the vehicle spent the last of its momentum bouncing up three steps and coming to rest with its front end on a small porch of an empty house.

The battering back and forth had awakened David and then things settled down so that he wasn't being flung across the back of the truck. He was completely disoriented and wanted to just go back to sleep. But some inner warning told him he had to move. Years of training took over and he loosened his hands from the cord they had been bound in. He then pulled off the black bag over his head and breathed real air for the first time in what seemed forever. He used his feet and forced the back doors open on the little truck. Falling out of the bed onto the street was only a matter of two feet since the back end was well below the front end on the porch.

David had to make three attempts to stand before he gained his feet. He didn't know who he was, where he was, or why he was where he was. But the urgency within him made him stagger away from the truck and turn the first corner he came to. His walking improved somewhat and he made better time to the next corner, which he turned the other way. Eventually he came out onto a major street with shops on it and people strolling along.

A wave of weakness caused him to hang onto a signpost. A young couple from Germany was walking by and saw him stagger. The man, Karl Ernhart, asked David if he was all right or needed help. Karl didn't speak Hebrew so he asked the question in German. David had studied German as a youth and had been training in the language in the Mossad. He had actually spent eight months in Berlin on assignment and spoke fairly good German, even if he wasn't aware of those facts at the present.

Responding in German quite naturally, he told Karl that he had apparently had an auto accident and wasn't feeling too well at the moment.

Karl, and his wife Elie, felt concern for a fellow German and helped him down the street to a small cafe where he could sit at a table. Karl asked the waiter to bring them some water.

David's mind was terribly foggy. He couldn't remember anything before falling out of the truck. His inner urgency told him that he needed to get off the streets and out of sight while he worked out what was going on. His years of Mossad training and experience were too well ingrained to be ignored.

Karl was about to use his cell phone to call the police to help him. Not knowing why he didn't want that kind of help he asked Karl not to do that just yet. He told them that he was feeling much better just sitting there and drinking the water. A feeling of hunger struck him and he asked Elie if the cafe they were at served Bratwurst and Cabbage. These were two dishes he had eaten while in Berlin and it seemed to him at the moment that he was probably German. Those two foods were comfortable in a German setting. Karl laughed and said that David must be feeling better.

The restaurant did serve a Jewish form of sausage and cabbage and they all dined on it. David had two stouts with his meal. The heavy, dark ales had another soothing affect on his psyche and his stomach. David made the comment that the meal didn't measure up to one in Berlin. Elie smiled and asked him if he was well enough to remember where he lived or was staying.

David thought about it and came up with an address, even though he couldn't remember how to get there. Karl called up a directory on his phone and located the address. Karl paid for the meal and put David into a cab. Paying the driver for the trip in advance he was saying goodbye when David asked him where he and his wife were staying. Karl told him the name of their hotel and that they would be there for three more days if David wanted to reach him. He then waved and the cab pulled away.

David wasn't sure why he wanted to know where the couple was staying, but it seemed important and he was simply working off of hunches right then. There seemed to be more information floating just out of reach in his mind but he just couldn't seem to catch it. Maybe he would recall more once he got to where he was going.

A mile behind the departing cab, the Israeli police were pursuing ten or more people who had simultaneously fled the firefight when the first cop car got there. Other officers were examining the damaged truck, several dead bodies, and a bunch of abandoned weapons. While being pursued, all ten of the people were looking for David Zahavy as they moved.

Severon's mercs had survived the ambush with only one wound and that was minor. They ran in the downhill direction that the truck had gone earlier. Finding the truck they checked it quickly and noted that there was no blood in the back. So, the Mossad agent was still alive and loose. Barton would not be pleased with this piece of work.

Back in Dallas, Jack fielded a phone call on his cell phone. The caller was anonymous but Jack thought it was a military aide to General Miles if he was right about the voice. "Jack, you, Mark, and your wives need to be somewhere other than in the U.S. for the next few days. The Senator has gotten several Congressional warrants issued so that he can have you held until he can tie you up for the next month in committee hearings. While he finds enough information he can twist or misinterpret to hang your team. There are things being started right now that will get these indictments squashed, but it will take about three days. In the meantime, if the indictments can't be delivered, then they have no effect. Leave now!"

The caller hung up without even saying goodbye.

While Jack was analyzing all the factors about the call, Sarah also got a long-distance call on her cell phone. She listened for two minutes and then made a comment in Hebrew. She hung up and turned to the men. "David's been kidnapped in Jaffa. The Mossad feels it's a band of Islamic radicals. There may be a tie to Severon's money, but, they don't have any real leads and have no clue as to David's whereabouts. The call was from an old friend who knows that time is short and all he's able to do is investigate. I need to help David and I need to do it quickly." The urgency in her eyes was bright and undeniable.

Jack told her. "Get packed. The four of us will take a short vacation and see if we can't help David."

Mark looked puzzled. "Guys, we've got less than three weeks until the bomb goes off here in Dallas, what are you talking about?

Jack quickly filled the others in on the warning call from Washington. "Since we're stymied for the next few days anyway, we owe it to David to help him.

Two hours later, the four Team members were airborne with Su Li as their pilot. Their Cessna Citation X was already outside the jurisdiction of the U.S., flying at fifty-one thousand feet heading for the Middle East.

The Team brainstormed what they could do to help their friend. Jack brought up a hiccup in their plans. "Being shut off from the NSA prevents us from tracking him with his locator chip. That would give us a real head start. I don't think the Mossad is aware of his use of the ID chip as yet."

Mark frowned and thought for a few minutes. "Don't sell us out yet. I think I know how to get the information we need." He turned in his seat and picked up the satellite phone. Dialing a number from his catalog of numbers in his pocket PC he waited out the third ring before the phone was answered. "John Michaels, how can I help you?"

Mark smiled at the thought of the high jinks John and he had done in an earlier life. "John, this is Mr. Gopher, I need a small favor." Mr. Gopher had been his somewhat innocent nom de plume during some of their activities.

John was quiet for a few seconds, then he came back with, "Well, well, Mr. Gopher. It has been a long time since we, talked. What can I do for you?"

Mark continued, "It seems Mr. Roche has gone missing and I need to find him. Could you tell me where he is? His number is 3X098788P1."

John laughed, I'd like to help but Mr. Manly has foreseen this event and I am being seconded. I'll see you when this has been resolved, ta-ta."

Mark disconnected the call. He looked at the rest of them. "Well, it seems the long arm of Senator Lorch has made it impractical for the Crossfire Team to get any help from the NSA on David's tracker ID.

Sarah dialed a number. When she got a response she spoke rapid Hebrew telling the person on the other end the information and number that Mark had just made available to his friend at the NSA. She also got several pieces of information from the agent.

Hanging up, Sarah frowned, "I don't know if the NSA will give the cooperation to the Mossad to locate David in time. When we get there, maybe there will be someone who can tell us where to find him." The look on Sarah's face indicated that the interview would not be graceful or pleasant for the interviewee.

Sarah looked at Mark and asked, "Why do think they grabbed him now? Is it connected to us and our involvement with Severon's operation in Dallas?"

Mark thought for a few seconds. "I don't know Spylady. We'll just have to wait until we get there and see what we find."

Mark started praying. Things were just not going right for the Team. Everywhere they turned they were being stopped. Mark worried about what could happen in Israel and if they would be able to return in time to stop Severon's plan to bomb the Jews and Arabs out of Dallas.

# CHAPTER TWENTY-EIGHT

The cab pulled up to the address David had given the driver and David got out. The cab pulled away and David stood there in the fading afternoon sunlight and looked around. Nothing he saw brought back any memories.

He mounted the five steps to the front door and rang the doorbell. Nothing happened for a few minutes and then the curtain on the door was moved aside and a man stared at David for several seconds before unlocking and opening the door. The man was physically in good shape and looked to be a weight-lifter from his build and bulging biceps. His Jewish features were darkly handsome and he wore a small beard and mustache. He stepped out onto the small porch and asked, "How can I help you?" The man spoke in Hebrew.

David was stumped; neither the house nor the man brought back anything he could use. He looked at the young man and said, also in Hebrew, "I'm not sure. I was in an auto wreck earlier today and can't seem to remember much. I did remember this address though."

The man smiled and stepped forward and hugged him. "I'm sure we can help you, please come in." He stood back and gestured to the open door.

David didn't have anywhere else to go so he went into the house. The other man looked carefully around and, not seeing anything out of the ordinary, went back in and closed and locked the door.

He took David's arm and showed him to the living room. Indicating a soft chair for David he sat down across from him and looked carefully at him. It was obvious that David didn't recognize him. Softly he said, "My name is Judah Marriz. Do you remember Dizengoff Square a year ago?"

The name was familiar to David and the square he mentioned brought back many memories. But it was still elusive. The confusion showed on David's face.

Judah got up and asked David to stay there for a minute while he got some refreshments. He was back in

109

several minutes with a drink for each of them. David drank some of his and noted a strange odor or flavor in it. It didn't seem bad, just different.

As they sat there, not talking, David felt pleasantly comfortable and more at ease with his situation. He looked at the young man across from him and it came to mind to ask him, "Judah, how is your assignment here in Jaffa proceeding?"

Judah smiled, "Very well, Director Zahavy."

As that name registered in David's mind with it came a torrent of memories and David shook his head. The recent incidents up to the cafe kidnapping came clearly back into perspective for him. He sat up and analyzed events that he could remember since then. Then he looked at Judah. "How did I come to be here?"

Judah laughed, "Welcome back boss. I don't have a clue. You just appeared on my doorstep, apparently drugged and lost. I suspect it was one of your memories of this safe house address that led you here."

David nodded. He remembered deliberately memorizing this address so that he could drop in and see Judah after his meeting with the cleric at the cafe.

He asked his agent, "Let me use your phone."

Judah pulled the cell phone out of his pocket and gave it to David. David dialed a number and talked to his headquarters for several minutes. Then he thought for a few seconds and dialed another number. It was answered on the first ring.

David said, "Sarah?" Judah dropped his eyes as he remembered the woman his friend was talking to on the phone.

After a few minutes of pleasant talking, David got down to business. "Listen, I'm sure that Severon's agents were involved in my kidnapping. They're probably still looking for me as are the men involved with Rabbi Abe Barzelai. We will have to attend to them ourselves. I look forward to your stay. Judah and I will meet you at the airport ourselves. I still have to make amends for the first time you four came to Israel."

Breaking the connection he gave the phone back to Judah. "Your assignment for the duration has changed. You are seconded to me as of now and will work with Sarah's

Team and myself until we find a way to eliminate Severon and his operations!" David took the phone back again and made a second call to his office and dictated the change in Judah's status and ordered another agent to finish Judah's work in Jaffa. He also had them disable his previous cell phone and put a trace on anyone that used it.

He held the phone down and told his top agent at the Mossad the details of his kidnapping. He learned of the death of the supporting agents and the three Arabs that had kidnapped him from the cafe, the gun battle, and the search for the guilty. David told his office to concentrate on the Temple operations and Abe Barzelai and his contacts. Then he told them to forward all leads and reports on the three non-Arab men that had been involved in the gun battle to Judah. Hanging up he thought out the scenarios and made plans.

Explaining what he was contemplating to Judah, while he packed to leave, David saw that they had time to reach Ben Gurion International Airport to meet the Team after their fourteen hour flight from Dallas.

David stood up and immediately sat down again. The room wasn't too stable for him.

Judah put his hand on David's shoulder. "The antidote I gave you will gradually eliminate the effects of their drugs but you must move slowly for the next hour or so."

They got out of the building with Judah acting as a walking crutch for David. They got Judah's van out of the garage it had been kept in and Judah drove for the airport. David was glad to let him drive because the lanes, cars, and roads seemed to change dimensions as he looked at them.

# CHAPTER TWENTY-NINE

Thirty minutes out of Tel Aviv, Jack got a phone call from Charlie Wu. "Jack, my software has finished analyzing the information from Severon's server and slave computers. Their cleaning was pretty thorough so there isn't very much to be gleaned from the data. But, I was able to isolate a trend and capture a huge list of apparently random number groups that they were using and communicating back and forth to a high-speed number cruncher site of theirs. I have some suspicions as to their use but I would rather let you figure it out to see if I'm right. I just sent you the file. Let me know what else we can do."

Jack opened the file and studied the number groupings. Sequential strings of numbers with slight variations marched down the file. Jack called Mark over to look at the data. Mark looked at three sheets and then at Jack. "Those are PAL codes. Permissive Action Launch codes for U.S. ICBMs. I've seen them before when I worked on missile launch strategies. I'd guess that Severon was looking for launch codes so that he could control one or more of our intercontinental ballistic missiles."

Jack called Charlie back and confirmed his suspicions concerning the data. After some more details, Jack thanked him and broke the connection. Looking at the other three members of the Team he said, "We don't have to guess too hard to figure out what Severon wants with intercontinental ballistic missiles. I'd say we're heading for ground zero right now."

Mark and Sarah exchanged looks. Sarah nodded her head. "Mark was right. This is weirdly like the Denver scenario. The devil is trying to repeat a pattern here. Severon is going to detonate his Pakistani bomb in Dallas as a diversion so that he can try to get control of an ICBM during the confusion and launch it at Israel. That's how he expects the world to believe that the U.S. has become Israel's enemy. If he does launch, I can assure you that many of the surviving people in Israel will believe that."

Laura asked Mark, "Where are there missile silos or storage places that Severon could attack and use?"

Mark shook his head, "There are roughly 200 ICBMs and 20 missile alert facilities deployed over 12,600 square miles of Colorado, Nebraska, and Wyoming. But, the 90th Operations Group has over 1,500 combat-ready personnel on continuous alert to operate, protect, maintain, and support those sites. Severon cannot take over one of the isolated ten-silo complexes with only a hundred men. It's been tried before and failed miserably."

Mark gestured with his hands cutting his throat to illustrate the stupidity of such an operation. "The 90th Op Group provides the North American Aerospace Defense Command and United States Space Command Consolidated Command Center with road mobile, survivable, and endurable command, control, and communications, and base support capability. They train constantly just for this type of possibility. Unless Severon has some kind of special "in" he isn't going to succeed."

Jack thought about that. "What if he has bought or blackmailed some of the launch personnel to get his people into the silo command area?"

Mark shook his head. "I wouldn't put it past him to arrange something like that. But he still needs Presidential authority to launch. Even the local silo specialists can't launch a missile until they get an authenticated PAL or until all signals from command and control cease. That would signify a first strike that took out our administration and Space Command control. Then they would still have to coordinate a launch with their base command."

Sarah said, "We must assume that Severon knows all this and has found a way to circumvent the command and control authority. His electronic hunting for PAL codes indicates he's aware of the requirements. He plans to take a missile and launch it at Israel and I doubt that Israel will be able to stop it." The thought of a fifty-megaton warhead detonating over Tel Aviv made her sick to her stomach. Everything would be destroyed and many of the Jewish nation would die. The effects would last for hundreds of years and worse yet; she would see the Arabs dancing in the streets of their cities in triumph like they did after the 9/11 strike against America. "This must not be allowed!"

Her comment had all the conviction and the sincerity she could generate.

As the wheels on the aircraft came down in preparation for landing, Jack asked Mark a question. "Do we have enough valid information to warn the President of Severon's apparent plan?"

Mark considered the interference of the Senator. "Actually, we don't have any hard evidence that Severon is going to bomb Dallas or Israel. Both of these possibilities are just supposition on our part. But, they need to be investigated. Why don't you quietly contact Gary Rhodes and let him bring it forth as an FBI warning through Homeland Security? That way we won't be involved and the military can get the information to act on in the event we are right in our thinking."

Jack nodded and placed a call to Denver. As the plane touched down on the runway at Tel Aviv, he hung up and nodded to the others. At least their suspicions were in play and they might head Severon off in his quest to destroy the world.

# CHAPTER THIRTY

A large, florid-faced man of sizable girth, Severon jammed his six-foot, three-hundred pound frame into the chair across the desk from Pickett. His eyes locked on those of the mercenary. "Are we ready?"

Pickett smiled and nodded. "Yes Sir! We've got the drill down perfectly. If those software wizard's codes of yours work, we'll be launching our missiles at Israel in less than two weeks."

Severon smiled a grim smile. "Does it bother you that launching those missiles will kill over four million Jews?"

Pickett slowly shook his head. "As far as I'm concerned, any guilt will have to be handled by you. I'm just doing the job as requested. I feel that everyone has to die sometime anyway. So, your operation is expediting some of them, so what?"

Severon didn't like that attitude. He wanted to gloat and dance over the impending destruction as the sweetest victory ever seen. He stared at Pickett for a minute. "Okay, just make sure everything goes as planned." He levered himself out of the chair and made for the door to the office.

Pickett watched the man leave and shook his head. He wasn't happy about the destruction of an entire nation. He knew the odds of his surviving the assault were a lot higher than escaping the wrath that would follow. He had his money squirreled away and his vacation retreat all stocked up. He was going to disappear from the face of the earth after this job. He thought of the terrible things that would drive a man to kill millions of people he never met. "Sometimes revenge isn't enough." he thought to himself.

He was pretty sure that Severon would try to eliminate him and his men after the launch. It made sense to cover your tracks and eliminate eyewitnesses. Pickett had done it himself several times. But, he was fairly sure that he could pull it off and escape Severon's housecleaning. He wasn't too sure that his men would make it though. Too bad. Changing gears in his mind, he knew he had to get the

Dallas operation ready to go. His elite troops here would be ready when he returned from Dallas.

Severon rode in his chauffeured limousine deep in thought. He was on the brink of doing what he had sworn to his dead son that he would do. "Needless to say," he thought, "I'm going to be an unpopular person after that." His plans had been laid for several years and they were still solid. He was going to a place of extreme comfort and watch the world twist in the wind in their grief. They all deserved it after what they had done to him. His son had been the bright, shining star of his world. They were going to conquer the world after he served his military duty.

Severon's mind played the sequence over again for the thousandth time. The memories were so worn by being played over and over in his mind they were predictable. But, oh, they were still so painful.

His son was flying a U. S. Air Force F-18 fighter along with four others in a protective flight over Israel. Jordan had threatened to launch massive air strikes against the Jews for some, already forgotten border dispute. The United Nations had stepped in to prevent the entire region from going up in flames. The U. S. had sent fighters to the area to help keep the peace. Jordan had sent two dozen bombers towards the Israel border. In the confusion of the confrontation between the American fighters and the Jordanian bombers an overeager Israeli had launched a ground-to-air missile. Inexplicably the missile targeted his son's fighter rather than the bigger Jordanian bombers.

The missile tore the plane to pieces and his son was killed without ever knowing what killed him. The Israelis denied their culpability or even involvement. Severon was sure that was because they didn't want the Americans to hold them accountable. The U.S. compounded the insult by agreeing that the missile had not been launched by the Israelis but by persons unknown.

Severon swore revenge on the Israelis, the U.S. Government, and the U. N.

Well, the U.N. self-destructed by defending the Arab Strike Force which had poisoned both Israel and American cities. The UN was disbanded and thrown out of the U.S. They were effectively destroyed.

That left Israel and the U.S. Government. Well, this operation should eliminate the former and probably be a death knell to the latter. He knew it wouldn't bring his Donny back, but it would make him feel better about his responsibility to support his son.

What the billionaire wasn't aware of was that the forces of darkness had planned on his involvement for years. The demons that had carefully nurtured his hatred and pain were bringing along their part in a vast plan to kill God's people.

Donny Severon had died in his fighter over Israel but the missile hadn't come from the Israelis. It had been fired by a small group of PLO carefully goaded along by demons. The Arab radicals that fired the ground-to-air missile were under the impression that it would ignite the Jihad between Jordan and Israel. The head demon didn't care what they thought. His assignment was to use a missile to kill Donny Severon. He accomplished his assignment and left the confused radicals to die in a retaliatory raid by the IDF.

The enemy had prepared the man contacted by Barton Severon about what really happened to his son. The soldier had been carefully prepared to seek a reward by telling the rich man what he had been told to say.

Severon remembered the conversation with the ex-Captain. After he had assured the man he would be well-paid for his information Severon asked him what had happened to his son.

Licking his lips over the amount of money he would get, Norman Catrich told the millionaire the story he thought he had concocted himself. "Well sir, the Israelis were itching and moaning about how the Americans were showing up the Israeli Air Force. They weren't at all happy about being second best at anything. One of the things that really chapped their butts was that your son was richer than their Generals. They felt it was wrong that he was using his money to make himself look better than them. You know how they can't stand it when someone other than a Jew is successful. Well, your son wasn't snotty or anything but just being there irritated them. One of the Jews decided to show us that we were just as vulnerable as they were, regardless of how much money we had. He ordered a missile to be fired at a laser identifier. He then locked the identifier beam on your son's F-18. Crap, Mr. Severon. Those identifiers and the missile were given to the Jews by us."

"After they blew your son out of the air, everyone pretended like they didn't have anything to do with it. But really, everyone knew or found out real quick. Secretly the whole nation had a quiet celebration of the fact that they were better than us. Your son was just a symbol to them. They didn't care how hard he trained or how much he wanted to help Israel. They deliberately killed him in cold blood just to prove they were better than us and now they're saying they didn't do it. But, I've got the radar tracks and the tape of the pilot ordering your son's execution." Unfortunately, as Norman Catrich left his apartment one of the Hamas missiles fell out of the sky and he was killed immediately after his phone call. He had done what he did for greed and he didn't understand that Satan only needs you for his purposes. After that, he wanted Catrich's soul.

As for Barton Severon, the confirmation of the callous murder of his only beloved son drove the rich man into a form of insanity. The demon assigned to Barton fanned the flames of indignation, offense, and insult until nothing but the utter destruction of the Israelis would satisfy him.

Barton was quite brilliant in business. That's why he was so rich. He knew how to set up organizations to accomplish a stated goal. He set out to do just that with the destruction of the Jewish nation. He had succeeded, but he had shadowy help he wasn't aware of helping to guide his efforts and using the greed of others to make the right things happen.

The enemy of mankind was pleased with the progress that the "Arrow of Vengeance" was making. The unnecessary and excessive destruction of most of Dallas would just be an unexpected icing on the cake for Satan. But the enemy of mankind was most pleased because God did not want the destruction of His "chosen people".

# CHAPTER THIRTY-ONE

Hassim looked carefully into Abdullah's eyes. He spoke slowly and carefully to the young man. "You have been well trained and know how to do what you must do for the glory of God. Praise Allah and be brave!"

Abdullah smiled nervously and climbed into the helicopter's pilot seat. Still smiling on the outside he was trembling with fear on the inside. Thinking to himself, "I have flown one of these three times but can I really do what must be done? Ah, there is no one but me to do it. And I must do Allah's will." He started the helicopter engine run-up. As the craft came to life he thought about their path to this point.

They had discovered that the infidel mercenaries who had killed their bothers were about to leave Israel from this airport. The four of them had raced out here and, with the help of a fellow countryman who worked on the grounds maintenance crew; they had gotten into the secure facility. This way they had bypassed the Israeli Airport Authority checks required to gain entrance. They had guns and were prepared to hijack the airliner the mercenaries would board. Then Hassim got a call on his cell phone informing him that the men they were after were going to leave in a private jet.

There was no way they could get to the private hangers in time to stop them. Then Hassim saw a pilot preflighting a commercial helicopter for takeoff. He saw a way to achieve their victory. The killers could not be allowed to just fly away. No! This could not happen. They must die and since Abdullah was the only one of the four with helicopter pilot training, he was the chosen one to stop the infidels.

The pilot was in the co-pilot's seat but already dead. He would not be a problem. Abdullah realized that his life was about to end and that made him sad. He was so young that he hadn't even had a life yet. Still, this is what the Prophet said they must do to reach Paradise. He waited quietly as Hassim watched the aircraft coming out of the hangers in the private hanger area. Hassim knew the correct number on the tail and when he saw the plane head for the taxi strip he told Abdullah which one. Abdullah nodded and applied lift off power to the helicopter. It lurched off the ground and started to ascent. Allah would be honored this day.

As the Crossfire Team's aircraft came to a halt outside a private hanger, Sarah spotted David and Judah standing beside a van next to the hanger. "Much better than the last time." she thought, recalling the team's first arrival at Ben Gurion. They had been set up and she remembered even getting shot that time.

As they disembarked Sarah ran to David and hugged him. He smiled and held her at arm's length to look at her. "Well, being married to Mark seems to agree with you. You look wonderful."

Sarah stared at her mentor with fondness. "You don't look so good, David. What happened to you? We were coming over to see if we could help find you."

David let her go and smiled a grim smile. "It seems that you have started something with Severon that has spilled over on me. We're still trying to determine exactly what took place. I was drugged and don't remember anything before finding myself crawling out of a smashed-up truck bed."

Judah's phone rang and he answered it in Hebrew. He looked up and motioned for David. David made it over to him in three steps, "What is it? Have they found the men that kidnapped me?"

Judah was nodding as he hung up. "Yes sir, they're right here at the airport and apparently already boarded a private jet with the insignia 2B6793. The service is attempting to have the tower stop them."

David grabbed a pair of binoculars from the van and studied the aircraft on the taxiway. "That's the one right there. We need to stop them ourselves." Everyone piled into the van and Judah burned rubber in a quick turn to chase after the slowly taxiing aircraft.

A quarter-mile away, the commercial helicopter veered out of the strictly enforced flight path and headed directly for the taxiing jet. Abdullah hadn't even bothered to put on the head set and couldn't hear the strident demands of the tower to identify himself. He didn't speak Hebrew anyway. He lined up his approach to the taxiway and powered the helicopter into a dive towards the jet. He saw that he was going too fast and would go behind the plane so he shut off the power and angled the helicopter steeply at the oncoming jet.

With no power the helicopter dropped like a rock. Abdullah realized his mistake and attempted to add power as the runway came at him with a terrible speed. Meaning to say something profound at the last second, Abdullah just screamed as the fully-fuelled chopper smashed into the ground in a massive explosion.

Although he hadn't hit the business jet squarely, the explosion shattered the front of the jet and collapsed the front landing gear. The force of the blast blew through the front windscreens and instantly killed the pilot and copilot. The closed security door kept the flames from going straight through the aircraft.

The van was less than three hundred yards away when the helicopter crashed and Judah was hard-pressed to keep it from flipping over. The heat wave from the explosion blackened the paint on the front of the van and darkened the windshield.

"Dear Jesus" was all that Laura could say as she watched the devastation. Jack looked at David, "We've got to see if any of the passengers are still alive."

Judah shook his head. "The fire is too strong. It will reach the fuel tanks on the jet in almost no time. If you go there, you'll be killed."

At the urging of the Holy Spirit, Jack opened his door and jumped out of the stopped van, followed closely by Mark and Su Li. Racing toward the plane Su Li took the lead and ran towards the back of the private jet. The front door was already involved in the quickly moving fire. Su Li reached the back of the plane and reached up to a handle recessed into the surface of the plane. Pulling on the handle she tried to get it to come out. It wouldn't budge. Mark moved her to one side and grabbed the handle. The muscles in his arm stood out as he applied maximum force and the handle popped out. He turned it to the left and the baggage door opened upward.

Jumping up into the opening Mark pushed the piled bags out of the way and reached the emergency entrance to the passenger compartment. It opened without a problem and immediately smoke and debris flew out to the darkened compartment.

Su Li had followed Mark and reached over to a bulkhead and got an emergency flashlight. Powering it on she turned the beam into the passenger compartment. Everything had been thrown around by the crash and explosion. There were three bodies jumbled up in the seats and other things like part of the headliner.

Jack pushed past Mark and checked the first man. He had no pulse. Leaving him, Jack checked the other two, one was unconscious but alive and the other was dazed but somewhat awake. Jack steered the man to Mark and grabbed the other one. They hurried as quickly as possible back into the luggage compartment and Su Li dropped to the ground to find David, Judah, and Sarah there. Mark passed the mercenary he was helping down to them and turned to help Jack. Jack let Mark lower the man to the others and watched as Mark jumped down to the ground. About to go out the door he noticed a briefcase that had the Severon logo on it. He grabbed it and bailed out of the back of the aircraft.

Supporting the two mercenaries, the six Team members ran as hard as possible away from the plane. Laura pulled the van up to them and they all climbed into it. Laura turned and drove away from the wreckage as fast as the van would go.

Expecting the fuel tanks to go at any second, Jack looked back to see the fire going out. Then he saw the huge airport firefighting truck spraying foam over the wreckage and snuffing out the fire. Laura slowed the van as David told her to stop. She brought it to a halt and everyone exited the vehicle. Two military personnel carriers were quickly heading for them with a variety of heavy weapons pointed their way.

As the soldiers disembarked the personnel carriers the Team was ordered to put their hands behind their heads and to get on their knees. Obeying the demands the Team was impressed by the absolute control the IAA exerted.

David spoke to the officer-in-charge and let the man see Judah's identification. David hadn't had time to replace his that he had lost during the kidnapping. The officer used his comm gear and talked to several people. He then nodded and told everyone they could get up and put their hands down. Then he began to have a serious discussion with David since the IAA had no clue as to what had just happened. David wasn't sure of the helicopter involvement but knew about the mercenaries and their recent rampage in Jaffa.

The military wanted to take control of the two men and the briefcase but David convinced them that it would in the best interests of Israel if the IAA and the Mossad worked jointly to find out what they could.

Bullets smashed into the armored personnel carrier and whined through the air around the van. Everyone dropped to the ground or sought cover behind the APCs. The van took a barrage of rounds as the military sought the source of the attack. David looked at Jack, Mark, and Sarah. "What is it with you people? Every time you come here there's death and destruction and you're giving Ben Gurion a bad name." He was smiling as he said it so they weren't offended.

Sarah offered him an answer. "Somebody doesn't like us."

Two more APCs came into the fray and used their TOW missiles to destroy the two trucks being used by the attackers. The explosions were much smaller than the one the helicopter achieved but just as effective. The three men in the two trucks didn't survive the missile fire.

David spoke to the officer with them. "It seems almost anybody can get in here with guns anymore. I would also suggest that this group was responsible for the helicopter crash. I'm guessing that these are the militants that originally kidnapped me and were attempting to eliminate Severon's men for some real or implied insult."

The huge cloud of smoke from the aircraft and the smaller ones from the trucks had been extinguished. The bodies had all been bagged and the wreckage was being removed. The sky was still bright and life was returning to normal. All seven members of the Team had gone through an extensive interrogation, called a "debriefing" due to the involvement of the Mossad.

The wheels of Israeli justice had begun to turn and the Team was allowed to sit in on the interrogation of the two surviving mercenaries. It was an enlightening experience for most of them.

# CHAPTER THIRTY-TWO

As the full meaning and implications of the statement sank in, President Bollen smiled. He asked the Attorney General to clarify his announcement. "Run that by me again, okay?"

The Attorney General smiled a bigger smile. "All right, Mr. President. When I got notice from Homeland Security that there was some substance to the rumor about Senator Lorch meeting with Severon and terrorists, I followed it up by assigning two agents to corroborate the information."

The Attorney General shook his head sadly, "It's a sad thing when a popular, long-time public official decides to turn his back on his country." Frowning, he continued. "Anyway, when the agents confirmed there was credible evidence of this infamy, I convened a federal grand jury to bring indictments. John Ross, Lorch's number one boy got word of the grand jury and decided to cover his own tail. He came to our office and offered to give Lorch up if he could get a deal to keep himself out of jail. When we told him that he would have to name names and be specific, he laughed and said "Wait till you see what I've got." We agreed to a plea bargain and he gave us a DVD. That disc shows Lorch, Severon, Ross and the top two leaders of our favorite terrorist group, discussing Severon's plan to overthrow the Government of these United States. Lorch gets to be President for life as reward for his involvement. That involvement included the stopping and defaming the Crossfire team. He did this to keep them from derailing Severon's operations. And, of course, the DVD is in full color and stereo sound and has been verified as authentic by our experts."

The President considered the political implications; after all he was a politician. There would be major ramifications of Lorch's downfall. The most important would be his seat as Chairman of the Armed Services Committee. The Grand Jury investigation would also probably turn up a whole slew of co-conspirators and payoffs. The President prayed that the Lord would direct his handling of this meltdown. He suddenly realized that there was a better card to play than simply removing Lorch. He looked up at the AG and said, "Issue the warrants and bring them in on terrorism charges. But leak it to the press just before the arrest of Lorch. Bust him with the cameras rolling."

The AG smiled and left the Oval Office.

The President called the Chairman of the Joint Chiefs of Staff to his office. When General Miles arrived, the President briefed him on the upcoming event and told him to prepare his staff for a period of limited Congressional oversight. He also told him to get all of Lorch's warrants and condemnations of the Crossfire Team struck down.

After the General left, President Bollen sat back in his chair in the cool, quiet office, and thought out all the possibilities. He slapped his leg in emphasis of his feelings. "Severon is going to have a stroke when he sees Lorch get arrested."

Senator Lorch was having a great repast at one of Washington's finest restaurants with his influential friends when the FBI agents swarmed into the restaurant and found him. His loud protestations were seen and heard throughout the restaurant and would be soon heard around the world.

Knowing the seriousness of his crimes and the concrete evidence they were based on, the agents weren't bothered by his venomous threats and carried out their duty. They got him up from the table, emptied his pockets, frisked him, and then handcuffed him and led him away in front of everyone who was anyone and a bank of cameras. His lunch partners were so stunned they were voiceless in the face of the federal agents and the press.

The Senator was booked and his possessions, including his shoe laces were collected and put in an envelope. Then the guards marched him into the cell block and locked him in a cell. When he demanded to be released because he was a United States Senator, he was told he was incarcerated under the Patriot Act's anti-terrorist laws and there would be no bail, no release, and no privileges due to the seriousness of the charges.

He was allowed one phone call. So, the Senator called his lawyer. Having already been apprised of the charges and the solidness of the case by the Attorney General, the lawyer resigned and suggested the Senator ask for a public defender since no reputable lawyer would want to represent him.

The Senator was scheduled to appear before a judge in three days. Until then he would remain in his cell. All his bluster spent, he sat down on the thin mattress and looked at the bars all around him Two hours earlier, he was on top of the world, and now, he felt that the world had caved in on him. Seeing the other prisoners around him he was glad that at least he had a cell to himself. He didn't like the way the rougher inmates stared at him.

Severon sat at his desk, stunned by the television reports showing Senator Lorch being arrested and led away. He listened to the commentaries and heard the words "terrorist" and "rogue industrialist" and knew that the cat was out of the bag. Somehow, someone had made the connection between Lorch, himself, and the terrorists. He shut off the television and tried to think. This was not good! He had to shut the Senator up before he talked to the Government. Severon didn't doubt that the Senator would give him up in a New York second just to save his own worthless hide.

Severon punched in a number on his phone and heard Pickett answer. "Tom, we have a problem. Have you been watching the news?"

Tom said that he hadn't and Severon filled him in on the arrest. "We have to shut that fat slug up before he sings and ruins everything!"

Pickett was quiet for a few dozen seconds. Then he answered his boss, "You're right about shutting him up. Any suggestions on how we do that? He's probably being held in a federal facility. I would probably have to use the Pakistani bomb to make sure we got him."

Severon thought for a few seconds. Pickett's comment gave him an idea. He explained it to Pickett and told the mercenary that after he found out where Lorch was being held they'd refine the plan.

After Severon hung up, Pickett went over the idea from every angle he could and decided that the Billionaire was fairly brilliant in some ways, diabolical, but brilliant.

The Attorney General was aware of the power and money Severon could bring to eliminate the Senator so he had the man moved to an "undisclosed" security lock up and made sure that it was an "undisclosed" location.

Pickett had the "undisclosed" location of the Senator in less than an hour.

# CHAPTER THIRTY-THREE

In Israel, the interrogations of the two surviving mercenaries had cleared up the questions about the kidnapping and the airport attacks. But, it hadn't provided any new information concerning Severon's target or intentions.

For the tenth time, Sarah went over all the information they had acquired and considered the things they had retrieved from the bodies on the aircraft. All of their clothing and their effects were professionally cleaned and devoid of any traceable information. The only exception was a scrap of paper that had been in the pocket of one of the dead mercenaries. It was a phone number that was simple to track down. It was a nightclub in Corpus Christi, Texas. In fact, it was a sleazy stripper bar. The man had probably gotten the number from one of the girls that worked there. So it was just another dead end that didn't get the Team any closer to determining what Severon and Pickett were going to do in less than ten days.

The briefcase that Jack had rescued from the mercenary's aircraft was another enigma. It contained several text books on ship construction. Nothing was earmarked or highlighted so they didn't have any clue as to how the books tied into Severon's schemes. In fact, they might not be a clue at all. It could be that one of the men was just interested in how tankers and container ships were made. There was no indication as to where the books came from or who owned them.

David walked into the conference room and flipped a switch on his desk. A section of the wall slid back to display a big-screen TV. The arrest of Senator Lorch and his top aides was the story of the hour. The newscaster's analysis indicated that the Government had an air-tight case against the man and that a plea bargain would probably be in the works.

Mark shook his head, "Severon isn't going to let Lorch talk to a grand jury. I hope the AG knows that little fact."

Laura frowned, "I'm sure they are going to be ready for Severon. This arrest was way too public and the press was obviously told beforehand. I think this is a trap for Severon's people."

Mark thought for a few seconds. "Pickett won't send a hit man to take out Lorch. He's more likely to nuke the whole building."

Jack said, "Do you think with Lorch out of the way, we could talk to the AG and warn him?"

Mark said, "It's worth a shot." Looking in his cellphone for the data, he punched in the number and got the AG's hot line responder. Asking to talk to the attorney in charge of Lorch's case got Mark the AG himself. Ron Bittleman knew Mark personally from before the recent bad times. "Hi Mark; see you're calling from the Mossad. What's up?"

Mark's eyebrow went up along with his estimate of the AG's technical capabilities. It was obvious that he had an instant lock on Mark's cellphone. "Well Ron, I'm wondering if the Crossfire Team is off the hook enough to offer a suggestion to the Attorney General in reference to Senator Lorch."

Ron grinned even though he knew Mark couldn't see it. "Well, you guys have been given a clean bill of health from the administration now that the Senator is out of the action. But there are a lot of Senators and Representatives that still are very concerned about you thanks to Lorch's efforts. What do you have for us?"

"What I have is just a personal heads-up for you." Mark continued, "I know Pickett fairly well and if Severon wants to silence the Senator I would be concerned that Pickett will take out the entire city block to do the job."

Ron nodded his head as he talked, "Yeah, which was pretty much our assessment too. I'm glad you concur because I'm dealing with some pretty entrenched attitudes that Severon and Pickett are powerless against the system. I've taken steps to reduce the effects and to prevent Pickett from achieving his goal. What are you up to in the Jewish anvil?"

Mark pondered what he should divulge. "We needed to get away from Lorch's pogrom and one of our friends over here had a problem. We came over to see what we could do."

Ron laughed, "Okay, I won't pry. I've got to go anyway. Tell David Zahavy that the action at Ben Gurion was spectacular. Bye." The line went dead.

Mark looked at the others. "They're on top of it."

# CHAPTER THIRTY-FOUR

The high-powered attorney sat across from Barton Severon and inwardly gloated over the gigantic fee he was going to receive for this case. It would be tough and he would be up against a lot of damning evidence but he would make a great fight out of it. Personally, he was fairly sure that he would lose. But it would cost Severon several million to realize that.

Severon stared at the man with anticipation. This man would be their salvation to the Lorch mess. He indicated the Moroccan leather and gold trimmed, three thousand dollar brief case on the desk containing the files concerning the case. "There are the files you'll need during your interview with Lorch. You can keep the briefcase as a token of my appreciation of your taking this case. You have defended some of the people with the least chance in the Government's eyes and won. I expect nothing less in this case. Senator Lorch has been set up and framed, just like the Government is attempting to do to me. "He looked at his watch. "How soon will you be able to see Lorch?"

Stratford Fliess smiled. "It took my office less than an hour to arrange a meeting for me with the Senator. I will see him at two o'clock this afternoon. Of course the Government will take me there without letting me know where I'm going to be. No matter, by the time it comes to trial I should have the Senator being portrayed in the press as the injured party and it will only go downhill for the Government from there." He stood up and closed the briefcase.

Severon looked at his watch. "I'll get one of my people to take you to the drop-off point for meeting the Government people. You'll just have time to get there if you leave now. If you decide to take the case after meeting with the Senator then I'll wire the first third of your fee to your office."

The thought of the seven-figure down payment made the lawyer smile. Severon smiled back and waved the man on his way.

As Severon's driver took him to the rendezvous, Fliess thought about the people he had been defending for the last eight years. A maniacal, drugged-out basketball star that had killed his wife and three other family members. He did this while on a mixture of cocaine, alcohol, meth, and doughnuts. Using a diminished capacity defense, Fliess had gotten him off with only community service and drug rehabilitation. Thinking about the case the attorney smiled. The man had killed them before he started the drugs, at least for that day. It was too bad the athlete didn't learn anything and killed his manager two years later. This time there was no defense, he was just mad at the man for not doing what he wanted. He had stayed away from drugs. Unfortunately it was drugs the state gave him that killed him in the death chamber. Fliess had made three million on that one.

The last defendant he represented was the reason that Severon had called on him. This time it was a traitor who was caught, red-handed, giving information to a terrorist group. He'd even confessed to everything. Fliess was able to convince a jury that he had been coerced into making a false confession. Fliess had impugned the star witness against his defendant because he was a former spy for the Iranians and had lied enough that Fliess was able to convince the panel of jurors that the man's word could not be trusted. After getting the case against his man dismissed, Fliess turned around and sued the U.S. Government for profiling and illegal privacy invasion. He'd shared in the seven million dollar settlement the liberal judge had awarded his poor, defamed client. Actually, the man was guilty and should have been hung. But thanks to Fliess' talents, he was back to spying for the same terrorist group again.

The van pulled over to the curb where a similar black van waited with two men standing beside it. Fliess climbed out and ignored Severon's driver completely. The man drove away.

After greeting the Federal authorities, Fliess was searched along with his briefcase and taken in a windowless van to a building several miles away. When he exited the van he was already in a closed garage. They took an elevator up several floors and then walked down a long hall to a small conference room. It was eerie in the building. No sound of other people, machines working, nothing. Fliess realized that they would keep the Senator isolated from everyone else to protect him.

Entering the room he found himself facing a wall of thick, bulletproof glass with a microphone and speaker arrangement. On the other side of the wall sat a dejected Senator Lorch. The lawyer turned to the agent that had brought him here. "I'm invoking the right of attorney-client privilege. No one is to be present at this meeting or to hear what we are saying. Is that understood?"

The agent didn't look happy about it but told Fliess that no one would be within hearing range and that there were no taping devices. They would be watched on closed-circuit television but the audio was completely disabled. Then he left and shut the door.

Stratford Fliess sat down in the comfortable chair and stared through the glass at the Senator. "Senator, how are you doing?"

The Senator looked frustrated but nodded. "I'm in a real pickle here. Can you really do anything for me?"

The lawyer stared at his ball-point pin and watched the band at the end of the cap. It stayed white. It was another gift from Severon. It could detect the slightest radio transmission in the area. No one was transmitting or monitoring their conversation. "Barton Severon has retained me to defend you. We will be attempting to destroy the Government's case against you and make them out as the villains in this case." He opened the case and took out the information Severon wanted the lawyer to explain to the Senator before they got into the particulars of the action.

Looking down the information he wondered about one line. "What does Severon mean here when he said to tell you "Pickett sent me"?"

The Senator's eyes opened wide and he started to say something when the world exploded and everything was fire and collapsing rooms.

A quarter mile away, Pickett put the radio detonator away and started his car. Lorch's case was closed and they could get on with their business.

As Pickett drove away from the scene of the explosion and fire, one of the Federal Prosecutors watched the entire wing of the abandoned building as it collapsed in fire and debris. He said quietly, "Well?"

A very much alive Senator Lorch shook his head. "Okay, you've got a deal. That SOB wants to kill me so bad, I'll tell you everything I know about Severon." He looked at the building again and wondered if the attorney ever realized that he was all alone in the building with a plasma screen image when the bomb went off.

# CHAPTER THIRTY-FIVE

Jack sat quietly in the darkness of his seat in the Citation X as it winged its way through the night back to the United States. Su Li was at the controls with a Mossad co-pilot for backup.

Jack's prayers had been fervent and long. He was beseeching the Lord of the Universe to prevent the death of His children in Dallas, Israel, and wherever else Pickett and Severon were going to attempt their takeover of ICBMs. He had pleaded with God to help all the unsuspecting people that would have their lives snuffed out in an instant by the nuclear horror that Severon was arranging to bring to Texas and Israel. The Lord had agreed that Severon had to be stopped and He made it clear to Jack that He was counting on the Crossfire Team to stop him

In the glow of the lights from across the aisle, Jack looked at his beautiful wife sleeping in the seat next to him. His heart ached when he thought of her going into battle after battle with him and risking everything. He realized the loss he was worried about would be what he would feel. It dawned on him at that point that he wasn't looking at their efforts through the eyes of the spirit but through the eyes of the flesh.

The fear of loss wasn't a thought from God or even himself. Jack confessed it as a sin and asked the Lord for forgiveness. He repented of the sin, and then he took the thought captive to the Lord. In his mind's eye he literally put the possible hurt and sorrow on an altar in his mind and raised it up to Yahshua. As he communed with the Lord he felt the burden lift and peace and love came from the Lord. He felt the truth and conviction of the Holy Spirit that it was right for Laura to be with him to face the dangers. He also felt the assurance that he would never be separated from his wife through all time. He leaned over and kissed her cheek. She stirred and smiled in her sleep.

Jack looked across the aisle and watched Mark, Sarah, and David as they went over all the information they had on Severon's ICBM operation. Jack thought about the thrust of Severon's obsession. He wanted to launch one or more ICBMs at Israel. They had talked to the commander of the 90th Operations Group and had been assured that steps were being taken to keep Severon from having any access or edge to any of the silos or the command centers. After listening to the precautions being taken it was obvious that five more bodies wouldn't add anything to the defense there.

Jack asked the Lord for assurance that their construction of events was the true possible future. He realized that no other agency had any such theory. This was a Crossfire Team concept that actually was made up of nothing but their expertise, Mark's knowledge of Pickett's operations, and guesses.

He tried to look at the situation through the eyes of another group that didn't explicitly trust each one of the Team members. It was an eye opener. They could be totally off-base and Severon might not be doing any of the things with which they had judged him. They were going to look really foolish if there was no Dallas operation or bomb, let alone any attempt for the ICBMs. But, the concept of being judged wasn't something that deterred Jack or any of the other Crossfire warriors.

True, Severon was doing everything he could to eliminate or muzzle them. But that could be revenge for eliminating their cash cow pastor. The Dallas thing was based on a bar-room rumor that Mark had pried out of a disgruntled ex-Jewish mercenary that could be only a figment of his imagination. Suddenly Jack wasn't so sure they had the right handle on this matter.

Across the aisle the other three Team members sat back and looked at each other. Mark turned and got Jack's attention and motioned for him to come over. After he took the fourth seat of the two sets of facing seats, Mark indicated the piles of data in front of them. "We've looked at the second attack and ICBM control scenarios every way we can think of and there is nothing we can add to the 90th's efforts to protect the silos. I think if Severon tries to get control of one he will be stopped and probably killed along with Pickett and all of his men. I really can't see any weaknesses in their coverage regardless how hard all three of us try. David, Sarah, and I have penetrated dozens of supposedly secure sites, many times with ease. All three of us are stymied by the system in place here. And, this worries me. If we can conclude this then so can Pickett. He's not going to charge into sure death. They have to have something else up their sleeves."

Jack nodded. "All right, if you three are positive the ICBM defense is as good as it can get, then we need to focus on the possible Dallas bomb. Let's shift all of our efforts to that problem, although I have to tell you I am beginning to believe that we may be misled in these efforts. I can't believe that we can be the only group that has gotten wind of this attack. Also, thinking back over the things that have led us to believe this I can't find any concrete leads or sure indications that Severon is really going to nuke Dallas."

Mark sighed, "I know. I've thought the same things. It does seem strange that the FBI, CIA, and David's group haven't even gotten a clue about either operation. I've prayed about this until my head hurts. I feel a peace about it; I'm just not sure we could convince anyone else.

Jack realized that the tables were turned from previous missions when he asked Mark, "Are you sure enough to bet everything on it?"

Mark nodded, "Yes I am. I believe we need to go forward as if both missions are real. I feel in my spirit as well as my gut Severon is going to nuke Dallas and Israel."

Jack felt a conviction that Mark was right. "Okay, then we proceed as before regardless of the other agency's determinations."

Mark realized the tremendous faith Jack was according to him. If he was wrong it would disgrace the Malones as well as the Crossfire Team. Mark nodded again, "Okay, I talked to General Miles a little while ago concerning the Miles Marauders. He has them in the middle of a messy situation and they won't be able to help us with either one of these operations. There are other military groups available, but it will take time to get them reassigned and I doubt that they could be in Dallas in time to help. It looks like we have to find the bomb by ourselves, and possibly with some help from the FBI. Even though we've been cleared from Senator's Lorch's recriminations it will take a few weeks to forever before some of the alphabet agencies will work with us or even trust us."

Jack nodded his head. "The Lord firmly confirmed that it is up to us to stop Severon. He is counting on us."

Mark, Sarah, and David looked at each other and realized the awesome responsibility that they had been given. Even though they had notified every agency concerning their assumption that the Pakistani bomb would be used in Dallas there was no real proof. No weapon signatures had been detected in that area of Texas, and until there was, none of the agencies wanted to stick their collective necks out.

In the cones of light from the overhead console, the four Crossfire warriors felt the weight and the incredible tiredness that comes with such liability. Then a hint of a soft perfume and the gentle touch of a hand on Jack's shoulder told them that Laura had joined the group out of the dark. She bent down and kissed Jack on the cheek. Looking at the four super-serious people she grinned. "You forget whose side you're on. I suggest that we ask God what we need to do and for his strength to do it."

As usual, Laura's calm insight cut through the heaviness surrounding the group. The despair fled into the dark as the Team sought the Lord and his counsel. The praise song they sang first was sweet and militant at the same time. It concerned the taking back what the enemy had stolen. Su Li lifted one of her headphones and listened to the singing and smiled.

The co-pilot saw her smile and grinned in return. He had heard some interesting stories of what happens after these people started praising their God.

# CHAPTER THIRTY-SIX

After the Team returned to their suite in Dallas, Mark got a call from John Michaels of the NSA. "Mr. Gopher, I presume?"

"Hi John, has Mr. Manly gotten off your back so you can talk to me yet?"

John laughed. "It seems the pressure has been removed and your image has been spit-shined and placed back in the "friends" category. I see you resolved your location problem since your two locators are showing as one dot right now."

Mark thought, "Boy, they are getting a little too good these days." He said, "Yes, we have. I assume that there is another purpose for this call?"

John's voice turned serious over the phone. "Yeah, my mom and dad live in Dallas and I prefer them the way they are rather than as crispy critters. Thanks to our illustrious past, I've been given the honor of assisting you in locating the Pakistani bomb. That is, IF it is in Dallas. Our equipment is pretty high-tech and dang accurate and we don't have a hint of that particularly nasty piece of hardware in the Dallas area."

Mark wasn't surprised; the same equipment hadn't found the bombs near Denver either. The new shielding technique that the ASF had acquired was still effective. He decided to give his friend a challenge. "If your equipment is so good then tell me where in the world that particular Pakistani nuclear weapon is at the moment."

John was quiet for a few seconds. "I see what you mean. The bomb in Denver was also hidden from our sight wasn't it?"

Mark said, "Both nuclear weapons were hidden so none of our equipment could locate them."

John whistled, "That's right! The missile head was also cloaked. Our scientists have the cloaking material for both of those weapons. I'll check and see if they've figured out how to penetrate the stuff."

Mark said, "You'd better hurry if you want to spend the holidays with your folks. I believe the information we have is righteous and we only have four days left before the conference."

John said that he would hurry and hung up.

Jack asked Mark, "Just how much damage will this bomb do to the city?"

Mark thought for a second. "The total destruction in the area of the bomb is about a mile or so. But, let's get someone in here who has the actual data and can give us a professional opinion."

Laura looked at Mark, "Like whom? We're still not too well liked in a lot of places you know."

Mark grinned, "This guy will be glad to talk about one of his hobbies to us. I'm talking about Mike White."

Su Li smiled at her teacher's name. "Mike's going to come here? Maybe he can teach me about the new Super-Raptor I've been hearing about."

Mark grinned, "He might."

Jack suggested that while the rest of the crew was working to determine the specifics of their challenge he and Laura would seek God's direction on how to stop the detonation. They went into the study of the suite and relaxed on two of the chairs there.

As they prayed Jack felt the heaviness of the Holy Spirit settle on him as he sought the Lord of the Universe. It was very pleasant and comforting to him. He let himself settle into the feeling and the rest of the world moved off into the distance. He prayed with a broken and contrite heart, knowing at last that he was powerless to do anything without God. He earnestly implored God to use him and the rest of the Team as His agents on Earth to do His will. He then cleared his mind of all distracting thoughts and listened patiently for God's answer. A concept came into his mind. No words, no angels, not even a scripture, just a concept. He saw an old haystack and watched a needle fall into it. No amount of careful searching could find the needle. Then a powerful magnet appeared above the haystack and the needle jumped out of the stack and stuck to the magnet. Then he felt the urging of God's Holy Spirit to get after it!

He opened his eyes and saw Laura still in prayer but with smile on her face. In a few minutes she opened her eyes and grinned at him.

Jack said, "What are you grinning about?"

She replied, "God was very specific in His solution to our problem."

Jack was amazed; maybe his vision didn't have anything to do with God's solution after all. "What did He tell you?"

She tipped her head to one side. "He told me that He gave you the answer on how to find the bomb."

Jack thought for a second and then told her. "Well, that is confirmation for sure."

Laura sat up, "What did He tell you?"

It was Jack's turn to smile, "It's just a needle in a haystack. We need to find a new solution to finding a hidden nuclear weapon in a city of over seven million people."

Laura thought that over. "Okay then, let's go tell the others."

Sarah chewed on the information for a while and then looked up. "You know there may be a different way of finding such a weapon than any we have used so far. The unique thing will be that it won't be something that Severon or Pickett have thought of so far. So, we need to think of everything they could of thought of and find something they wouldn't have thought of yet." She looked at Mark, "Well honey, this sounds like your forte."

Mark smiled at his wife, "Yeah, thanks a lot."

Jack asked Mark if he had been able to get in touch with the Air Force Major. Mark nodded, "He'll be here tomorrow morning at nine."

Sarah came over and sat down across from Mark. "Okay, you play like you're Pickett." She looked at Jack. "You play like you're Severon. Now let's brainstorm all the possible ways that the U. S. Government could detect our leaky old Pakistani ten-kiloton nuclear weapon."

The session lasted well into the early morning hours but didn't resolve their problem of locating the bomb if it really was in Dallas.

# CHAPTER THIRTY-SEVEN

The next morning Mike White sat at the table and listened to the Team as they discussed what they felt the possibilities of damage and death would be if the ten-kiloton Pakistani nuclear weapon went off in the city of Dallas. Clearing his throat he got everyone's attention. He smiled grimly at the people in the room. "You all have been discussing what you've heard about a nuclear strike. But, you need to be educated on the actual damage even a small-sized nuke like that can do in a crowded metropolitan area."

Every eye was on him as he talked. "Nuclear detonations of any size are extremely devastating. Remember Hiroshima or Nagasaki. A nuclear detonation generates and maintains a severe environment including blast, thermal pulse, neutrons, x- and gamma-rays, radiation, electromagnetic pulse, and ionization of the upper atmosphere. Depending upon the environment in which the weapon is detonated, blast effects are manifested as ground shock, water shock, cratering, and large amounts of dust and radioactive fallout. All of these factors pose problems for the survival of the local population."

The Major got up and paced back and forth as he recited the details from memory. "The energy of a nuclear explosion is transferred to the surrounding medium in three distinct forms: blast; thermal radiation; and nuclear radiation. The distribution of energy among these three forms will depend on the yield of the weapon, the location of the burst, and the characteristics of the environment. If Severon is planning a low altitude atmospheric detonation of the ten-kiloton weapon, the energy will be distributed roughly as fifty percent as blast and thirty-five percent as thermal radiation. The thermal radiation is made up of a wide range of the electromagnetic spectrum, including infrared, visible, and ultraviolet light and some soft x-rays which are emitted at the time of the explosion. Another fifteen percent of the energy will be emitted as nuclear radiation; including five percent as initial ionizing radiation consisting chiefly of neutrons and gamma rays emitted within the first minute after detonation, and another ten percent as residual nuclear radiation. Residual nuclear radiation is the hazard in fallout."

He looked at the assembled crew. "Got it so far?" Everyone nodded or said that they understood him.

Mike pulled out several documents from his briefcase. Referring to them he continued. "Considerable variation from this distribution will occur depending upon the location Severon chooses for the detonation.

Because of the tremendous amounts of energy liberated per unit mass in a nuclear detonation, temperatures of several tens of million degrees centigrade develop in the immediate area of the detonation compared to the few thousand degrees of a conventional explosion. At these very high temperatures the nonfissioned parts of the nuclear weapon are vaporized. The atoms do not release the energy as kinetic energy but release it in the form of large amounts of electromagnetic radiation. In an atmospheric detonation, this electromagnetic radiation, consisting chiefly of soft x-ray, is absorbed within a few meters of the point of detonation by the surrounding atmosphere, heating it to extremely high temperatures and forming a brilliantly hot sphere of air and gaseous weapon residues, the so-called fireball. Immediately upon formation, the fireball begins to grow rapidly and rise like a hot air balloon. Within a millisecond after detonation, the diameter of the fireball from a ten-kiloton air burst is only twenty meters. This increases to a maximum of roughly 1100 meters within 10 seconds, at which time the fireball is also rising at the rate of 100 m/sec. The initial rapid expansion of the fireball severely compresses the surrounding atmosphere, producing a powerful blast wave."

Everyone in the room could picture the fireball in the heart of the city. The Major let them think about it for a few seconds before he went on. "As it expands toward its maximum diameter, the fireball cools, and after about a minute its temperature has decreased to such an extent that it no longer emits significant amounts of thermal radiation. The combination of the upward movement and the cooling of the fireball give rise to the formation of the characteristic mushroom-shaped cloud."

"As the fireball cools, the vaporized materials in it condense to form a cloud of solid particles. Following an air burst, condensed droplets of water give it a typical white cloud like appearance. In the case of a surface burst, this cloud will also contain large quantities of dirt and other debris which are vaporized when the fireball touches the earth's surface or are sucked up by the strong updrafts afterward, giving the cloud a dirty brown appearance. The dirt and debris become contaminated with the radioisotopes generated by the explosion or activated by neutron radiation and fall to earth as fallout."

"This causes tremendous suffering over a long period as it gets into the people that survive, the animals, the plants, everything. As observed in the Hiroshima blast, which was a relatively small blast, the thermal radiation increases the level of thermal energy in all physical structures for miles. The intensely hot air rising rapidly over the site of the explosion sucks a hurricane force of inrushing cooler air at ground level, towards the point of the explosion. This creates an intense fire-storm surrounding ground zero."

"Again, the relative effects of blast, heat, and nuclear radiation will largely be determined by the altitude at which the weapon is detonated. Nuclear explosions are generally classified as air bursts, surface bursts, subsurface bursts, or high altitude bursts. I'll describe each of these but I would bet that Severon is planning a surface burst."

"An air burst is an explosion in which a weapon is detonated in air at an altitude below thirty kilometers but at sufficient height that the fireball does not contact the surface of the earth. After such a burst, the blast may cause considerable damage and injury. The altitude of an air burst can be varied to obtain maximum blast effects, maximum thermal effects, desired radiation effects, or a balanced combination of these effects. Burns to exposed skin may be produced over many square kilometers and eye injuries over a still larger area. Initial nuclear radiation would be a significant hazard with Severon's smaller weapon, but, if he was to use an air burst, the fallout hazard can be ignored as there is essentially no local fallout. The fission products are generally dispersed over a large area of the globe unless there is local rainfall resulting in localized fallout. In the vicinity of ground zero, there may be a small area of neutron-induced activity which could be hazardous to anyone required to pass through the area."

Mike sat down again and referred to the documents. Locating the article he wanted, he continued the lesson. "A surface burst is an explosion in which a weapon is detonated on or slightly above the surface of the earth so that the fireball actually touches the land or water surface. Under these conditions, the area affected by blast, thermal radiation, and initial nuclear radiation will be less extensive than for an air burst of similar yield, except in the region of ground zero where destruction is concentrated. In contrast with air bursts, local fallout can be a hazard over a much larger downwind area than that which is affected by blast and thermal radiation. I would think this would be Severon's first choice even though it requires the bomb to be more exposed and therefore more vulnerable."

"A subsurface burst is an explosion in which the point of the detonation is beneath the surface of land or water. Cratering will generally result from an underground burst, just as for a surface burst. If the burst does not penetrate the surface, the only other hazard will be from ground or water shock. If the burst is shallow enough to penetrate the surface, blast, thermal, and initial nuclear radiation effects will be present, but will be less than for a surface burst of comparable yield. Local fallout would be very heavy if penetration occurs.

He shook his head at the prospect of a citizen turning on his nation like this. Especially if the Crossfire Team was right and he was only using it as a diversion. He looked up at the people in the room. "I am pretty sure there will be no way Severon could drop his bomb without being detected with it on an airplane. But to round out the descriptions, a high altitude burst is one in which the weapon is exploded at an altitude above thirty kilometers. Initial soft x-rays generated by the detonation dissipate energy as heat in a much larger volume of air molecules. There the fireball would be much larger and would expand much more rapidly. The ionizing radiation from a high altitude burst can travel for hundreds of miles before being absorbed. Significant ionization of the upper atmosphere (ionosphere) can occur with larger weapons, say over a megaton.

Severe disruption in communications can occur following high altitude bursts. They also lead to generation of an intense electromagnetic pulse (EMP) which can significantly degrade performance of or destroy sophisticated electronic equipment. There are no known biological effects of EMP; however, indirect effects may result from failure of critical military or medical equipment. "

He thought for a few seconds and then dug out a different article. Scanning it he found the part he wanted. He read from the paper. "Although thermal radiation, EMP, and ionizing radiation from a nuclear blast are all damage producing, Severon's stolen Pakistani bomb is five times as powerful as the normal field-tactical nuke. At yields below a megaton the blast and shock produced by a nuclear weapon cause the predominant damages."

"The intensity of thermal radiation decreases as the inverse square of the distance from a nuclear detonation, while blast, shock, and prompt ionizing radiation effects decrease much more rapidly. Thus, small-yield weapons are not primarily incendiary weapons, able to start fires and do other thermal damage at distances well beyond the radius at which they can topple buildings or overturn vehicles. With the size of his weapon I would say that Severon is not intent on completely destroying the city of Dallas. He probably does want to kill all the Arabs and Jews at the conference and create a major disaster to draw everyone's attention. Therefore I suspect that he will center the bomb on or near the site of the conference building."

The Major sat back in his seat, "That, ladies and gentlemen is the definition of what a ten-kiloton nuclear explosion will do. As far as the actual damage his bomb will do to Dallas I can give you the approximate radii of the effects. The actual blast will cause a minimum of fifty percent casualties in a circle a quarter of a mile across. The ionizing radiation and thermal radiation will do the same in a circle one-half mile across. If this was set to detonate at the American Airlines Center you would completely lose all of downtown Dallas and a hundred blocks of the suburbs in all directions. The fire and radiation damage will be extensive for about three miles for anything that isn't knocked down by the initial blast. If this goes during the business day I would guess that you'll kill roughly a hundred thousand or more people in that area if they are not evacuated first."

The gruesome facts sank in on everyone. After a few minutes Mark asked the Major what documents he was quoting his data from.

Major White said, "This is information adapted from a document called "Nuclear Weapons Effects Technology (MCTL) Part II: Weapons of Mass Destruction Technologies", and two papers, "The Effects of Nuclear Weapons" and the "Effects of Nuclear War" from the Office of Technology Assessment, May 1979. I'm also quoting from the "NATO Handbook on the Medical Aspects of NBC Defensive Operations Part I - Nuclear" and the "Nuclear Attack Planning Base 1990, the Final Project Report, Executive Summary dated April 1987. That should give you any backup data you need."

Mark nodded as he wrote down the titles of the papers. "Thanks, Mike; if we survive I'll use these in my summary report to General Miles."

# CHAPTER THIRTY-EIGHT

Jack had worked hard in the on-going guessing-game to determine how to find Severon's bomb before the next thirty-six hours passed and the whole question would be unnecessary.

He was resting in the bedroom he and Laura shared. Lying on the bed he ran the whole list of possibilities over in his mind for the tenth time. There just wasn't any new way they could think of that Severon wouldn't have countered already. The man was warped for sure, but still brilliant.

Something tickled the back of Jack's mind. He relaxed and let the thought emerge. Severon was brilliant but that was also his weakness. He could have created his own flaw. "But what would that be?" The question bounced around for a few seconds and Jack asked the Holy Spirit to grant him wisdom on this subject.

A truly original thought came to his mind. Jack manipulated the thought and looked for loopholes. Then he thanked God for the "wisdom" and jumped up from the bed. Striding back into the living room which was acting as a war room for the moment he startled the Team by slapping his hand on the table.

Noticing that everyone was now looking at him, he announced. "I think God has shown me the way to find Severon's little package of joy."

Mark dropped his pen on the table and said, "Enlighten us, please."

Jack walked over to the white board they had set up and erased everything that was on it. He then drew out his concept. Pointing at various parts of the drawing he explained. "Which of you are familiar with Gamma radiation?"

Mark, Sarah, David, and the Major nodded.

Jack explained to Su Li and Laura, "Gamma rays are not actual particles but photons. The rays are high energy and therefore, have high penetrating power. Lead shielding can provide protection, and I'm pretty sure that Severon's shielding can stop them also. That is the key that will let us locate his bomb. The fact that he has shielding that will stop Gamma radiation!"

He grinned, "Since Gamma radiation can be directed in a straight line, what we will do is sweep the suspected area with Gamma radiation and then see if the "transmission" is blocked at any point between the generator and the receiver."

Mark nodded his head. "That would work if we had a generator and a receiver for Gamma radiation."

Jack smiled again. "I know of a DARPA project in the Carrollton area that has an extremely high energy Gamma emitter. They also have a computer-controlled detector that records the Gamma radiation as a straight line as seen from above. It has only been used in the confines of a laboratory. What I'm suggesting is that we "borrow" those two systems, mount the receiver in a helicopter and the generator on a truck. Then we start at the Reunion Arena and sequentially generate Gamma beams in a radius from the arena in all directions. We'll watch the lines from the helicopter and if the line stops or is broken then we may have a possible location of the device."

Mark said, "Won't that be a little hazardous for the people in the way of the beams?"

Jack shook his head, "Not really because we all have Gamma radiation that passes through us every day. Also, assuming Mike's right about Severon using a low altitude surface burst, we'll do our search starting thirty feet above the ground and it shouldn't affect anyone on the ground. Remember, we expect the device to be near the Arena. Once we find one or more locations. We can move the truck and cover the suspect point or points from a ninety-degree angle and triangulate the position. Then we will vary the height of the transmitter until we know about how high it is. After that we can determine what we can do to get to it."

The Major added, "That is, if it really is in Dallas." Mark frowned. He was sure that they would find it in Dallas. This wasn't pride on his part. He knew in his spirit that it would be there.

# CHAPTER THIRTY-NINE

It had taken the direct intervention of the DOD ordered by the President of the United States to get the company to allow the Team to use their Beta test Gamma Ray beam generator and detector. But it was accomplished with the agreement that engineers from the company could accompany both parts and monitor the operations.

Mark chuckled inside as he remembered the two engineer's faces when he had handed them their Kevlar vests and pistols. They both had big eyes when Mark had told them, "There are certain risks to this operation and you need to be prepared. Hopefully nothing will happen during the tests, but just in case the person who has the equipment we are looking for catches us looking, "He had let their imaginations take it from there. Their original, "better-than-you" attitudes had shrunk to minimal size as they strapped on the gear and realized they could be going in harm's way.

Su Li and her engineer had the monitoring equipment loaded onto a Bell Jet Ranger helicopter and had already lifted off to their scanning position two thousand feet above the Arena.

Jack and the other engineer had placed the beam generating head on the basket of a cherry-picker hooked on a power company truck. They acted like they were working on power lines near the front of the Arena. They were above the top of the structure. Jack called Su Li on his combat phone. He spoke into the miniature boom microphone next to his mouth. "Su Li, are you ready to copy?"

Su Li looked at her engineer and he nervously nodded yes. "Yes Jack, we are ready to copy."

Jack nodded and the engineer started the beam generation. The power being used caused the head to hum heavily and then quiet. Each time the beam was finished being generated the head was rotated one degree clockwise. The entire operation took six minutes. The engineer shut down the generator and started running diagnostics on the system. Jack checked in with their aerial force. "Su Li, did we locate anything?"

The engineer superimposed an outline graph of the buildings of Dallas over the graph of the scan. After eliminating all known shielded positions only three unknowns showed up. He pointed them out to Su Li. She relayed them to the ground. After looking at his map Jack quickly eliminated two of the remaining locations. That left only one place.

They climbed down and pulled in the cherry-picker. They moved the truck to the intersection of Memorial Drive and Hotel Street. They set up for the detection again and only did three degrees in the direction of the first unknown location. The location was narrowed down to a ten-foot area.

Jack then had a crane brought to their location. They mounted the entire assembly on a large pallet and hooked the power cables to a portable generator. They had a problem staying on the proper coordinates because the platform swayed in the strong breeze blowing across the area. The sun was setting directly west of their location by the time they had gotten a complete beam through the position. That meant that they were above it at four hundred and fifty feet.

Returning the Gamma radiation equipment and the engineers to their company, the Team took their information back to their suite. Examining the scans and the pictures Mark had Sarah take of the supposed location they made several interesting discoveries. The location of the supposed bomb was three-fourths of the way up the Reunion Tower next to the Arena.

Mark used his computer for information about the tower. He gave the Team this summary. "It's part of the Hyatt Regency hotel, and houses both an observation deck and a revolving restaurant. At night, the bulge that makes up the actual building is dotted with lights which can form patterns. The top level observation deck is above the restaurant which revolves once every fifty-five minutes. The whole structure is six hundred feet tall and weighs 23,600 tons. The "maintenance" work being done on the structure at the four hundred and fifty foot level is the location of the shielding we've detected.

Laura looked at the picture of the tower and asked, "How are we going to get to it? It looks like it would take a crane to lift you to it and if it is guarded they won't have much trouble picking you off or setting off the bomb early."

Mark smiled, "There's several ways to get to that position, and without anyone noticing us. But there are other problems we need to think about. I told you that Pickett is a fanatic about planning down to the last detail, right? My guess is that he has spread out his twenty-some men. Some will be on the platform, some in sniper positions, and some at a remote location. They will all be interconnected by radio and or phones. There will be some form of constant checking going on to insure one group doesn't fall off the map suddenly. We will need to find each and every one of them and take them all down at once to make this thing work."

Jack looked at his watch. "We've got less than thirty hours and there are only six of us. Mark. How do we do it?"

Mark thought for a few minutes. "Well, I think we are about to test Gary Rhodes belief in us. We need to put more men on the job."

Jack reached for his phone to call Denver.

# CHAPTER FORTY

Gary Rhodes used the Presidential authority he had been given to both clear the impending action with his counterparts in Dallas and to use their people and assets. He listed the last assignments as he flew into DFW, Dallas and Fort Worth's giant airport. His superiors had been persuaded by the President and the Chairman of the Joint Chiefs of Staff, General Miles, to authorize the assistance requested by the Crossfire Team. Everyone involved realized that their careers were on the line on this operation but that paled in comparison to the possible death and destruction such a weapon would cause to the United States and the city of Dallas.

Two hours later the FBI teams and the Crossfire Team held their final briefing. Mark had spent the last ten hours devising a plan that hopefully would have the success they would need to avert a detonation. David and Sarah had scouted the area near the Reunion Tower and spotted one of Severon's mercenaries going for food at a nearby restaurant. Making a command decision they had tailed him until he had the food and was headed back to wherever he had come from. Sarah distracted him and David took him from the back, quickly and quietly. Thirty minutes later they had the information they needed. David's little bag of drugs provided the necessary confusion and the auto-suggestion implanted in the man's mind would make him think he had been mugged. They took his wallet and the food so it would look like a robbery. Dumping the wallet and food in a trash bin, they called the police anonymously and told the dispatcher that a man had been mugged and his location. Hopefully that would defer any suspicions until after the coordinated raids.

After listening to the information from the Mossad operative, Mark pointed out the remote control room in a suburban hotel to the FBI assault team. According to their Intel, there were ten men in the control center which was far and away from the blast area, and six snipers which left approximately nine on the bomb platform. The Crossfire

Team would storm the platform at the same time the FBI took out the snipers and the control room. This all had to happen with split-second timing or it could result in horror for the city of Dallas not to mention the death of everyone assembled there. Moving on to the FBI snipers he then pointed out the six sniper positions and what he thought would be good counterfire positions.

The FBI teams agreed with Mark's assessment and moved out to get into their positions. Mark, Sarah, Jack, and David were going to repel down to the platform from the bottom of the dome while Su Li and Laura were going to provide fire support from the Jet Ranger.

As the four of them got ready to leave, Jack called them altogether and prayed for success and protection for everyone on their Team and on the FBI teams. He looked at them after the prayer. "If anything goes wrong, we probably won't know it. If that should happen, I'll see you all in heaven."

Everyone realized he was right. If the ten-Kiloton nuclear warhead was detonated they would all be within the initial fireball and would be vaporized in less time than it would take to realize it.

Mark said, "We aren't going to fail, I've got too many car payments left. Let's do it!"

The FBI had arranged with the Dallas Police and the management of the tower to implement the team's access to the platform. Even though they were in deadly danger, the patrons of the tower weren't told of the bomb or evacuated. This would have been a sure sign to the mercenaries that they had been located and they might set off the bomb. A lot of people were going to share the risks tonight and not even be aware of their heroism.

As they waited to go, Mark shook his head. Jack looked at him. "What's the problem?"

Mark frowned, "These guys on the platform and the snipers are all mercenaries, right?" At Jack's nod he continued. "Mercenaries aren't suicide bombers. They aren't going to set off the bomb while they could still be killed. What is their strategy to live through the explosion?"

Jack thought about it for several seconds. "Most likely they'll all abandon their positions after setting a timer to set off the bomb. They probably have some high-speed transportation to let them get away before the bomb goes off."

Mark thought about that. "Okay, that makes more sense. Not even Severon's money would convince a Mercenary to die for the cause."

As the four Team members crawled out of the service hatch at the bottom of the dome the night was pleasantly warm and the breezes light. They were only sixty feet above the platform. Each member was dressed in black combat gear including the head and face coverings. Their armament consisted of a silenced MAC-11 machine pistol with laser sighting and two extra, twenty-round magazines, a .45-caliber pistol with two clips, a KaBar fighting knife, and a flash-bang grenade. They were wearing Kevlar vests which would stop bullets but not nuclear explosions.

Mark seemed totally unfazed by the five-hundred foot drop to the ground. He signaled the others and as one they stepped off into the night. The rappelling ropes ran through their hands quickly and they used the hand brakes to bring them lightly to the edges of the platform. Mark felt that the wind would create enough other noises that they could land without being detected.

The platform was made out to be a typical repair station with a plywood floor and roof, each supported on four cables to the dome above and fastened to the leg of the tower where the "maintenance" was supposedly being done. Mark had used a high-powered thermal imaging scope and determined that there were three more plywood walls behind the canvas sides. After studying the layout he had set each of the four raiders at a place they could go through the canvas without running into the plywood walls. This was to be a "hard" raid. There would be no tranquilizers used this time. The stakes were too high. Even Gary Rhodes had agreed to that after David and Sarah told them that the man they had interrogated had confirmed that the bomb was here and was primed to be detonated at the first sign of attack.

Eight miles away the control room Team moved carefully into position. Due to the seriousness of the threat the hotel structure was expendable if needed. Gary Rhodes checked the det cord placements on the hall wall and the two rooms on either side of their target. The FBI agent was imposing in his black combat rip-stop uniform. He had an H&K MP5KA on a sling under his right arm and a .10mm autoloader on his hip. He was wearing full Class 4 Kevlar body armor and face shield to deflect any blowback from the det cord explosions. He confirmed the three team's readiness and pushed the comm button to let Mark know they were ready.

In each of the positions of the counter-snipers the sight picture was locked in and each man pressed his button to announce his readiness to shoot.

Seeing the ready lights from the other seven positions, Mark looked at the dark blurs of the other three and at a head nod from each one he pressed the button that activated the FBI teams. Cutting the canvas in front of him he tossed in his primed flash-bang grenade through the cut. Each of the other Team members did the same. Stepping over behind one of the plywood walls helped prevent the concussion from knocking him off the platform. All four of the grenades went off almost as one. It must have been sheer hell inside with the super bright flares and the tremendous noise of the grenades. Mark didn't have time to wonder about how the scene played out to the people on the ground.

The six counter-snipers fired and confirmed six kills. Gary Rhodes pushed the command squib and all three det cords detonated as one. The walls crashed into the control room and flash bang grenades exploded. The three teams stormed into the room but discovered that they were just there for mop-up. The det cord explosions and flash-bang grenades had disabled everyone in the room. The FBI agents quickly disarmed and cuffed the men. Gary pushed the "mission accomplished" button on the comm unit.

Mark slit the canvas the rest of the way and surged into the room. There were three men near him; all were in agony or unconscious. All were also heavily armed. Mark took all of them out with one figure eight of the rapid-fire MAC-11. Changing his magazine he stormed through the platform to the other end. He found the other six men already dispatched by Sarah, David, and Jack.

Mark pulled off his hood and goggles and checked the readouts on the comm unit. That made seven green lights. He also pressed the mission accomplished button and then keyed his microphone. "Bomb squad, target is clear, move, move, move!"

Three other men landed, none too gently, on the platform and made their way into the room. Ignoring the bodies and the blood they focused on the large gray structure in the center of the platform. The concussion of the grenades had deformed the soft shielding around the warhead and every detector on the platform, in vehicles, and on satellites had lit up with the signature of the Pakistani ten-Kiloton warhead.

The experts began removing the covering as quickly as possible and the man in charge used a fire-extinguisher to freeze several circuits. He then traced two wires and cut one. He turned and smiled.

Gary Rhodes called over the communications net and confirmed the elimination of the danger of an explosion. Mark thanked him and turned to the bomb expert. "Is that thing really safe now?"

The man looked introspective for a few seconds. "As safe as a nuclear weapon can be. It can't be detonated by any means right now. Not even if we wanted to do it. His booby-traps and fail-safes were defeated when we froze them and I've completely eliminated the firing capability of the primary charge. What we need to do is to get this out of here and to a safe facility until it can be given back to Pakistan."

Mark gathered the Crossfire Team together and checked them for post-combat stress. He actually was only worried about Jack. He knew that Sarah and David had taken lives before and had learned to cope with the emotions that are generated by doing that. Jack was at peace with what he had had to do. Knowing what was coming he had simply prayed to the Lord before the action and afterward asked Him to forgive him for the two people he had to kill. He never felt any burden because it had to be done to save thousands of innocent lives.

Mark heard from Gary Rhodes that a crane had been brought into position and would take the entire platform to the ground in the next twenty minutes. He told the others and then told Su Li and Laura to land and meet them back at the hotel.

After the crane was connected to the platform and the other cables removed, the connections to the leg of the tower were severed. The entire assembly was lowered to the ground. The Dallas Police had cordoned off the area and plastic walls were being erected to keep the onlookers from seeing the bomb being removed to a large truck.

# CHAPTER FORTY-ONE

Gary Rhodes accompanied the Team back to their suite. While he coordinated with the Washington office, David checked with the Mossad back in Israel for any updates on Severon or Pickett. New rumors abounded of attacks on the Jewish nation but none that applied to this situation.

In the suite's sauna Mark and Jack let the tensions of the last few hours drain off with the hot water as it ran off their bodies. Jack decided to seek the Lord for what to do next and Mark joined him. As they prayed they asked the Lord to guide them in their efforts to locate Severon and his team.

Jack looked up at Mark and said, "I get the feeling that the Lord has it all in hand and we just need to be obedient."

Mark nodded his agreement. "I share some of the emotions that Sarah and David are going through right now. I wish we had something to go on. If Severon was using the Pakistani bomb to occupy everyone's attention then he has to be doing his main act right now."

Jack was thinking about that when Sarah stuck her head into the sauna room. "Mark, it's John Michaels at the NSA and it sounds urgent."

Mark jumped off the seat of the sauna and took the phone from his wife, "Thanks spylady. Hello?"

"Hey Mark! I finally got my boss to watch the Dallas video of your team. We watched you guys taking that bomb platform. I actually found myself praying for you. Well, you and my parents. Anyway, I think you have a new fan. She'd like to meet you sometime soon to "evaluate" you in more detail."

Mark laughed. "I'll let my wife evaluate her first. You can tell your boss that Sarah was one of the "guys" that took that platform. But seriously, you did call me for some real purpose didn't you?"

John was quiet for a few seconds. "Yeah, we can't give you a location on Severon but we do have an associated report that might help you. It seems that an ex-military type had a gall-bladder go bad on him and he ended up in the hospital at the Naval Air Station at Corpus Christi, Texas. Even though he had really good fake identification, a corpsman there thought that he had met the man before under another name. What with the war on terror he felt he had to check out his suspicions so he ran a DNA ID check and surprise, it came up with the man's real name and shady history. It also included the fact that he had last been listed as wanted by the FBI, CIA, Interpol, and several agencies in Pakistan in regard to working for Barton Severon and Tom Pickett. The technician notified his supervisor who called it in as required. The FBI will be there tomorrow to interrogate the man. I think you should be there for that, don't you?"

Mark's mind was spinning with possibilities and schedules. "You're right John, Thanks a lot. I'll let you know what we find out."

They said goodbye and Mark called the others together. He put on a robe to cover his swim trunks and sat down in the living room as they gathered. Looking around to see that everyone was there he composed his thoughts. "Look guys, John just gave us a heads up on one of Severon/Pickett's men who is hospitalized in Corpus Christi. The FBI will be there tomorrow to pry what they can out of him. I suggest we beat them to it. We've got sixteen hours until nine a.m. tomorrow. What do you think?"

David summed it up for the rest of the team. "What are we waiting for?"

Five hours later the Bell Jet Ranger touched down on the hospital Life Flight pad just outside the hospital and five people got out of the chopper and walked into the ER entrance. Checking with the ER desk they made their way to the convalescent ward. There was only one room there with a policeman outside the door. Jack stopped the Team and pulled out his cell phone. Five minutes later they walked up to the officer and asked to be admitted to the man's room. The officer wasn't intimidated by the size and obvious hardness of the group facing him. "I'm sorry sir, only authorized police and FBI agents are granted access to this room."

Jack said, "We're about to be authorized."

The officer lowered his eyebrows and slid his hand back towards the pistol on his gun belt. His radio crackled to life. "Harris, this is Grover. You are going to have five people asking to enter the room. Let them in. This is straight from the Governor."

The cop nodded and moved to the side. The Team entered the room and approached the figure lying on the bed. He was either asleep or faking it. There was no talk and no wasted motion. Jack and Mark locked the man's arms to the bed and Sarah injected him with an Israeli truth serum.

Five minutes later they started getting answers that made some sense. They finished up their questioning and put a band-aid over his needle mark. They left him quietly sleeping off the drug.

Exiting the hospital they lifted off from the helipad and headed back to Dallas.

Looking at the transcript of the meeting, Mark shook his head. "Let's go over this one answer at a time. I don't think we have much time left."

Jack indicated the first answer. "Well, he admitted that he was with Pickett when they got the Pakistani bomb. That rings true with what we know about his record and the FBI files."

Sarah indicated the fifth answer. The question had been, "Where is Severon going to get his ICBMs?" The answer had been, "He already has them."

David's next question had been, "Where is he going to fire them from?"

The man didn't seem to know the answer to that. So, David probed further. "How is he going to launch them?" The man said, "Like normal, right up the chute."

David had become somewhat exasperated by the evasiveness. "How many missiles does he have?" The man said, "Three". David asked him what type they were. The man said, "Trident D5s."

Mark moved David out of the way, "The Trident D5 weighs 130,000 pounds and only has a range of 4,000 miles. How can Severon hit Israel with them?"

The man took the question as literal as people under truth serum tend to do. "He will take them within striking range and launch then."

Mark asked, "You were important to the program, how can he do it without you?"

The man seemed confused for a few seconds. "I'm just one of several launch officers. I'm not necessary if the truth be known."

David asked, "When did Severon leave with the missiles?"

The man thought for a few seconds, "The missiles left a couple of days ago, I guess."

Mark asked, "How is he traveling?"

The man seemed confused again and said, "Who is traveling?"

Mark caught on, "How are the missiles traveling? The man responded, "With the launch platform, how else?"

David looked at Mark, and then he asked the man, "What is the name of the launch platform?"

The man thought for a while and then muttered, "The Phoenix."

After that the man had refused to answer any more questions.

Mark sat there shaking his head. "I should have guessed that Severon wouldn't try the 90th. He looked at the others as Su Li piloted the chopper to the northeast. "The man is brilliant; you've got to give him that. He somehow arranged to get his hands on three SLICMs. Trident D5s are multiple warhead ICBMs that are launched from a "boomer", a missile submarine. He apparently has built his own launch platform and is going to get it within the D5's range and launch them on Israel. We need to stop him soon. If the guy in there was telling us the truth, then Severon's missiles have a two day head start and if they're on anything that has sea legs, they may be close to a launch point already."

Laura asked, "Why are you differentiating between Severon and the missiles?"

Mark frowned, "Because Severon isn't with the missiles according to that launch officer. He couldn't understand who I was talking about when I asked when Severon had left with the missiles. The only thing that makes sense is that he is somewhere else than with the missiles."

David picked up his global cell phone and called the Mossad. He explained the situation and told them to search for any surface vessel headed towards the Mediterranean or the east coast of Africa. The vessel had to have the size to house three missiles forty-five feet in length. The assumed name was "The Phoenix" but that could be a code name and not the name of the actual vessel.

Mark called John back and gave him the same information including the probable ship date of two days ago. He added, "We just have to pray that Severon didn't get himself a used submarine to launch them from. I really doubt that because he'd almost have to have a boomer and those aren't for sale."

Jack called the office of the President and waited while they patched him through to the Chief Executive of the United States. When he got an answer he said, "Good evening sir. I hope I haven't disturbed you too much. But we have a definite lead in the nuclear threat to Israel by Barton Severon."

The President asked what the news was and Jack brought him up to date. "The good news is that we have identified how he is going to launch the missiles but the bad news is that he already has three missiles and has a two-day head start on reaching the launch point."

The President asked what the missiles were and how Severon had gotten his hands on them. Jack answered, "The missiles are Trident D5s but we don't have an answer to the how as yet sir. Sarah has briefed NCIS (Naval Criminal Investigative Service) and Naval Intelligence on the assumed theft. They will get to the bottom of the how. We need to locate this launch vessel and stop him before he launches those missiles."

The President agreed and hung up. After calling the CIA and NSA to start an all-out search for the ship, he called General Miles. The President asked, "Howard, if Severon can get within four thousand miles and successfully launch these Trident D5 missiles can they be stopped?"

Howard Miles didn't even hesitate. "It is unfortunate, but, No Sir! We've put millions of design hours into these things so that once you give the order and they are launched they can't be stopped. If someone doesn't prevent that launch, there is no power on Earth that will save the nation of Israel."

The President sighed and thanked the General. He hung up and sat back in his chair in the Oval Office and started praying for God's intervention.

# CHAPTER FORTY-TWO

The feedback from the alphabet agencies was that there were over one hundred vessels moving across the North Atlantic Ocean towards Africa, Europe, and the Mediterranean Sea. It was reduced somewhat taking into account the two day sailing time but that was uncertain and it still left over eighty vessels of a size sufficient to house missile tubes for the Tridents.

Ten minutes later Commander Bill Johnston of NCIS called Mark. Mark took the call and walked over to the window of the suite to hear better. "Mark Connelly."

"Mark? This is Bill Johnston, NCIS. Our investigation into the theft of three Trident D5s is almost complete. There are three missing Tridents and they disappeared in the right time frame for Severon to have taken them."

Mark asked, "Bill, can you tell me how he did it? We both know that the sub launched ICBMs are one of the most well guarded missiles in the world."

Bill sighed, "Yeah, they are but we got conned by a terrific slight-of-hand. The best we can figure out is that Severon arranged to swipe the three missiles when they were unloaded from a damaged boomer."

Mark thought back, "What damaged boomer?"

Bill thought about the security ramifications of telling Connelly the classified data. Considering what they had just done in Denver and Dallas it seemed appropriate to him. "The Harpoon was just off Galveston when they had a strange reactor leak. They SCRAMMed the core, abandoned ship except for a suited skeleton crew, and were towed into the Naval Station at Corpus Christi. There was a civilian nuclear disaster Team training there that had the qualifications and the clearances to check out the problems."

Bill took a big breath, "The Captain was against civilians taking over the ship no matter how many clearances they had. But he took violently ill and the Executive Officer approved the team. They examined the reactor and told the Exec that they needed to get the

166

nuclear missiles off the ship immediately to prevent a possible contamination by the leaky core. The Exec agreed and had a missile transport crew remove the missiles and take them to a secure storage depot. Only problem was that there were three missiles missing when they got there. It seems that somehow, Severon was able to have three practice missiles loaded into the transports before they got to the ship. Then someone in the transport Team handled the switch and didn't load three of the active missiles. The rest of the Team thought every missile was accounted for and double checked to make sure each transport tube had a missile in it. It wasn't until they reached the depot and unloaded the birds that the training missiles were discovered. Even then they thought that the training missiles came from the ship. They had the ship checked and there were no missiles there."

Shuffling his papers he read a report and summed it up for Mark. "What the cameras caught was that as soon as the transport trucks had left, another three trucks showed up and proceeded to remove the three missiles left in the sub. The cameras caught the Exec overseeing the operation. An hour later the civilian Team left the sub saying they had found the problem and it was corrected. The Team came from one of Severon's companies."

Mark asked, "How's the Captain doing?"

Bill sighed again. "He died this morning apparently from arsenic poisoning. We've arrested the Executive Officer and he has confessed his role in the theft, poisoning, and disablement of the ship. A mitigating factor was that Severon's men had taken the officer's wife and children hostage and threatened to kill them if he didn't follow their orders. He says that he thought that the drugs they gave him for the Captain were only temporary, not lethal."

Mark shook his head and asked, "Did his family get released alright?"

Bill was quiet for a few seconds. "No, our agents found their bodies two hours ago."

Mark's anger was hard to control. "Do you have any information as to what ship they were loaded onto and what port they left from?"

The Commander understood Mark's reaction. His had been very much like that also. "We matched the trailers with two keyhole satellite series and were able to track them from the base to a dock only three miles away. They were loaded on a container ship called the Fire of Allah which is flagged out of Algeria. Now get this. Two days ago the owners of the Fire of Allah called the U.S. Coast Guard. They complained that their ship had been stolen in U. S. waters and they want the Coasties to get it back for them."

Mark thought about the implications of all the new news. "Thanks Bill, I'll get this info to all the groups immediately." Mark hung up and turned to an obviously rapt audience waiting to hear the news.

Mark looked at David. "Apparently the missiles were loaded onto a container ship called the Fire of Allah. The ship was reported stolen by their Algerian owners two days ago. I find it hard to believe that Severon would steal a ship to haul Trident D5 missiles unless he had time to build launch tubes and controls into the ship. The owners were probably bought off a long time ago and are acting the innocent party. Anyway, how do you think we should handle it?"

David said, "Why don't you get the NSA to locate the ship and I'll get my people to get it stopped." It was obvious by his tone he meant stopped forever. It was the only way. Severon wouldn't respond to reason or threats, he'd just fire the missiles anyway.

Jack listened to all of the events and information happening and prayed about it. He asked for wisdom concerning Severon himself. It wouldn't do any good to stop the ship if they couldn't find the head of the snake and eliminate it once and for all. An elusive bit of information they already had tugged at his mind and he relaxed into a passive mode of thinking. The data bit surfaced and he recalled it. Looking around he called Sarah over and asked her, "Do you remember the phone number we got off of the dead merc at the Ben Gurion Airport?"

Sarah stared at Jack attempting to discern his line of thinking. Failing that she said, "It was a strip bar in Corpus Christi, Texas. Why?"

Jack nodded, "I thought so. All the missile theft activities have been in that area. I'll bet that Severon is somewhere in the Corpus Christi area running the missile launch remotely. I sincerely doubt that he or Pickett is on that ship."

Sarah agreed. "But how are we going to find him with almost no time left?"

Jack smiled, "Simple, a new complex of communications dishes. The town isn't that big and it should be easy to find out where a new set of comm dishes has been put in during the last six months. The size he'd need would require a permit. Call the Corpus Christi Chamber of Commerce and see who we need to talk to concerning permits for that sort of thing."

Sarah went over and sat down at a phone and started punching buttons. She rolled her eyes when the information message cautioned her that the call would cost a dollar and a half.

Mark walked over and asked what Jack was researching. Jack filled him in and he nodded. "They'd also want to have a backup power capability in the event of a power out. Pickett would insist on that. Those things are only made by one or two manufacturers in that size. I'll see if I can track that down."

Jack said to Su Li, "Get the corporate jet ready." She grabbed her jacket and headed for the door.

Laura continued to pray for God's favor and protection for Israel.

# CHAPTER FORTY-THREE

Actually, it only took seventeen minutes to confirm the location of both a new power backup generator and a recent permit for large communications dishes in Corpus Christi. There was only one building and the company was owned by a subsidiary of one of Severon's shadow companies.

Jack called the FBI and told them where the building was and what they thought it was being used for by Severon. The agent told him that they would coordinate with headquarters and assign a Team to check it out.

Jack slammed down the phone. "It's going to take too long for the FBI to get there. We may only have hours left. Get the weapons and let's see if we can't disrupt Severon's operation."

Laura said, "If that is really the one. He may have set it up as a dummy to draw us away from the real location."

Jack sighed. "It's the only lead we have that we can track down in time. We've given everything else we have to the NSA and the FBI. We need to shut this door or at least check it out."

No one disagreed and action was better than just waiting.

The four hundred mile trip took only ninety minutes from the time the Team loaded onto the plane until they disembarked at Corpus Christi International Airport.

Su Li had called ahead and rented a large business van without windows. A quick trip down the 358 brought them to the location on Yorktown Boulevard. Pulling up in an alley to the rear of the tall, single-story warehouse like building, Jack noticed the large communications dishes behind the building. By then everyone except Su Li had their full combat gear on, including helmets and goggles.

Su Li looked at the building and said, "I'll scout it out first. We're going to look really silly if it turns out to be only a cable TV company." With that she climbed out of the driver's seat and walked around to the front of the establishment.

Opening the glass door to the reception area, Su Li approached the young girl at the desk. "Could you tell me if your company is hiring?"

The girl smiled back. "No, they're fully staffed, thank you for asking."

Su Li pressed the issue. "Could you tell me what they do here?"

The girl continued to smile at the pretty Asian woman. "No, I can't. It's classified as corporate information and not available to the public. Now I'll have to ask you to leave."

Su Li feigned a hurt look. "But, Tom Pickett said I could find a job here."

The knowing look in the girl's eyes was all the confirmation that Su Li needed. The girl said that she didn't know of a Mr. Pickett and insisted that Su Li leave.

Su Li left and casually walked back to the van. "I think we have a winner. The girl up front lied when she said that she didn't know who Pickett was. She knew all right. Also they wouldn't t..."

Laura yelled, "Out of the van NOW!" No one questioned her direction. The double doors on the right side and the back flew open and the five people inside bailed out and ran to cover. Su Li was two steps ahead of them when the van exploded in a huge fireball. The noise almost deafened everyone.

Throwing himself behind a concrete wall, Mark turned and scanned the roof of the building across the alley. He spotted a man with a LAW tube. Using gut instinct he snap-aimed and fired his CAR-15 full auto. Ten .223 caliber rounds flew across the space at four thousand feet per second. Four of the rounds impacted the body of the man on the roof. All four rounds were absorbed by the Kevlar body armor the man was wearing. The Kevlar didn't do anything to stop the two other rounds that hit him in the head. He fell from sight as the smoking remains of the van slammed back down onto the concrete of the alley.

Jack looked at David. "I guess that takes most of the guesswork out of our target identification." Flipping the fire selector switch to full auto Jack ran a zig-zag path to the side of the building owned by Severon. Su Li stayed behind to warn any police that showed up as to the nature of the battle and the danger involved. The other four warriors dashed across the alley after Jack.

Jack looked around the corner and jerked his head back. "They've got the entrance covered four ways from Sunday."

Mark slapped two bricks of C-4 against the side of the building on the alley side. "Okay then we will make our own entrance." Putting firing squibs into both blocks he ran to the far end of the wall. When the others joined him he pushed the remote control. Both charges went off and a whole section of the wall blew into the building.

The Team ran to the edge of the hole and peeked around the corner. They had opened an access into a large warehouse area with various crates now spilled across the floor. Climbing over the debris and charging across the space the five Team members reached halfway across the bay when gunfire drove them all to the floor behind whatever crates they could find for cover.

Bullets seemed to be whining through the air everywhere. Pieces of the crates exploded into wood chips. Bullets tugged at their clothes and nicked their hair. Everyone had several hits to their body armor by direct gunfire or ricochets. The mercenaries were attempting to surround them by moving up the sides of the room, angling to get a killing shot.

Mark's accuracy under fire took out two of the more aggressive ones and slowed the advance somewhat. Sarah also shot one man with a definite head shot and wounded another through the leg.

Still the odds were heavily against them as more and more of the mercenaries poured into the far end of the room and added their weapons to the defense of the building.

Laura suddenly felt a heavy conviction to pray. As she was praying her praise turned into a powerful song of praise to the Lord.

As the song grew in adoration, the battle dimmed to her senses and was lost in the wonderful communion with God. David heard Laura's singing and he joined in singing the song in a rich tenor. Jack and Mark picked up the hymn and joined in praising God. As the hymn of praise grew in intensity, Laura couldn't believe the peace and joy she knew they all felt in the middle of a combat zone with fifty or more people trying to kill them.

As the closeness of the Lord enveloped her completely, she gave voice to love she felt in a pure and beautiful melody. God's love wrapped around her and swirled through time and space. Laura sensed the infinite power and control of God. Fear of death for her or the others evaporated as a tiny, worthless worry when seen next to the glory of God. She gave herself completely over to pure worship of the Lord.

Sarah took a solid round to the body armor that stunned her. She turned around and sat with her back to the crate. Amid the bedlam of combat the singing swirled around her and flooded over her. It touched her heart. She relaxed into the worship and gave voice to the love she felt for the Lord in a contralto of such purity she was amazed that she could sing something so beautiful.

In heaven, God released power from heaven into the battle as He listened to the worship and communed with them.

Laura's golden armor flared into visibility. As she continued to sing, she risked a peek around her crate and snapped her head back as several bullets tried to fill the same space. Several demons had manifested into the human dimension from behind the mercenaries and were moving toward Laura and Sarah to stop their praise and worship. Satan was committing a large force to win this battle.

Even with her armor, Laura wasn't led to battle the demons. Instead she was captured by the joy and power of the song and melted into the sheer sweetness of the closeness of God's Holy Spirit.

One of the mercs had crept far enough along the right side of the room to get a clean shot at Sarah who was on Laura's right side. He took aim and fired at her head. Halfway there the bullet hit something that resembled a faint diamond in the air and ricocheted into the ceiling of the room. The merc flipped his fire selector to full automatic and emptied all of the rounds in the magazine at Sarah. All of the bullets hit that same faint diamond substance and were deflected. Two of the rounds were deflected directly back and struck the mercenary in the head.

A large, fierce angel appeared wielding the diamond surfaced sword in such a swirling pattern that none of the rounds being fired at the women were getting through. The angel was dressed in flowing white robes girded by a golden belt. He was dark haired and every inch a warrior in appearance. The robes he was wearing glowed as if with an inner light. The wrath of God was in his eyes and on his face. As the fear of the Lord struck deep into their very being, to a man the mercenaries threw down their weapons and fled into the other part of the building, many of them screaming in terror.

As the mercenaries fled the room a flood of demons entered it. They were afraid of the angel of the Lord with the diamond sword but were compelled to attack him and the people behind him. Laura got up and, still singing, joined into the fray with her golden sword slashing into the demons next to the angel's diamond weapon.

Sarah and the men started praying for Laura and the angel, empowering them to greater efforts. But it was quickly obvious that it was a lop-sided battle as more and more demons surged into the battle against the two defenders.

Suddenly, all across the southern half of the state of Texas, intercessors were given an extremely urgent burden to pray. Most just dropped to their knees where they were. It didn't matter if it was at the kitchen sink or in the board room of a corporate meeting. The burden was undeniable. As thousands prayed, the gigantic upsurge in prayer power released tremendous power from heaven and several hundred angels were released into the battle in the building in Corpus Christi. The demons were dispatched so quickly it was hard to comprehend. Suddenly all the spiritual beings were gone and Laura's armor disappeared. The Team was alone in the room which was still full of gunsmoke and the smell of cordite and blood.

Regrouping and reloading their weapons the Team still softly sang or hummed the song they had been singing. They moved quickly but carefully into the next major room to confront any mercs that hadn't seen the angel. The urgency to find Severon drove them on toward a small room that had been built into the larger area.

The Team kept to covering and were rewarded for their caution as shots again flew by them and smacking into the walls. Pickett's voice rang out over the shooting. "You losers are too late. The birds are already in the air!"

The missiles had already been launched at Israel.

# CHAPTER FORTY-FOUR

The three Trident missiles had been programmed and launched correctly by Severon's technicians so that their multiple warheads would strike against all the cities of Israel.

The President watched the tracks of the missiles on a screen in the Oval Office. He was physically sick because they were American missiles and they were about to destroy one of America's staunchest allies and kill millions of innocent people. Despite all their technology and best efforts, neither the U.S. nor Israel had been able to find and stop the ship before the launch.

The technologically-advanced ballistic missiles rose on pillars of fire towards their apogee, the highest point in their arc before coming down towards their targets. Traveling at a third-stage speed of thirteen-thousand miles per hour, the fifty-million dollar missiles were beyond anything man could do to stop them.

Flashing in at speeds exceeding one-hundred, sixty thousand miles per hour, or roughly twelve times the speed of the missiles, body XA12435, the small cloud of meteors, slammed into the Earth's atmosphere and into the three rising missiles. The kinetic energy of ten tons of loose gravel traveling at interstellar speeds instantly vaporized the three missiles.

$$$$$

The majority of the meteor cloud was also vaporized by the encounter with the missiles. All the remaining fragments burned up in the sky except for a single piece that had been big enough to start with and survived to reach the surface of the planet.

Back at the Corpus Christi launch building and not realizing that God's plan of many thousands of years in the past had just eliminated the missiles, the Crossfire Team continued to battle through the mercenaries to get to the control room.

Pickett was starting to worry. He was down to three men besides himself and this five man Team was chewing up his little army at an alarming rate. They seemed to have unlimited ammunition! He ducked as several rounds struck the up-ended desk he was behind. Looking behind him he saw a path to safety. Crawling quickly through the partially open door to the control room he abandoned the remaining mercs to their fate and ran for his life to an outside exit. He was sure that after they launched the missiles, Severon and Lutz had gone out this way following the path of all the frightened mercenaries that had fled the building.

He pushed open the door and stepped outside. He took one step towards freedom when a young Chinese woman blocked his way. That she was serious about stopping him was evident in the Light Anti-tank Weapon she had pointed at him. He knew that his body armor was useless against such a weapon.

Su Li said quietly, "Put your hands on your head and get on your knees, NOW!

Pickett grabbed for his sidearm and threw himself to the left. The pistol had just cleared the holster when the missile struck him at the waist. The explosion effectively ended Pickets' career and also eliminated any hope for an open-casket funeral at the same time.

Su Li tossed the LAW launcher to the side and drew her own handgun. No more people were getting out of that rat hole.

The last two mercs died fighting to the end. The Team closed on the control room and found it empty. Checking the exit, Jack saw Su Li guarding it. He waved at her and told her to come in.

David was on his cell phone and was saying, "What? What are you saying?"

When the man on the other end told him for the third time that the missiles had just disappeared off of their radar at apogee he laughed a huge laugh of relief. He turned to the others, "It looks like God stopped the missiles from ever reaching Israel!"

Laura was hugging Jack when she heard the news. Together they sent a silent prayer of thanks to the Lord of the Universe for his mercy. Sarah was dancing with glee. Mark smiled but didn't look completely happy. Su Li was grinning as she asked Mark, "What's the matter?"

Mark waved his had around the control room. "Severon got away."

That sobered everyone up quickly.

Several miles away, on Interstate 37, heading North for San Antonio, in a silver Mercedes Benz 500 SL coupe, Severon had been gleefully gloating. He had repaid Israel for his son's death. After the world found out it was U.S. missiles that destroyed the Zionist nation, the United States could possibly fall. He had escaped free and clear. Pickett and his men were going to be killed by the force that had attacked them. Life was good. He would quickly get to his extremely well-stocked and plush island hideaway and savor the world upheaval from luxurious comfort.

His thoughts vaporized along with the majority of the car as the remaining two-pound fragment from body XA12435 slammed into the silver car. The fragmented wreck rolled to the side of the road and burned furiously. God's judgment had just come to Severon for his attempt to destroy God's chosen people.

# CHAPTER FORTY-FIVE

Looking outside, Jack told everyone to disarm and walk out of the building with their hands in plain sight.

Dozens of policemen, the FBI, and SWAT had arrived and were laying siege to the building. The Crossfire Team exited the building and was held by the SWAT Team for investigation. The fire department showed up to prevent any possible fire. Parts of the building were smoking even though there were no flames to be seen anywhere.

As the investigators entered the building they found bodies laying around although the majority of mercenaries had continued to flee the wrath of God and had left the building completely. The FBI took control of the situation and directed the police to start sweeps of the area to find any of the mercenaries that could still be there and to look for Severon at the same time.

In Washington, the Director of the FBI had just had a short meeting with the U. S. Attorney General. Contacting the local FBI Team he told them to take a statement from each of the Crossfire Team and release them immediately. They were operating with the authority of the President of the United States. For the second time on this mission they were allowed to retrieve their weapons and communications equipment.

One of the mercenaries that had been apprehended by the Corpus Christi Police was brought over to where the Team was finishing their statements. He was held in arm and leg shackles until they could talk to him.

Mark took him to one side and told him. "I can make it a lot easier for you if you'll tell me what you know."

The man knew he was in deep trouble and it looked like his employers had fled the scene so he wasn't even going to get paid for this. "I'll tell you what I know, but it probably isn't much."

Jack and Laura walked over to the two men. Mark shrugged and told him to speak his piece.

The soldier's name was Hugh Miller and he had only been with the operation since last week. He'd been brought on as a replacement for the attrition that the Crossfire Team was causing Severon and Pickett. Su Li walked over to hear what the man was telling them.

Miller looked at Mark and said, "You'll get a lot more information out of Pickett if you can catch him."

Su Li laughed a grim laugh. "That'll be tough. Pickett is scattered over the whole end of the building and won't be giving a statement."

Miller sighed, he'd liked the Colonel. "All I can really tell you is that Lutz advised Severon to get away after the missiles were launched. I went out the door with Severon to protect him all the way to his car. He got in and left real fast. I was headed back when fifty or sixty of the guys came racing out of the building like the devil was on their heels. I took off with them."

Jack asked Miller, "What type of car was Severon driving?"

Hugh thought and said, "A new Mercedes Benz two seater, all in silver."

Mark looked at Jack and asked Miller one more question. "What did Lutz look like?"

Miller thought about that. "A thin man, about forty years old, graying hair, lean skull and burning black eyes. No facial hair or scars. He always dressed neatly in a suit and tie."

Mark led the man over to the lead FBI agent. "Would you do me a favor? Cut this one some slack. He didn't fire a shot and only ran away because the others did. He was more of a non-involved security guard. He'll cooperate with you. Okay?"

The FBI man smiled, "Sure, we'll check him out". He called the police sergeant over and had the man's leg shackles removed. Then he had him placed in a squad car for transportation to the police station for interviewing.

Jack and the other Team members asked for transportation to the airport. Once there they got on the plane, Su Li flew them back to Dallas.

On the flight they heard the news of Severon's freaky death by a meteor. Laura laughed, "I wouldn't doubt that God knew a million years ago exactly where Severon would be at that instant.

Jack sat back and wondered who this Lutz character was and what his part in all of this meant.

# CHAPTER FORTY-SIX

Hermann Lutz stared out of the window of the jetliner as it flew over Germany. His eyes were sharp and he could pick out the tractors in their fields as they tilled the fertile German soil. They didn't really register because his mind was so enraged that Severon's mission had been ruined by God and His agents. After all his careful planning and development, the Jewish homeland had not been destroyed and his mission was again defined by that failure.

The pain being applied to him for this latest failure was intolerable and unending. He had to find a way to use these weak, spineless people to bring about the extermination of the Jews! He felt his best hope still remained with the Germans. They were pliable and effective once trained. He had worked with them to almost achieve his goal in the last Great War. But, it didn't matter how many millions of them he killed, they bred like rabbits and kept surviving. This happened regardless of the efforts he had made over the last decades to eradicate them.

Now God had raised up this "Crossfire Team" of combat specialists to defeat his efforts around the world. They had interfered in his last eight efforts to reduce the Jewish population. They had kept his agent in Denver from acquiring the crucifixion nail. Same with the effort to inflame Houston so that America would be distracted and he could have other agents attack Israel. This accursed Team had almost single-handedly stopped a nine-year effort to poison the Jewish homeland. Then they destroyed his effort to end the world at the Arctic Circle. That would have been his finest hour except for these meddlers. They had interfered in his arrangements in Zyngola and now they ruined his efforts in the southern United States! This was intolerable!

He could fan the hatred of the radical Arabs into murder and war against the Jews quite easily. They were always ready to kill the "Zionists". But because of their theology or philosophy they tended to think small and even if they won a battle now and then they eventually lost the war. Some countries, on the other hand, could be counted upon to rally behind almost any cause, especially if it boosted their pride.

His thoughts returned to the Team that was hounding him. He knew that God was directing them against him. This was so unfair. It was time to deal with these upstarts. He would apply himself to eradicating them and their interference once and for all! He thought through the list of people and groups he had contact with or control over. He had one group that was set up in the U.S. that could mount a serious effort against this small team.

"Hmm" he thought. "These people could put together a serious effort against the Crossfire Team in their home country. They would throw themselves at the Team without regard to their lives. Still, they would probably all die in the effort. But, there was several other upsides to this idea than just that. It could possibly kill them all and would definitely occupy the attention of the pesky Denver-based group for some time. This would give him time to prepare a truly fatal strike against Israel that wouldn't fall apart due to poor execution like the more recent failures."

He considered all the angles about the coming war against the Crossfire Team and added some embellishments to it. He decided it would take several weeks to prepare a trap and bait it. He preferred one massive initial strike that would kill them all at once. A major effort with two, or even three, additional waves of attacks to ensure none of them survived.

Seeing that he had a workable plan to eliminate the Crossfire Team he made two calls on the airphone supplied by Lufthansa. The local representatives of the Soldiers of Zultar would meet him at the airport. He would give them their marching orders. Of course he would be paying them and supplying them with weapons and transportation, but it was for a good cause. This group of fanatics was the ultra zealots of that particular religion and as a plus; they had a score to settle with the Crossfire Team for disgracing their god in front of the world press. They felt if they got rid of the Team that led the disgrace, they will have erased the event from everyone's memory. At least it would serve as an abject lesson on why one shouldn't mess with Zultar.

Lutz then turned his mind to his main goal. This would be even more complicated and involved. He found he couldn't focus well because of the constant barrage of insults for failure and the pain of that failure. He shouted in his mind, "Leave me alone if you want this to work!" The doubt and fear and condemnation faded away and were replaced with the single thought. "This is your last chance. Fail again and it will be the end for you." There was great power in the thought and utter assurance that if he failed again the punishment would be severe beyond comprehension.

Back in Dallas, the Team said goodbye to David at DFW as he headed back to Israel on a commercial jetliner. They had shipped the bulkier stuff and loaded everything else on their corporate Citation X for the short trip back to Denver and the Fortress.

Su Li took the jet smoothly up to thirty-two thousand feet and headed north-northwest towards the mile high city. Sarah was in the co-pilot's seat taking lessons from Su Li. She never knew when she might be called upon to fly a plane again. She wanted to learn how to land without leaving most of the aircraft on the ground behind her.

The rest of the Team discussed the events of Dallas and Corpus Christi and wrote up a summary of everything they knew and a list of what they didn't know. The top item on the list was Hermann Lutz. David had assured them that he would see that Joey Goldberg's last request was acted upon as soon as he returned to Tel Aviv.

One of the other items that they needed to check on was the climate in Washington as far as they were concerned. Did they have to work alone or could they count on the power and resources of the U.S. Government to battle any future threats?

Jack said that he would go to Wonderland on the Potomac and test the waters. Laura said that she would go with him. Thinking about the Malone's last foray into D.C. Mark nodded and said that after some research at the Fortress, and maybe a couple of days of rest, he and Sarah would accompany them. Mark really didn't want to find the two of them in a hospital again anytime soon.

Charlie and Linda Wu decided that they would remain in Denver and see to their investigation business.

Su Li wanted to return to Washington to see more of it and since she had to go as the pilot it would all work out nicely. Also, it would be a good time to continue Sarah's flying lessons.

At two a.m. the Citation X touched down at DIA Since there had been no one at the Fortress to bring their cars to them, Jack rented two GMC Tahoe SUVs to get all of their gear in and ferry them home.

The trip was uneventful which was fortunate because only Jack and Mark were awake because they were driving. The Fortress was as they left it and since it was so highly automated, it was actually improved since they left.

Everyone crashed into their beds letting the tensions of the last few weeks drain away in sleep.

# CHAPTER FORTY-SEVEN

After an exhausting trip to Washington where they had to explain what happened in Corpus Christi and in space over Israel several times, the Team returned from Washington D.C. to the Fortress. Since there were no urgent requests for the Crossfire Team, everyone tried to remember what they used to do when they weren't involved in terrorism, combat, or investigations.

After a week of rest and waiting, Mark and Sarah began doing investigations for Mark's company. Jack went back to his manufacturing company, Technical Alternatives, and Laura spent her days praying and making archive records of their operations in a data base. "More like adventures she thought". But then, they had a lot of notes, research information, and photos and video for each of their "assignments". It was enough to keep her busy for several months.

Su Li took a two month leave for more advanced fighter training under the teaching of Major White and approved by the Air Force.

After settling into their normal routines, Jack had started teaching martial arts again at the dojo. His dojo style instruction had changed considerably since his first run-in with Don Miland. He dropped all the flourishes and showmanship movements from his techniques. His style was functional, effective, and terse. Opponents that went for the flashy, head-high, spinning back heel kicks found themselves on the ground and already hit three times before they knew what had happened.

He showed his students how to achieve real focus. His experience was actual combat, life-and-death Kaumate without any wasted effort. This excited the students and his classes grew in size as more people wanted to learn what he had to teach. For he himself, Jack didn't want any of these people to get caught in any form of street combat with only dojo fighting skills.

Winter had arrived in Colorado. Many days were short, dark, and cold like this one. The snow was dropping in small flurries and the roads were slick. Jack had started getting used to being home by six for dinner and was grateful to reach the warm, solid protection of the Fortress. It had become home to all of them and they had added a barracks compound on the land next to the granite mountain for the troops that were training on their property. The Crossfire Team paid for the construction and outfitting of the barracks and they provided Class-A housing for the one hundred troops that rotated through the training facility.

It had become known as Camp Crossfire and was highly desirable duty. There was a considerable waiting list for the various branches of the military to use the facility for training.

As he walked through the living room he felt the solid protection and comfort that one could only get with a half mile of granite between them and the storms outside.

It came as a slight jolt when he found the kitchen dark and Laura and the Connellys in the war room. Hanging up his overcoat he joined them and asked what was up.

Mark pointed at the email on his console which was marked URGENT! Reading it Jack could tell it was written by someone who learned English as a second language because of the poor wording. It said,

*"Crossfire Team - We has the nine children captive. You will bring the crucifixion spike to us or dead they will be. You have six hours to be at the following coordinates or we kill them slowly.*

*SOZ."* This was followed by a set of GPS coordinates.

Jack dropped it back on the table. Looking at Mark he shrugged. "Do you think this is a real message?"

Mark shook his head. "It's hard to tell. There are nine kids missing off a school bus near those coordinates. The Sheriff has teams out looking for them but isn't sure they're really lost or just not accounted for by the bus driver. It just happened a couple of hours ago."

Laura was silently praying as she listened to the chatter. In her mind's eye she saw a huge bear trap snapping closed. Its bright metal teeth smashing together with enough force to cut a bus in two. She said, "It's a trap. They may have the kids but they are just bait for us."

Jack said, "Okay, we know it's a trap to either get the nail or to get us, or both. But, since children's lives might be at stake, we need to ask God on how we respond".

After the Team prayed for a while, Jack noted that he wasn't getting any leading in this matter. No one else was either. Laura said, "The Lord has been training and maturing us and expects us to be his hands on Earth. Why don't we proceed as we have in the past and listen for God's directions as we go? I believe that these people will torture and kill innocent children if we don't respond within their time requirements. Do you agree?"

Mark nodded, "I checked the GPS coordinates and they want us to show up with the nail in a mountainous area south-southwest of Alamosa. The area is approximately twenty-five miles from the New Mexico border and is at nine thousand feet in altitude. I've ordered a satlink photo series of the area and it should be here any minute."

Mark took a drink of coffee and continued. "The only reason they would pick a deserted location such as this would be an ambush. Only the Lord knows how long they've had to prepare it. I believe that is the reason for the short response time. So that we can't overcome their preparations in the short time allotted."

Jack thought about the situation. "Okay, we assume they have nine innocent children they are using to bait a trap. If we ignore them or don't follow their demands, they'll kill the kids."

Sarah added, "If they haven't already killed them."

Jack looked at her with compassion knowing that she had been through situations like this before when she was in Israel. "There is that possibility too. But we can't work with that until we're sure they have done it. If, like Mark says, they've had weeks or months to set this up then we can be sure we won't be able to walk into it and then fight our way out. They will have the place locked up six ways from Sunday to prevent that."

Sarah said, "If we don't walk into their trap, the kids die, if we do, we all die and so will the kids. They won't leave any witnesses behind."

Laura frowned, "Then what can we do?"

Jack had an idea. "Let me pray about this for a few minutes. We'll need to get Su Li back because we'll need her helicopter skills. Would you see if you can arrange that for us Sarah?"

# CHAPTER FORTY-EIGHT

While Jack was praying, data and Intel on the area came in from the NSA scans of the ground and sub-ground in the area. Mark took the images and studied them. Looking at them for the fourth time he slowly nodded. "Hey, the meeting spot west of Alamosa is surely a fake. There are no installations, no people, nothing except a small metallic object that could be a box no bigger than the traditional bread box."

Jack frowned and walked over and looked at the screen images. "Could they be hiding their forces, like Chun did in China?"

Mark shook his head. "Not from this type of scan. No, I'll bet my next month's check that this is a test to see if we'll cooperate. We'll probably be required to go to some other place with absolutely no time to research it or to scan it. That's what I would do anyway."

Jack thought through the idea. "Okay, I'm going to go there and see what the situation is. If it is a trap, then you guys will have to get me out. If it is just a test, I'll relay the information to you and meet you at the next place. Now, do you think they'll do this several times?"

Mark considered the possibility. "No, and why I don't think so is because it isn't a game to them. They probably have some form of observation on the first place, satellite, long-range visual, or something else. They are wary of what has happened to our adversaries before this. They probably are expecting a massive show of force so that they can threaten to kill the kids if we do that again. It's a good way to shape the conflict and shows a high-level of military organizational skill. We can throw them off by acting one way here and a different way the next time. Now, why you? Why is it not me or Laura or Sarah?"

Jack smiled, "Because I think the Lord wants me to confront this and by going by myself, I limit the damage they can do to us, if for example, that thing explodes in my face."

Laura laughed, "Oh no, you're not getting out of this that easy. I'm going with you."

Sarah was nodding her head. "We are too. The message was to the Crossfire Team not just one individual."

Jack checked his watch. "Okay then, we have got three and a half more hours to the deadline." He looked at Sarah, "What's the ETA on Su Li?"

Sarah shook her head. "She can't be here before tomorrow morning at the earliest. They were training on a carrier somewhere in the Atlantic. She's leaving immediately but it will take her at least eight to twelve hours to get here."

Jack turned to Mark, "Can you get a helicopter pilot from the Army or Marines to get us there ahead of schedule?"

Mark picked up his console phone and made a call. After talking for several minutes he hung up and nodded. "The Army has a specialist in helio-warfare at the barracks. He'll be landing on the pad in less than ten minutes. He's bringing a Black Hawk so we'll have plenty of room and more than enough speed to get there in time."

Mark thought back about the S-70 Black Hawk and remembered a time, not too long ago, when he owed his life to the abilities of crew and craft.

-----------------------*****-----------------------

He had been assigned a "snatch and grab" mission, which meant they had to find the person they were assigned to, take possession of said person, and get them out of whatever situation they were in at the time. The person could be friendly, hostage, or hostile. Before they left on the mission Mark had the opportunity to examine the, then, new S-70A Black Hawk and find out about its capabilities.

The Black Hawk had low delectability and outstanding nap-of-the-earth flight capabilities. The aircraft was considered tolerant to small arms fire and most high explosive, medium (23mm) caliber projectiles. The flight controls had been ballistically hardened and the crew was provided with redundant electric and hydraulic systems.

Hoping that he wouldn't have to use them, Mark knew that the helicopter had the ability to absorb high crash impact velocities. The fuel system was crash resistant and self-sealing. The crew seats and the landing gear are energy absorbing.

The helicopter was flown by a crew of three, the pilot and the copilot at the flight deck and one crew member in the cabin. The S-70A helicopter was equipped with a glass cockpit and digital avionics. This meant that it was very high tech. The S-70 was a launch platform for sixteen laser-guided Hellfire anti-armor missiles, using the External Stores Support System (ESSS). Mark learned that the ESSS had the capability of carrying a 10,000lb payload of missiles, rockets, cannons and electronic countermeasures pods. The helicopter could also accommodate additional missiles, supplies or personnel inside the cabin.

The S-70 mounted 7.62mm caliber machine guns in the side windows. This was one fact that Mark really appreciated because of their immense cover fire capability.

The cabin was equipped with ventilation and heating systems and provided accommodation for eleven, fully equipped troops. Since he was only taking five other people there would be plenty of room. He learned that the cabin could also handle four litters (stretcher patients) with a medical officer for medical evacuation missions. Again, something he hoped he wouldn't have to use.

The helicopter was equipped to handle secure voice communications, satellite communications, and a special ground Team comm system for this mission. Satisfied with his transportation Mark went to collect his strike team.

In his memory, Mark remembered studying the mission profile which was sketchy at best. Their target was hostile, in a hostile nation, which thankfully didn't have an air force. The target was important enough to warrant a bevy of security guards and measures, but not so important that he got military protection. He was going to be at a Hacienda located on a low hill, surrounded by a tall rock and concrete wall topped with glass and sensor wires. His security Team numbered roughly eighteen men with access to everything from pistols to Stinger missiles. That fact worried Mark in regards to their evacuation from the site.

The only reason they were authorized to snatch this known terrorist was because he had just recently fallen out of favor with the ruling Junta. So recently that he didn't know about it as yet. He would know tomorrow morning when it broke on the morning news. They needed to get to him while he still thought that he was immune, protected by the nation he had settled into after killing over one hundred innocent civilians with a truck bomb. The only reason he was wanted alive was because he had information on other cells that could lead to some major victories. Still, the mission profile clearly stated that he was to be brought back alive, if possible and not at the expense of U.S. soldier's lives, if possible.

Having planned his strategy he called the guys together and told them what he expected they would run into, how tight the time schedule was, and what the odds were, for, and against them. The men he had selected were all veterans of this type of operation, real professionals. They stoically accepted the information and prepared themselves mentally for the upcoming strike.

Loading onto the helicopter, Mark met the pilot for the mission. He knew that the man had flown helicopters in the original Gulf war and battles since then. He only knew him by his "handle" which was "Spud". When he asked the man how he got that nickname, he smiled and said, "I'm from Idaho, you know, the potato state? Well, during the Gulf war I was flying an Apache and had knocked out several tanks and APCs when we raided an advanced radar site."

"Our orders were to knock out the radar and to interdict any other operations at the base. I'd used my Hellfire missiles on the radar installation itself and was about to return when I saw a truck scurrying across the base in a big hurry. It was pitch black night and I saw him in the FLIR. I couldn't tell what it was carrying because it had a tarp over the back. Checking my weapons stores list I found that all I had were missiles with fleshettes in them. You know those things that look like children's jacks except that they're sharp at the points rather than round."

Spud smiled thinking back to the attack on the truck. "So, I selected eight missiles, four from each rack and fired them off. They shredded the truck and tore the tarp off of it. About that time we had another target and had to engage it. But before I left I made another pass over the truck to make sure I had destroyed it and to see what it had been carrying."

"You know that there are cameras that take pictures of everything we do and see on the helicopter, right? Well, in the FLIR all I could see was stacks of sacks which had been destroyed. Anyway, when we reviewed the tapes, my Crew Chief laughed and told me I had just shot up their food supply truck and the sacks were sacks of potatoes. Everyone had a good laugh at that and when I went to fly the next time I had a new entry in my "kills" markings on the side of the chopper. There were two tanks with diagonal lines through them, three APCs the same way, and a large potato with a line through it and my new nickname was printed below my window, "SPUD". That's how I got the name. Welcome aboard, now tell me how we are going to risk our lives to help you accomplish your mission."

Mark had outlined his plan and the chopper took off into the gathering darkness as night fell over the land.

# CHAPTER FORTY-NINE

Reviewing his previous mission, Mark remembered that he had learned from the Intel on the target that the host country had helicopters that made frequent trips over the city and country. This traffic was mostly military choppers ferrying troops. Therefore, the sound of a chopper passing overhead would probably not attract much attention from the guards at the property. Based on that assumption Mark had gotten creative.

As the helicopter neared the property it was flying with the wind which was about fourteen miles an hour. At four thousand feet the five-man strike Team went out the open rear loading ramp and jumped into the darkness. Five seconds later a black parawing popped out of each man's backpack and the Team formed up on the small flashing light on the top of Mark's helmet. Twenty seconds later the three guards on the roof died without firing a shot, cut down by silenced rounds from the sky.

The five man Team landed and fanned out across the roof, shedding their chutes and using night-vision goggles. Each man had on a black, ripstop nylon combat suit with all the necessary weapons and supplies hung on belts, harness, and backpack. Each man also had a silenced Colt CAR-15 with a laser aiming device. Opening the roof access they quickly descended the stairs and found the right bedroom door. Mark and his second went in quickly and quietly. The man asleep in the bed matched the picture of their quarry right down to the scar on his neck. Mark carefully shot him with a tranquilizer dart that was loaded with a quick-acting and powerful narcotic. The man tried to slap at the sting of the small dart but lost control of his muscles before he could do it. The woman in the bed hadn't noticed anything and she also got a dart to keep her quiet.

The two raiders tied their quarry up and put him into a body sack for transportation. Carrying him out of the room, Mark got another soldier to help carry the man back to the roof. He took the other two men and went to nullify the possible Stingers. Somewhere on their journey through the house they must have tripped a silent alarm system. A bunch of guards were rushing towards the bedroom when they noticed the three-man Team of raiders. The raiders broke into a room to the side of the hall they were in to avoid being bracketed by guards at both ends of the hall. They had stumbled into a large sunroom with windows above and all along one wall. There was a three story drop to the ground outside of the windows which didn't offer much in the way of escape.

The guards were shouting and firing AK-47s at the door which splintered but resisted disassembling. Mark was on the radio to the chopper while he set up a firing solution for the three of them. The heavy oak doors of the sunroom continued to resist the guard's attempts to shoot it down and they resorted to using an axe. On the third strike of the axe, Mark fired a metal-piercing round through the door and there was a scream and a thud. The axe stayed in the door for the duration. Knowing what was coming next; Mark gestured to the other two men and got down behind a heavy sofa. Opening his mouth to equalize the pressure he was proven right when an explosion tore the doors apart and sent chunks of the doors and splinters throughout the room.

The three raiders had arranged for a crossfire pattern through the door that piled up guards in the first rush they made to get in the room. Apparently there were more than three dozen guards at the villa because there were at least that many left outside the door. Using wooden and metal shields the guards worked their way up to the sides of the door and prepared to rush the three men in the room. It wasn't hard to estimate the odds of their surviving this many rifles. Mark clutched his silenced Colt AR-15 and waited for the rush.

It came suddenly and there was a tremendous volume of rounds in the air, splintering the furniture and punching out through the window panes. Suddenly, all three of the raiders heard two words on their combat radios. "Spud, duck". All three men dove to the floor as what was left of the sunroom windows blew in from a storm of 7.62mm rounds that shredded everything above two feet. Every fifth round from the three machine guns was a tracer and there were enough of them going overhead Mark could have read a newspaper. There wasn't even time for any screams. It was over in seconds. Mark popped his head up and looked for any active enemies. There weren't any to find. The holes from the machine guns on the chopper had walked both ways down the walls from the central door and if anyone had still been behind them, they were history. The building was making serious creaking sounds from above. The machine guns had cut two load-bearing walls almost in half. The heavy thump of the helicopter rotor blades above the roof wasn't helping the situation.

The three raiders shook the glass and debris off of themselves and padded over and around the bodies to check the hall. Nothing moved. Mark called the chopper. "Thanks guys. I think you may have finished them all off. But should we check for the odd man out who might send a missile up our tail?"

Spud answered, "Not tonight Captain. While this terrorist isn't in favor with the Government, our flight over their territory is very illegal and we need to be gone, now!"

The three black-clad raiders ran back to the stairs and up to the roof. The Black Hawk was hanging less than a foot off of the roof and kicking up a sand storm of tiny bits of roofing material. Mark made sure the two men were on board before he jumped into the open doorway. The pilot pulled pitch and lifted quickly away from the roof. Gathering speed, the chopper dropped almost to the deck as the pilot flew by NVG and the co-pilot watched the FLIR for possible enemy activities.

After several miles the crew brought the chopper back up to cruising altitude and Mark breathed a little easier. At the low level they had been flying, a farmer's silo could have brought them down if it hadn't been for the skill of the pilot and crew.

Crossing out of the country and back to their base the chopper settled lightly to the ground. A Team of doctors and Intelligence Agents met the chopper and took their suspect away in an ambulance. Afterward, they were examined by the medics and debriefed. After their mission was determined to be a success, Mark gave each of his men an assurance they would get a commendation. Only the people important to their military careers would every read about this mission. Other than that, very few people would ever know how this terrorist came to be in American hands. He then remembered taking the three-man crew of the helicopter and his guys out for a drink to unwind.

------------------------\*\*\*\*\*------------------------

Mark finished packing his gear and ran for the elevators which went to the top of the Fortress. It dawned on him that God had reminded him of that mission because it could help them on this one.

# CHAPTER FIFTY

Sarah was the last person boarding the Black Hawk as Mark ran up to it. He climbed in behind her and took a seat. The chopper lifted off the platform immediately. The platform descended back into the mountain as the chopper flew away.

Mark put on his headset and switched it to intercom. He was surprised to hear the pilot say, "Hey Captain, still kidnapping terrorists from foreign countries?"

Mark knew the voice. "Hey yourself Spud! What are you doing here?"

As he controlled the aircraft and aimed it at the San Louis Valley in the south central part of the state, the pilot replied, "I've been assigned to teach Army helicopter pilots advanced techniques here at Camp Crossfire. I didn't know you were here until I got assigned to this mission. Glad to see you're still functioning."

Mark grinned at the others, "I've kinda changed management companies though. Nowadays I'm a member of the Crossfire Team rather than a U.S. Navy SEAL."

Spud laughed, "Yeah I heard, different suit, same guy doing the same things. I'm a Colonel now but like all good ol' race horses I've been put out to stud rather than running races. I got this because everyone else is off for the Thanksgiving holiday and it was urgent. Can you fill me in on the profile of this mission?"

Mark thought for a few seconds. "Yeah, sure Spud. Apparently there is a radical group out there that doesn't like us and probably for good cause. I think we made their god look bad in Zyngola, or we may have prevented them from blowing up Dallas. Anyway, it seems that they want us at a particular rendezvous and to make sure we're there they've kidnapped nine kids and are threatening to kill them if we don't show up. However, it might just be a test and they want to see if we'll respond. So we're going to make an appearance and see where it leads."

Spud whistled, "That was you guys in Dallas? I am impressed. Well, you've certainly graduated from kidnapping terrorists. Now you're dealing with nuclear-armed terrorists that kidnap kids. Okay, we'll be your transportation and your backup. We should be there in forty-nine minutes."

Mark responded with, "I couldn't think of a better backup than you Spud."

The Team discussed their responses to a variety of possible scenarios while they zipped through the sky waiting patiently for their drop-off time.

Spud eyeballed the meeting place and checked it through FLIR. It was completely deserted as expected. He brought the chopper down two hundred yards from the spot and the Team disembarked and headed in on foot.

Spud took the chopper back up to eight hundred feet and watched over the team.

The Team approached the GPS location warily. There was a military field phone sitting on a tree stump. Jack walked up to it and picked up the handset. There were two minutes left until the deadline. The phone rang for six rings and then a man answered. "I see that you made it in time. I've sent the order to release the children as I promised. Now, if you survive this meeting then we will be in touch soon. Time to die." the line went dead.

Dropping the handset, Jack said, "Let's get out of here." The four of them ran back the way they had come as fast as they could.

Spud's radio came to life. "Crossfire flight this is AWACS. Be aware there is a falling object headed for the GPS coordinates from twenty-five thousand feet. It looks like an airdropped bomb or missile."

Spud rotated the chopper to the south and tipped it up. His ECM/Radar man scanned the heavens above them. "I have it, coming in at 125 feet per second. Free falling."

Spud knew what he had to do to protect the team. He imposed the helicopter between the bomb and the team. The helicopter would intercept the falling body to keep it from killing those on the ground.

Fighting to hold the heads up position, Spud said, "Lock on if you can." He keyed up a Hellfire missile and locked it to the helicopter's radar. A falling bomb doesn't have much cross section for radar to lock onto, especially one coming head on.

The ECM man said, "The signal is getting stronger. Hang on, OKAY! It's locked."

Spud fired the Hellfire missile straight at the descending bomb. The missile stayed locked onto the falling object and intercepted it at six thousand feet. The combined explosion was huge and the shockwave bounced the chopper around. Spud not only fought to keep the chopper airborne but to move it away and avoid any falling pieces that could destroy his rotors.

Bringing the nose down below the horizon and letting the helicopter fall off to the right side, he tilted the rotors that way and applied full power. There were bangs and pings as shrapnel from the explosion impacted the rotor blades and the aircraft body. After the debris was finished falling he swung the aircraft around and landed near the team.

Shutting it down, he and the crew examined the rotor blades and the body for any serious damage. Not finding anything that would cause problems in their return trip, Spud started the engines, ran the checklists, and gave the Team the high sign. The four warriors clambered onboard and they lifted off for the trip back to Denver.

As they reached cruising altitude, Jack got on the radio to the Conejos County Sheriff's department and explained the explosion and that no one had been injured and no fires had been started. Spud was doing the same explanation to the troops at Cheyenne Mountain in Colorado Springs. The people at NORAD (North American Air Defense) had detected the explosion and were concerned. Spud was more concerned that there was no trace of the aircraft that launched the bomb. NORAD speculated that it was a small private plane that went up to the launch height and then went back down out of radar range as soon as it released the bomb.

Laura had been praying to God about the attack and the children. The Lord impressed on her the importance of the part the helicopter pilot and crew had played in their survival. As Jack was talking to the Sheriff, she unbuckled her safety harness and made her way to the cockpit. She put her hand on the pilot's arm. When he looked at her, she smiled and simply said "thank you" which conveyed all the sincere appreciation of the Team for the heroic effort the helicopter crew had put forth to protect the team.

Spud smiled back and said, "All in a days work Ma'am. I seem to get these opportunities every time I'm around Mr. Connelly."

The ECM/radar man had listened to the exchange and added. "Could we do that again? I wasn't watching close enough." At which point the third crewman began to beat him on the helmet with his gloves. The release of tension was effective and everyone laughed.

Landing back at the Fortress, Spud told Mark as he was ready to disembark, "I appreciate the chance to work with you guys. Ask for me the next time you need air support."

Mark had watched the chopper put it's self between the on-coming bomb and himself and was proud of the courage it took to do something selfless like that. He smiled at his friend, "Have no fear buddy, you are now on our "A" list for air support." He shook the pilot's hand and jumped to the ground.

After they had cleaned up and re-convened in the war room, Sarah brought up the question that had been bugging her since the flight back. "I am concerned about our next response to these people. They said that they released the children. What lever are they going to use to get us to put our lives in danger the next time?"

Mark shrugged, "It doesn't really matter because we aren't going to wait for them to bait us again. We're going to take the war to them!"

# CHAPTER FIFTY-ONE

Mark and Sarah began a serious search for the resource components and people that make up the Soldiers of Zultar. They sought the assistance of all U.S. Federal agencies and a select group of international ones such as Interpol. Within four hours they had compiled a comprehensive list of the known operatives within the borders of the United States. It was a surprisingly large number of suspected terrorists.

Jack looked at the list and raised an eyebrow. "There are sixty three probably spies or saboteurs. Seems like a major security risk for America. I wonder why no one has moved on these people."

Mark sat back in his chair, the weight of his muscular body made the structure creak. He smiled grimly, "Because they haven't really done anything as yet. You know our rules; you can't bust em until they show their true colors by doing something you should have prevented in the first place." It was obvious that Mark wasn't pleased with this arrangement in some cases.

Sarah added, "Remember, some of these are questionable. They meet the profile but there is no evidence that they are a part of SOZ. That leaves thirty-two absolutely positive members. From the latest FBI report on the surveillance of these particular people, it seems that this group has been galvanized since about the time we got back from Dallas. They've gotten together a dozen times and have started slipping out from the net the FBI has had on them for the last three years. I would say that they got an order about us and have been in the planning and preparation stage until yesterday."

Laura asked, "Do we know where we can find them?"

Sarah smiled, "We've got a really good starting point. It seems that they tend to meet at three different locations. The pattern indicates that they are going to meet tomorrow night at the exclusive country home of Amal Hasan, one of their members, His house is located northeast of Phoenix, Arizona in the Fountain Hills area. It's a rather exclusive area and he lives in a gated community with his own armed security on his property."

Mark quipped, "I wouldn't have expected any less."

Laura shook her head. "This is so much like some of our other sorties. We have no real proof that this is the group that is attacking us. We don't know that this meeting will be for terroristic purposes or for a major card game. We will be in the wrong if we go in there in force without justifiable cause."

Jack nodded, "Everything you say is true and I agree that we would be breaking the law if we did it on the evidence we have now. Therefore we need to make sure Amal Hasan's meeting isn't innocent before we get down on them. How are we going to make sure before tomorrow night?"

Sarah held up a piece of paper with a man's picture on it. "I suggest we ask this man. He's here in Denver and has been at every meeting over the last two months. His name is Sadiq Kaim and he works as a truck driver. He is a truck driver who also happens to own a Masserati."

Jack made a wry face. "So much for the lowly-paid truck driver status. Okay, let's find him and extract enough information to determine if this is the group that attacked us or not."

Sadiq had finished his route for Thursday and parked his truck at the loading dock for the next day's load. Leaving the day's chores behind him he put on his sunglasses and headed for the parking lot. Now he could enjoy himself for a couple of hours before he called in sick on Friday and made the flight to Phoenix. He rounded the corner of the building and stopped. There was a darkly beautiful woman admiring his Masserati. He sauntered over and asked, "Do you like it?"

The well-built woman looked up and smiled at him. She quietly spoke in Arabic, "It is a beautiful car. My uncle hasn't shown up for me yet and I wanted to look at it. I hope I'm not in trouble."

Sadiq's libido went into high gear and he answered in the same language. "No, no, you're in no trouble. It is my car." He was enchanted by the big smile she gave him as the owner of such a car. "Would you like to go for a ride in it?"

That seemed to excite and scare her at the same time. She looked around and didn't find her uncle anywhere. Then she looked back at him and smiled coyly. "I probably should wait for my uncle, but sometimes he gets to talking and forgets about me." She bent over to look at the inside of the car and gave Sadiq a good look at her cleavage at the same time. "Yes, I would like to go for a ride, but where shall we go?"

Sadiq deactivated the alarm system and unlocked the doors. "Don't worry, I know of several great restaurants where we could have dinner. Are you hungry?"

She nodded vigorously which made her superstructure do all sorts of interesting movements. Sadiq couldn't take his eyes off of her blouse. "Come on then, get in."

They got in the car and he powered out of the lot and headed for a really good Arabic restaurant. He looked over at the woman and saw that she had some really great legs. The Masserati was very powerful and he accelerated away from everyone else at the lights. As he pulled into the restaurant's parking lot the woman got out her perfume and then playfully squirted some at him. It was a wonderful aroma. Sadiq passed out with a smile on his face while he was thinking of the heavenly delights awaiting him.

Sarah pulled her cell phone out and pressed a preset code. A few minutes later a black van pulled into the lot and stopped in front of the Masserati. The van doors on the side opened and Jack and Mark pulled Sadiq from the sports car and into the van. Sarah finished wiping down the car to remove any of her prints and jumped into the van as the doors shut and the van pulled slowly out of the lot.

Finding a deserted stretch of highway outside of Denver, Su Li steered the van behind some trees so that it was no longer visible from the road. Mark had already injected the serum into Sadiq's veins. Sarah continued to talk to the drugged man in Arabic. She steered the questioning towards causes and let him take the ball and run.

In twenty minutes the Team had their proof positive that this group was the one that had been tasked to eliminate the Crossfire Team and secure the crucifixion nail if possible. The only surprise they got was that the person ordering the attack and paying for everything was none other than Hermann Lutz.

Sarah looked at the quietly sleeping Arab. "What do we do with him now?"

Mark said quietly to Sarah so that Sadiq couldn't hear. "Give him an autosuggestion that your uncle saw you get in his car and followed you to the restaurant and made you go with him. Let Sadiq figure out why he fell asleep. Then we'll put him back in his car.

That accomplished they left the sleeping man in his expensive sports car.

As they headed back to the Fortress they considered what they had learned. Mark was shaking his head. "I can't believe they would actually put a bomb in a school and really detonate it if we don't respond on Saturday. It's inhuman."

Sarah patted her husband's hand. "You have no idea how inhuman this form of people can be. Yes, they'd gladly blow up every child in America to hurt just one Israeli. But, just threaten their children and they'll declare holy war on you. It's a big demonic double-standard. We've got to stop them before they put the bomb in the school."

Jack mused, "Legally we are still on really shaky ground. This could easily go against us in any court of law. Should we turn this over to the Government?"

Mark laughed a bitter laugh. "Yeah, and I know just who to turn it over to." He picked up the phone and called the office of the Chairman of the Joint Chiefs of Staff. He got connected to General Miles immediately.

General Miles came on, "Mark, how is it going for your Team after the Corpus Christi action? Didn't I just read a report about a bomb in southern Colorado?"

Mark chuckled, "Boy, we can't keep anything from you, can we, Sir?"

The General also chuckled, "I hope not, what is it that you need?"

Mark responded, "That bomb in Colorado was a part of a plot to destroy our team. It was bought and paid for by Hermann Lutz, probably in repayment for our taking Severon's operation down. Unfortunately it's not over. A radical group known as the "Soldiers of Zultar" was behind the bomb and has been commissioned to destroy us by Lutz."

"Our investigation has gathered proof positive that the next phase for these radicals will be to put a bomb in a Phoenix grade school in an effort to blackmail us into walking into another death trap. We have no authority to attack an armed private residence in the U.S. Sir. I was wondering if your office could energize the ATF or the FBI to raid Amal Hasan's place tomorrow night. They will definitely have serious fire power and bomb making materials. Our informant indicated that this is the last meeting before they place the bomb in the school."

The General trusted Mark and therefore the information. "I doubt that the ATF could get the job done. But, I know a group that can and the Patriot Act gives them the authority to do it!"

Mark replied, "Yes Sir, if you're talking about an elite Team of military types, beware that there are thirty-two suspects and a small army of armed guards and that these are religious radicals that want to die for their cause."

The General took the address and information on numbers and timing from Mark. Then he asked, "Do you want to be there with this group?"

Mark grinned, "You bet we do. Leave reservations for four more people."

The General said, "I'll get in touch with you as to where and when." and then he hung up.

Mark explained what had transpired over the phone.

Jack looked at his best friend. "How do we explain an armed assault on U.S. soil when our only rationale for attacking them is information we got from an illegal interrogation by drugs of an uncooperative captive."

Mark looked thoughtful, "We don't have too. This is now an anti-terrorist operation by the federal Government. The authority is there and I'm betting dollars to doughnuts that the SOZ aren't going to meekly give up. Therefore, we need to secure at least one leader that can give us directions to find Hermann Lutz."

# CHAPTER FIFTY-TWO

The following evening, just outside of Phoenix, the Crossfire Team joined the secret USMATS, or United States Military Anti-Terrorist Squad

USMATS was made up of selected military personnel that volunteered for operations that only targeted hostile terrorists or groups of terrorists within the United States. The selection process was very careful to include only those warriors that were seasoned veterans with experience in urban warfare and a through knowledge of the limitations on their activities.

This USMATS group was led by Major Thornton. He was a veteran of three conflicts, Serbia, Desert Storm, and Enduring Freedom. He was very knowledgeable on car bombings, roadside IEDs, and house-to-house fighting. He also had a legal degree and knew what lines not to cross.

As he explained to the team, due to the Patriot Act provisions and the reasonable expectation that the target included heavy weapons and explosives, this would not be a knock and desist encounter. The one hundred troops here tonight would be going in as softly as possible until there was any resistance. At that point the gloves came off and it was an all-out assault by a superior military force.

The CJCS had been pointed about cooperation with the Crossfire Team and the Major wasn't about to step on the Chairman's toes. He asked them what part they wanted to play in the raid.

Mark told him, "We are interested in one of the leaders, possibly the owner of the property, Amal Hasan. We want to ask him why he tried to bomb us out of existence two days ago in southern Colorado. We will give you any support you need other than that one request."

The Major liked the way that Mark didn't use their special status for anything. "Okay, I've got an extremely well-trained unit here. We've practiced this hundreds of times and actually done it several times. I'll explain what I've got planned and then ask you to let us handle the first stage of the assault proper. You watch the phase one assault against the guards and then join us for the attack against the actual members of the SOZ. This will give me peace of mind of not having to tell the CJCS that I lost one of you needlessly.

I've had observation posts around the property since yesterday. There have been over twenty-five cars arrive in the last two hours. We have video records of several people with suspect packages that look like high-powered rifles and possible satchels of C-4. Therefore, with suitable cause, I'm going to take out the guards as silently as possible and infiltrate the buildings. I'll call you on this unit." He handed a small cell phone to Mark. "And tell you to join us. Then we will attempt to take the suspects as they are meeting. Hopefully it will be a surprise and they won't fire a shot. That's the plan, and this is the reality.

The Major indicated a small map of the property. "We don't know what fortifications they have on the grounds or in the buildings. We also don't know what alarm systems are in place. We've found an electronic fence and sensor wires from a distance but we don't know if those wires go to an alarm or to a Claymore mine. The house has been extensively rebuilt on the inside and no plans are available. Thermal imaging last night indicates that there are more guards inside than out and they are probably in communication with each other."

After he said that, the Major looked at the property in the dark. "I'd guess that they'll start firing back before we're halfway to the buildings. At that point I'm going to use some armor to breach the place."

Mark looked up, "Armor? What type of armor?"

The Major indicated to his left, I've got two M1A1 tanks and four Bradley Fighting Vehicles just outside the wall. If things go hard, I'll blow the wall and the tanks will lead the way."

Jack asked the Major, "Could you get anyone in there last night to reconnoiter?"

The Major shook his head. "They've got six guards with NV scopes on top of the main building that would have seen our men easily. They are going to be the first to go tonight."

Jack motioned to Mark and the two of them walked a short distance away. Jack sighed and looked at Mark in the dark. "You know that it was our information that set this up, right?" Mark nodded and Jack continued. "Then we had bettered be right or this thing will be a massacre and on our heads."

Mark asked him. "Do you doubt the Intel? You were there during the interrogation of Sadiq. There is no way he could have had the information he had about us, about the bomb in Colorado, or about Hermann Lutz unless they are doing what we say they are doing. Jack, get a grip. This is the way things are done in the world. There are no guarantees. Now, we all prayed about this and I believe that the Lord was in agreement that we should act against this group before they act against us again, right?"

Jack thought it over. "Yeah, you're right. The thought of tanks attacking a home on our word rattled me. Heck, they might not be enough."

Mark chuckled, "If they're not, the Major isn't worth his salt as an officer if he doesn't have air power to back his tanks up."

Jack said, "Wow."

They walked back to the group just as the Major was about to start the festivities.

Even silenced, the .50 caliber sniper rifles made a heavy pffft when they fired, especially when there were six firing at once. The contingent of guards on top of the building went down hard, all at once.

At the same time, troops began to flow over special ladders that avoided the wall and its electronics. As a squad formed up it fanned out and moved towards the buildings. Specialists took out the guards as they found them. The entire group was on the grounds and moving towards the building when the first contact was made by the other side.

Like normal, it was a rarity. One of the guards had gone to the bathroom and had exited right behind a squad. Before they detected him, he grabbed his rifle and fired three shots at the troopers. Two silenced rounds took him out but not before the damage was done. The troops got up, bruised but unharmed thanks to their body armor.

Lights started coming on around the property and were snuffed out by bullets almost as quickly as they lit up. There was an alarm sounding inside the buildings and guards were running to the defenses at the doors and windows. The volume of fire increased constantly as more and more forces joined the fray.

The Team watched the battle for the grounds. It was obvious that the Major's men were far more capable and professional than the defenders. The defenders were going down all over the place while the assault Team had only lost one or two men. Mark noticed a light in a remote part of the open field next to the walled property. He snapped his NV binoculars to his eyes and saw a man in civilian clothes peeking out of a doorway built into the wall of a creek. The door was quickly closed and the light disappeared.

Mark told the others that he had seen a probable rat hole for the property. There were no other men from the USMATS group around. Mark made a command decision. "Come on, we'll close the hole for the Major." He moved out at a run. The others grabbed their weapons and chased after the ex-SEAL. They slid down into the creek and quickly waded to the location of the hidden door. Mark searched for the door and found it without too much effort. He tried the door but it was secure. Mark took out a small quantity of C-4 from his web belt and put a detonator in the small block of C4. He pressed the block against the door frame. Stepping down the creek about thirty feet he checked on his mates and pushed the red button on the detonator.

Someone was just opening the door when the C-4 exploded. This cleared the way and removed the upper part of the person opening the door. The Team ran back to the door and entered, carefully avoiding the remains scattered around. As they advanced in the dark using their NVGs they made good time reaching the next portal. This one was unlocked and opened at a touch. Still there was no one evident. The four Team members moved through the door and started further into the hall. The door behind them slammed shut and another panel slammed closed the hall in front of them.

For several seconds nothing happened. Then the small section of hall that they were in was lit up brightly causing them to pull off their NVGs. A voice said, "See, I told you that they would take the bait!"

# CHAPTER FIFTY-THREE

Mark frowned, "Who are you?" he shouted at the hole in the ceiling.

His reply was a laugh. "We are the poor little radicals that your vaulted military machine is trying to beat three floors up. They think they're winning but they won't get here for hours. You on the other hand are going to be dead long before that and we will be gone."

Jack said, "How did you know that it would be us at the door?"

Again the laugh sounded. "We knew because Mr. Lutz told us so. He knew you'd be left behind during the attack on the property. He also knew you'd attempt to take the credit by charging in here. But the best part is that he knew that Mr. Connelly's pride would keep him from telling the commander of the force upstairs because then he would lose the credit."

Mark didn't say anything. He looked at others and made three subtle hand signs. At the same time he looked at the ceiling and asked, "Just how does this mysterious Mr. Lutz know so much about me?"

"He knows because he's studied you for years, came the answer. "But that is enough chitchat, time for you to die."

Mark yelled one more question, "I expect that the mighty Mr. Lutz is too cowardly to do this himself, he'd probably hiding halfway around the world and allowing you to sacrifice yourself and your people, right?"

The voice came back, "Well, Germany isn't halfway around the world but, no, he is not afraid of you, he simply trusts us to take care such easily fooled people as you."

Mark and Sarah had slowly changed the position of their weapons. As the voice stopped, Mark said, "Now."

All four Team members triggered their M-49, 40mm grenade launchers that were part of their assault rifles. Two of the 40mm minibombs flew from the launchers held by Jack and Laura. These covered the twenty feet to the panel blocking their advance. Mark and Sarah's grenades flew directly up the hole above them. The combined explosions blew the blocking panel to pieces and all four members of the Team ran as fast as they could. There was a heavy "thud" behind them. Mark looked back and said, "Down!"

Everyone dropped to a prone position. A heavy explosion went off behind them but the force blew by them without any real damage. The charge had been dampened by the body lying on top of the package. Behind them the hallway collapsed as part of the house fell in amid clouds of dust and debris.

Jumping up, the Team charged up a ramp towards another closed door. Everyone had reloaded their M-49s and Mark fired his on the run as he said, "Knock, knock!"

This door exploded off the hinges and blew into the room behind it. A flurry of bullets flew back through the opening. Jack fired another grenade through the opening. He fired long and low. Laura fired one down the middle and Sarah fired one high and short. The triple explosions tore the room to pieces and knocked out all the lights. The Team moved cautiously past bodies and checked them; there were no signs of life. As they moved farther into the building trading fire with defenders, Mark kept up a running commentary with Major Thornton through his headset connected to the cell phone. There was a pitched battle going on just above them with explosions and an occasional scream. The USMATS were working efficiently to clear that floor of the building.

A group of the SOZ terrorists were holed up in a conference room near the end of the second floor. As soon as anyone neared the door they let loose with a dozen rounds or more. Mark debated just throwing a series of grenades into the room and taking them out. But they wanted at least one of them alive and talking. He got an update from the Major that the guards were just about eliminated and the top floor was in his control. So, this must be the last of the rats. A group of five tried to bust out of the room firing in all directions. Sarah was behind an upended sofa and fired a figure eight that expended all thirty rounds in the magazine. But it was sufficient to stop all five of the attempted escapees dead in their tracks.

The Major told Mark they were coming down the stairs. Mark apprised him of the situation with the conference room. The Major said, "Just keep them in there for a few more minutes. I'm sending a specialist down."

A soldier crept down the stairs and took a small backpack off. He pulled a fuse on the backpack and expertly threw the backpack into the conference room. Mark sent a dozen rounds into the room to keep everyone's head down. An orange-tinted cloud blew out of the backpack and filled up the conference room. Some of it leaked out of the door but blew away in the breeze from the stairs.

After five minutes the soldier on the stairs put on a gas mask and made it to the door frame. He used a mirror to check out the room and then went in himself. After a few minutes another cloud, this one blue, filled the room. In seconds both colors disappeared and the soldier, without his mask, came to the door and waved the Team into the room.

Entering the room they found eight people unconscious on the floor, their weapons forgotten. The Team and several more soldiers that came into the room put riot cuffs on each person and searched them thoroughly. Then they put a soft black bag over each man's head and two soldiers quickly carried them out of the room and up the stairs.

The Team stood down and went to find the Major. Major Thornton was happy to see them all alive and well. He shook Mark's hand. "Your plan worked. I really liked the thing with leaving the phones open so I could hear that overconfident blowhard tell you everything you thought he would. You called it when you said that the door in the creek was a trap for your team. Didn't quite work out the way he thought it would."

Mark grinned, "No Sir, it certainly didn't. Most of these people have never been in the military and have no idea of the amount of firepower each person can carry."

One of the troopers came up to the Major and gave him a sheet of paper. He scanned it and gave it to Mark. "Okay, which one do you want to "discuss" things with for a while?"

Mark looked at the pictures with the DNA confirmation next to them. He picked the one that said "Amal Hasan".

They repeated their interrogation technique with Amal and got some more surprising information. They turned the punch drunk and confused man back over to the USMATS Team and packed up to go back to Colorado. Mark went to look for the Major and congratulated him on an excellent job.

Mark told the Major that a commendation would be given to the CJCS for him and his team.

There were two soldiers that were wounded but thanks to their body armor, those wounds weren't life threatening. The SOZ lost forty-five people. There were no wounded on the SOZ side. The trap they'd set up had boomeranged on them badly.

On the flight back to the Fortress Laura hugged Mark and told him, "I never doubted your assessment of the SOZ's purpose. You live up to your reputation Mr. Connelly. Mark actually blushed.

Mark said, "It was a little obvious that they were trying to draw us in with this setup. First, the availability of Sadiq, and his being right in our neighborhood. Second, was the fact that they would completely miss the evacuation of all their neighbors. Third, that they missed the insertion of over a hundred military personnel. But, fourth, the real kicker was when Major Thornton moved the tanks right up to their wall. So they had to know we were out there. The only possible reason was to get to us. I just didn't know how they were going to do that until the door opened away from all the action, but still where we could see it. Even the dumbest person knows that you don't open a door with a light on behind you when it is dark outside."

Sarah smiled at her husband's explanation of the events.

# CHAPTER FIFTY-FOUR

As Su Li guided the Citation X towards Denver, the Team discussed Amal's answers. Mark cautioned that the man was repeating information he'd heard, not something he was involved in himself. Still the information was intriguing.

Jack said, "What do you make of his assertion that Lutz was also the guiding light behind not only the holocaust but the assassination of Archduke Ferdinand?" That would make him well aged, over a hundred and twenty years old at the least.

Laura noticed a glow appearing before her. None of the others seemed to notice it. She watched as the glow grew and the angel Rose appeared. It was obvious that this vision was only for Laura. Rose floated in the air with her robes gently swirling around her. Her color was more muted gold than fierce white this time. Rose smiled at Laura, "You have matured as a warrior in the natural as well as in the spiritual. The Lord is proud of all of you and your actions to resist those that defy Him."

The angel raised her hands and Laura felt the power flowing through her. Rose shifted more towards the fierce whiteness in color. "You and the rest of the Team are about to face your most severe challenge in His service. The demon that controls the being you know as Hermann Lutz is ancient and very cunning. He has destroyed millions of people on the Earth in his quest to eliminate the Jewish race. Beware of his guile and his misdirection. He is a master at deception. That is one reason he has been functioning on Earth for as long as he has. Events have come to require your Team to confront "Vorbleg" directly to rid the world of his foulness. Seek out Minister Throman for guidance in this matter. Be strong and courageous Laura, God is with you." Rose faded from sight along with the glow.

Laura interrupted the on-going conversation. "I just had a vision and a brief conversation with the angel Rose. Hermann Lutz has been controlled by a demon named

Vorbleg since he was born in the late 1890s. The demon is keeping Lutz from aging. Sort of like the portrait of Dorian Gray. He has been directly or indirectly involved in all the situations we've been in since the start. It's a secondary mission of his to get control of the crucifixion nail but, his primary mission has always been to eliminate the Jewish population of the world. To destroy God's chosen people. God is directing us to find Lutz and destroy the demon Vorbleg."

Laura sat back and watched the reactions of the other three. Mark immediately accepted the challenge and was starting to figure ways to find Lutz. Jack was trying to consider all the angles involved in both the hunt and the logistics involved. Sarah had the look of a huntress and a definite gleam of satisfaction that they were going after a demonic being that was trying to kill her people.

Laura herself just thought, "Here we go again."

The Crossfire Team will return in **_Dark Crossfire_**.

If this story has awakened your spirit or moved you to seek the love of Christ and His power for your life, whether you've never accepted Jesus as your savior or you've fallen away, repeat the following prayer and begin a most wonderful journey into eternal life with Him today.

Father God in heaven, As You said in Your Holy Word, (Romans 10:9) that if we confess the Lord our God and believe in our hearts that God raised Jesus from the dead, we shall be saved.

(The prayer on the next page is a sample prayer when asking Jesus into your heart as your Savior. You can also pray this in your own words.)

## Salvation Prayer

*Dear God in heaven, I come to you in the name of Jesus. I confess to You that I am a sinner, and I am sorry for my sins and the life that I have lived; I need your forgiveness. I believe that your only begotten Son Jesus Christ shed His precious blood on the cross at Calvary and died for my sins, and I am now willing to turn from my sin.*

*Right now I confess Jesus as the Lord of my life and my soul. With all my heart, I truly believe that your Holy Spirit raised Jesus from the dead. Today I accept Jesus Christ as my personal Savior and according to Your Word, right now I am saved.*

*I thank you Jesus, for your unlimited grace which has saved me from my sins. I thank you Jesus that your grace that never leads to license, but rather it always leads to repentance. Therefore Lord Jesus, transform my life so that I may bring glory and honor to you alone and not to myself.*

*I thank you Lord Jesus, for dying for me at Calvary and giving me eternal life.*

*Amen.*

If you just said this prayer and you meant it with all your heart, believe that you are now saved and have been born again.

You may ask, "Now that I am saved, what do I do next?" First of all you need to get into a spirit-filled, bible-based church that teaches the Scriptures, and you need to study God's Word.

Once you have found a church home, you will want to become water-baptized. By accepting Christ you are baptized in the spirit, but it is through water-baptism that you publically announce your obedience to the Lord Jesus. Water baptism is a symbol of your salvation from the dead. You were dead but now you live, for Jesus Christ has redeemed you for a price! The price was His atoning death on the cross. May God Bless You!